PURGATORY
KEY

A DEL SHANNON NOVEL

PURGATORY KEY

DARRELL JAMES

MIDNIGHT INK
WOODBURY, MINNESOTA

FIRST EDITION
First Printing, 2013

Book design and format by Donna Burch
Cover art: Man: iStockphoto.com/Nathan Jones
          Misty swamp: iStockphoto.com/Stuart Grant-Fuidge
          Sky: iStockphoto.com/Paul Senyszyn
Cover design by Ellen Lawson

Midnight Ink, an imprint of Llewellyn Worldwide Ltd.

This is a work of fiction. Names, characters, places, and incidents are either the product of the author's imagination or are used fictitiously, and any resemblance to actual persons, living or dead, business establishments, events, or locales is entirely coincidental.

Cover model(s) used for illustrative purposes only and may not endorse or represent the books subject matter.

Library of Congress Cataloging-in-Publication Data
James, Darrell, 1946–
  Purgatory key : a Del Shannon novel / Darrell James. — First Edition.
      pages   cm. — (A Del Shannon Novel ; #3)
  ISBN 978-0-7387-2371-6
  I. Title.
  PS3610.A429P87 2013
  813'.6—dc23
                                2013002524

Midnight Ink
Llewellyn Worldwide Ltd.
2143 Wooddale Drive
Woodbury, MN 55125-2989
www.midnightinkbooks.com

Printed in the United States of America

ONE

LEGGETT DENOUX WAS THE first to spot the kayak—a two-person inflatable, coming in from East Bayou, out of the swamp. This morning, the fog had not materialized and the day was already warm. There were two occupants in the craft. Teenagers it looked to be. Girls, both of them. Maybe eighteen, nineteen. Paddling with intent, closing fast on the shoreline.

"Ah, naw, naw! Pischouettes!" Leggett said to himself. *This is no good.* "Naw come to Terrebonne Key!"

It was a little after ten a.m., not the best time for trespassers—not that there was ever a good time. *But morning!* He had just rounded up one of the two white tigers. Gigi, the female—better trained, more gentle, generally she was not so much the problem. The problem was that the big male cat, her brother, Java, was still out there in the mangrove following their nightly, nocturnal prowl. Java was not to be trusted around people, particularly when Leggett wasn't around to command him, clap him down, talk to him, keep him under control. *Naw!* Grasping his gris-gris, which hung about his neck for good luck, Leggett tried his best to wish the teens away,

1

put all his power and thought into making them turn around—*chat!*—go back.

But they were coming—still coming—bent on making the island's eastern shore.

Leggett thought of Payton, now, the mistress's *Boo*. And Payton's brother, Teddy. He hoped for the girls' sake that neither of these two had spotted them this morning. He feared for these pischouettes, them. Java was still loose in the bush—for certain a danger, yes. But, if they should stumble upon the brothers. *Oo ye yi!* That would not be good, either.

Leggett led Gigi quickly to her pen, closed her in, and looped the rope-shank in place to secure her. Putting aside his duties for the time, Leggett headed out from the tiger pen and into the mangrove. His hope was that he could reach the girls before they made landfall, turn them back. Failing that, head them off before they made their way to the inhabited, western end of the island. Failing, that, yet again, well…

Leggett didn't want to think about what might come next.

———

The eastern shoreline of Terrebonne Key was gnarled with cypress. Bony, armlike roots reached out into the water's edge. Spanish moss dripped from wide-spreading branches. The island itself appeared to be nothing more than woods, and massive thickets of tightly tangled mangrove. It was dark and secretive. But was it all like that? Or was there more to the island than could immediately be seen?

All these things Lissa Rogers was thinking and wondering about as she blocked her paddle in the water and guided the two-man kayak into a small inlet waterway and landfall.

"Well, this is it. We made it," she said. "Didn't I tell you we'd find it?"

It was just the two of them. Lissa and her friend Kendra Kozak —kindred spirits since grade school, now teens, alone, having driven some fourteen hundred miles to get there.

They were in southern Louisiana at the outer reaches of East Bayou, the swamp, having arrived at Terrebonne Key—a private island at the end of their journey, through twisting, tangled waterways. Signs along its shoreline read: *Private Property! Do Not Enter! Keep Out!* It was a place alleged to harbor secrets—even more secrets than the swamp itself.

They had left, at first light, from Cocodrie—a town just south and down the bayou from Houma. Departing from the marina there, the boat ramp, where they'd launched their kayak. Laboring under the bright sun, the suffocating humidity, they had paddled out into East Bayou, on a search-and-find mission. They'd crossed the treacherous waters of the swamp, turning this way and that. At times feeling lost and desperate. They had already witnessed, this morning, more strange and awesome beauty than two girls from the desert were used to seeing. Encroaching into a water wilderness harboring all types of unusual wildlife—predators and prey alike. They had seen egrets, pelicans, and spoonbills sitting somberly in the trees. On the sketchy patches of firmament, amid the reeds and swamp grass, they had witnessed large ratlike rodents, and snakes and alligators. The alligators had witnessed them— eying them with cold, dead reptilian eyes—as they paddled past. The snakes had slithered off, to find even darker, more secretive locations in which to hide.

Lissa had been wishing she had remembered the printouts, the Google maps she'd researched. But despite the dangers of becoming lost, despite the dangers of becoming victims of the swamp itself, they had made it after all. *They had.* They had found the island where she had anticipated it to be. Now there, Lissa allowed them to float idly—kayak half in the water, half nosed onto the land—taking time to take it all in, indulging in a proud breath of fresh air while letting the gentle, westerly gulf breeze cool their brows.

"You still haven't told me what we're doing here," Kendra said. "Why it's so darned important to find this place. Haven't we seen enough? I mean, look at it! Look at where we are! We're the middle of nowhere, beyond the swamp! I'm not even sure we know how to get back!"

Lissa turned in her seat to look at her friend. Kendra was not the adventurous type—not anything like she was really, in any way—and Lissa now saw that her friend had come to the verge of tears. The sweltering humidity, the exertion, the fearful nature of the swamp … it had all gotten to her. Her long, red curls were hanging into her face. Sweat had soaked through her top. Mosquitoes buzzed about her face—squadrons of them—executing landings on her neck and arms. Limbs apparently too worn out to bother shooing.

"It'll be better once we're on dry land," she said. "This is going to be so awesome! I promise! You'll see!"

"That's what you said the last time. Remember? 'Oh it's gonna be great!' What was it that time? … Oh, yeah! … Little green men! You dragged me all the way up Camelback Mountain looking for evidence of UFOs you were sure we were going to find."

"There were sightings! Strange lights over Camelback! It was in all the newspapers, wasn't it? I think the aliens just left before we got there, that's all! Besides, this is different."

"Why? Because you read something in a book?"

4

"No," Lissa said, reaching into her hip pocket and withdrawing an aging tintype photo, displaying it for her friend to see. "Because, this time, I have proof."

"What's that?"

"Something that's just been sitting in my grandfather's collection, gathering dust all these years."

"You stole it?"

"Not stole. Borrowed. And it holds the secret I told you about. Something really fantastic!"

"You're nuts!"

"You can tell me that when I show you why we've come," Lissa said, returning the tintype photo to her pocket. "Come on! As Rooster Cogburn says … 'We're burning daylight.' We've got an island to explore."

———

Payton Rickey had just stepped naked from his bungalow—one of two that were originally intended for guests—to have a smoke, when he heard voices, a pair of them, coming up the path from the deserted end of the island toward him. His first thought was that it was Ivess, come to check up on him, and for a moment his blood ran cold. *Shit!* But then … No. Ivess would be in the other direction, down on the beach with her morning tea—her daily rituals so predictable you could set a universal clock by them. So, maybe his brother, Teddy, or the little coonass, Leggett. But, then, Teddy never ventured beyond the bungalows in that direction, and Leggett would be busy with morning chores. *So, who?*

Payton threw a quick glance back through the open doorway of the bungalow, where one of the main house's cleaning staff, a maid named Alonda, was still lounging about, wallowing in the afterglow of sex. The sheets were pulled over the lower half of her wide body, but her well-used breasts were visible, splayed out like pancakes. The two of them had practically sprinted from the main house to get there. Had rushed through their efforts to knock one off. And, now, she was lounging—*what women did, he believed.*

Payton reached over and pulled the door closed just in case.

Before Payton could consider his own clothing, two figures appeared on the path.

They were girls, teenagers, eighteen, nineteen years old perhaps—*the fuck!*—dressed practically alike, in shorts and running shoes, sleeveless knit tops. One of them was a pretty little thing, long dark hair and a slim figure. The other was a redhead, something less than pretty, but with a body that was more filled out in places, the way Payton preferred them.

The sudden appearance of the teens—Payton standing naked—caused him to fumble his cigarette. He grabbed in an attempt to catch it, burned his finger, and yelped at the pain.

The girls hadn't seen him yet, but now stopped abruptly, looking up to see him there—his hairy-man arms, legs, and chest bare, his spent genitals dangling. They froze. The redhead let out a scream.

There was a half-second, where no one spoke, no one moved. Then, "*Run!*" the slender one said. And both spun and broke back in the direction from which they'd come—the redhead shrieking as they fled.

"*Hey!*" Payton called after them, pitching his cigarette in the process. It had been his instinct to give chase, but as he pushed off in their direction, his bum leg—the one he'd injured in the plane crash—gave out on him. It buckled, and Payton had to catch himself to keep from going down.

The maid, Alonda, appeared in the doorway, now, a sheet wrapped around her middle. "What's going on?"

"Get your clothes on and get back to the house," Payton said.

"But, what is it?"

Just then, his brother, Teddy, happened onto the scene, coming along the path from the cabana, perhaps to see what Payton was up to. "I thought I'd find you here."

Now he spotted Alonda in the doorway and gave Payton a salacious grin.

"Don't worry about her!" Payton said. "Two girls! Teenagers! On the island! They ran off that way. They got a good look at me!"

"You think?" Teddy said. A rhetorical question, he was giving his brother's nakedness the once-over.

"Just get them! We can't let them get away."

Teddy gave his brother a sly grin, lifting a handheld radio from his belt. "That shouldn't be a problem," he said. And pressing the talk button, he said into the radio, "Leggett!"

Payton didn't wait to hear the reply. He turned back inside the bungalow, pushing past the maid, to gather his pants and shoes.

When he was dressed, he went back out, buttoning the final button on his shirt in the process.

"He's already on it!" Teddy said to him. "They won't get far."

———

The girls ran—Lissa leading the way—thrashing through overgrowth that cut into them as they fled.

"Don't stop!" Kendra cried, as she worked to keep up.

Lissa was setting a record pace. "The kayak!" she cried.

"I thought you said no one lived here?"

Lissa didn't answer. And, soon, their breath ran out and they were forced to slow their pace to a fast walk.

"Is he coming?" Kendra asked, on the verge of hysteria.

"No," Lissa said, coming to a complete stop now, hands on knees, to catch her breath. "We can relax, I think we've lost him. I was sure no one lived here. Nothing I read said the island was occupied."

"Well, maybe they don't write about hairy, naked men? Did you see that guy? He looked like somebody you'd see on a wanted poster or something!"

Lissa caught a last long breath. "Come on. Let's find the kayak and ... Wait!" she said suddenly, hearing something that sounded out of place.

"What? What is it?" Kendra threw a glance at the trail behind them.

"Listen! Don't you hear that?"

Kendra listening intently. "What? You're scaring me, Lissa. Let's just go ..."

"Shhhhhush! There it is again! Don't you hear it?"

"Don't do this to me!"

"Oh, God!" Lissa muttered, understanding now exactly what it was she'd heard.

The low, resonant rumble came again, making itself clear to both of them now. And a massive white tiger stalked out of the mangrove toward them. It was beautiful and terrifying all at once, moving with slow, liquid ease, stalking slowly forward, shoulders lowered, lips peeled back across dripping teeth. Its ice-blue eyes were locked on them with deadly intent.

"Lissa?" Kendra whined, clinging to her for protection now.

"Don't move!" Lissa said, keeping her voice low and non-threatening. "Stay very still!"

The tiger drew nearer, muscles working beneath its smooth, striped coat. Only steps away, now, it arched its head and raked off a mighty *ROWWLLLLL!*

It was Lissa who shrieked this time. Birds—that had gone oddly quiet before—now erupted into a cacophony of panic. Some took flight, others found deeper foliage in which to hide. Lissa stumbled backward, tripping on Kendra, who was struck speechless now, and both went down, in the rich, damp soil, a tangle of arms and legs.

The tiger unleashed another mighty *ROWWLLLLLLLL!*

Lissa was sure it was over for them. She clinched her mind and muscles tight, closed her eyes against the coming terror.

Just, then, a man's voice, interrupted the inevitable. "*Java!*" he called. His command was accompanied by two sharp claps of his hands.

Nothing happened, no terror came. Lissa reopened her eyes.

The big cat had suddenly, obediently, quieted. Its fierce snarl had dissolved into a sulking, suspicious glare.

The man clapped his hands again—"Java!"—and the beast relaxed its stance and dropped down on all fours and began to idly lick its fur with a broad, wet tongue.

Lissa let her breath out. Tears of relief flooded down her cheeks. Her heart was still mercifully beating. She could hear Kendra sobbing—the two of them still entangled.

From the mangrove, the man—their savior, as Lissa thought of him now—stepped into the clear. He was small in stature, dark-complected. He wore matching tan work pants and work shirt, the pockets were of the button-down type. His shiny black hair was slicked back, oily looking. A little cloth bag hung from a leather string about his neck—a charm of some kind. He squatted next to the tiger and hooked a heavy chain leash to its collar. He wrapped the other end of the chain, several times, around his hand and closed a strong grip around it. "Gar ici!" the man said to the cat. "Pischouettes don' read signs so good!"

9

Lissa wasn't sure if he was still talking to the tiger or to them. He spoke in an odd accent that Lissa recognized as Cajun—a cultural dialect they had encountered many times over the past two days in Louisiana bayou country. In particular among the shrimpers and fishermen at the marina where they rented their kayak. It wasn't clear, just yet, if he was friend or foe. But Lissa was grateful, nonetheless. Thankful he was in control of the tiger.

But now a second man suddenly appeared along the path.

He looked much like the naked man they'd seen outside the bungalow, Lissa thought, only younger, maybe, a bit taller, more oafish. He had blond hair that was buzzed short on the sides, but spiked taller on top. His skin was pale. His eyes were hooded—sleepy looking, almost colorless. Without saying anything, he gave them a smile that chilled her, made her blood run cold. This was not a nice man, she could tell.

They waited, all of them looking at each other, saying nothing.

Then, at long last, the naked man appeared—clothed now—limping, favoring a right leg that seemed somewhat misshapen beneath his pant leg. He was only slightly shorter than the younger brother. Perhaps even more powerfully built. He was ruggedly handsome, Lissa thought, for an older man, but seemed to have a hard edge. He looked far more intelligent than the brother. And where the younger brother's eyes looked sleepy, this ones gaze was sharp, penetrating. He approached now, angling directly for Lissa. An angry scowl on his face, he dragged her to her feet.

Lissa could smell the sour morning mix of whiskey and cigarettes on his breath as he pulled her close.

"What the hell you think you're doing, coming here like this?"

"We're sorry," Lissa said. "We were just out, kayaking. We saw the island and thought it looked interesting. We just wanted to see what was here."

"Is that right? Curiosity?" he sounded skeptical.

"Can't you just let us go?" Kendra asked, climbing to her feet and laying on a little schoolgirl charm despite her fear.

"You can't do that, Payton!" Teddy said, sharing the older brother's name now. "They've seen you, gotten a good look at you. They'll go back to the mainland and start yakking up a storm about the man they saw on the island. Describe you to authorities, right down to the wart on your penis, now that they've gotten a look at it."

"We'll leave!" Kendra said, bargaining. "We'll go back the way we came! We'll forget we were ever here. We won't say anything. We promise, don't we, Lissa!"

"We didn't mean any harm! We just wanted to see the island!" Lissa added, her voice pleading.

Payton withdrew a gun from his waistband and pressed it to Lissa's temple and cocked the hammer back. "You made a mistake coming here," he said.

"No, don't! Please! Why are you doing this?" Lissa felt tears welling in her eyes.

"Brother, brother," the younger brother said, shaking his head. "You don't want to waste these girls. I mean, look at 'em." He reached out and drew the back of his fingers gently along Lissa's cheek. The touch, alone, felt slimy, degrading. It gave her the creeps.

The brother named Payton seemed to consider the remarks. He eased the hammer down on the gun and lowered it. "Maybe you're right, Teddy," he said, giving away the second brother's name. "Maybe we shouldn't waste them."

Teddy grinned.

"But not because of what you're thinking," Payton added. "I've got another idea. Maybe something even more worthwhile. Shake them down!"

The brother Lissa now knew as Teddy came forward to grab Kendra around the neck with one big arm. He held her there, tight against him, as he ran his hands over the front of her, and down her shorts, letting his fingers linger in forbidden places a bit too long. Now, he pushed her away, and it was Lissa's turn to be man-handled.

He repeated the process, Lissa feeling his hand slide between her legs before he concentrated on her front pockets to find car keys, along with her laminated driver's license. He removed the license and studied it. "It says they're from Arizona?" he said, handing it over his shoulder to the brother.

"A long damned way from home," Payton said, studying it for himself. "What else have they got?"

Teddy continued his search, this time running his hands crudely along the back curve of Lissa's shorts. Finding a bulge in the hip pocket, he retrieved the tintype photo she had placed there. "Now, what's this?"

"It's just an old photo," Lissa said. "A souvenir. It's nothing."

"Hmmm…" Teddy said, pondering the image for a moment. Then, unimpressed, he returned it to her pocket and stepped away. "They're clean," he said. "Real clean."

"Can I have my driver's license back, please?" Lissa said.

"I think we'll hold on to it for a while," Payton said.

"What are you going to do with us?"

"For now, you're going to be spending a little time with us… Leggett!" Payton called to the Cajun. Who had remained quiet during the exchange, stroking the tiger, keeping it calm. "Put them in Teddy's bungalow. Keep them out of Ivess's sight."

"Where's him gonna sleep?" the Cajun asked.

"Teddy's going on a little trip. You won't have to worry about it," Payton said.

"A trip? Where?" Teddy asked, seeming not so anxious for whatever his brother had in mind.

Payton turned his gaze on him. "Why...Arizona! What do you think?"

Leggett stood now, the cat's chain leash still strongly wrapped in his grip.

Arizona, Lissa thought. That was not good news. She was starting to understand that this man, Payton, had thoughts of holding them here, possibly for ransom. They had her address from her driver's license. And could find their way to her grandfather with no trouble at all.

Her grandfather, back home in Tucson, in a wheelchair.

"No! Please!" she pleaded weakly.

"Can't you just let us go?" Kendra tried again.

Payton leveled his eyes on them, and with a jerk of his head, ordered them away.

"Allons!" the Cajun said, taking Lissa by the arm to lead her. "The man tell me for to do this." He nodded Kendra ahead.

Reluctantly, Kendra moved off, and Lissa allowed herself to be led away. Her concerns were on her grandfather, now, and on their own immediate safety. All the fanciful illusions about the island, about the Jacob Worley tintype in her pocket, and about the fortune that it revealed...

Were all forgotten for the time.

TWO

It was a Saturday, but Randall Willingham was in his office, nine a.m., pushing papers around his desk and nursing a hangover, when the phone rang.

Normally, it would be up to Patti, his receptionist, to answer it. But the offices were closed for the weekend. She and his investigators were off doing their thing—whatever thing that might be. Randall had nothing better to do.

The phone was still ringing.

Randall gave a sigh. And answered.

He'd been the owner of Desert Sands Covert for more than fifteen years, his firm specializing in finding and recovering missing persons, fugitive apprehension, other selective investigative cases. All this on top of the twenty-two years he'd spent in naval intelligence. He was starting to feel the wear and tear of it. Still . . .

"Desert Sands," he said into the phone.

"Desert Sands Covert?" a man's voice said.

"I'm Randall. What can I do for you?"

The caller was an elderly gentleman, Randall could tell—elderly by the sound of his voice; gentleman by the tone of it. The man went on to tell him that his name was Edgar Egan, and that he lived in Tucson, on the northwest side. He told Randall that the reason he was calling was that he was worried about his granddaughter—the girl's name, Lissa Rogers.

"How old?" Randall's first question.

"She's eighteen. Finished high school just this past spring," Egan said.

He went on to say that she'd been gone several days past the time she was scheduled to return, and calls to her cell phone had gone unanswered. He was inquiring about one of Desert Sands female investigators, Del Shannon, and wanted to know if she was available.

"And what exactly do you want done?"

"Why, to find my granddaughter, of course."

Randall pinched the bridge of his nose between thumb and fore finger, feeling a migraine coming on. Del Shannon was one of his top investigators. Possibly his best. If the man on the phone was asking for her by name, it was probably because he'd heard of her by reputation. Being a woman in a man's job and all, she seemed to get her picture in the newspaper every time he turned around. So, Randall wasn't altogether surprised the man was asking for her by name. No, what bothered him was the age of the granddaughter.

"With all due respect, Mr. Egan," Randall said, "I've heard this story before. Teenage girl goes off, fails to call home, comes slipping back a week later with her hair dyed orange and a new tattoo on her bumpkus. Isn't it possible your granddaughter has just gone off somewhere? Maybe with friends? Sleeping over someplace?"

"Well, in fact she has gone off with a friend of hers, sort of a summer adventure you might say. But it's not like her not to call, not to answer her phone. She's a good girl. Doesn't even have a regular boyfriend."

Randall pictured some Ugly Betty, fat and squat with a bad case of acne.

"You may have seen her," Egan said. "She was runner-up in the Miss Teen America Pageant last year."

Hmmm ... Randall thought ... so much for judgment.

"Well, Del Shannon is not in at the moment," Randall said, remembering that it was Saturday and that he'd promised Del the day off. "I have two other investigators. Both top-notch. I'm sure we could find someone to help you out."

Actually, Randall had to think, then, if that was true. He had two other investigators on staff, yes. There was James "Willard" Hoffman. But he was somewhere in Ohio tracking down a man wanted for questioning in a corporate fraud case, probably wouldn't be back for days. And Rudy Lawson, his other investigator, was currently laid up at home with his leg in a cast—the leg getting itself broken by a baseball bat, Rudy coming out of the Indian gaming casino on Ajo, the woman Rudy'd been sleeping with married and the husband not liking it so much. Randall didn't tell Mr. Egan all that.

"Yes, well, I was really hoping for Ms. Shannon. Do you know when she'll be available?" Egan's tone was saying he was willing to wait for her in particular.

Randall wasn't in the mood to object. He could smell the fresh coffee he'd started brewing just after coming through the door. It was ready, screaming for him to join it. He said, "If you're sure it's gotta be Del. It's Saturday, I'll have to see if I can track her down. If I can, I'll have her come talk to you. But, either way, I'll let you know."

The man still seemed unsatisfied, but sighed his resignation. "I suppose it will have to do."

Randall took down Egan's address and phone number. "No promises," he said, and ended the call.

Randall wasn't thrilled about going back on his promise to give Del the day off. While she approached her job with dedication, she was equally loyal to her privacy, often turning her cell phone off, weekends, to ensure such. Still, he shouldn't jump to conclusions. She could be out working—she sometimes did that on her day off, too. Either way, he believed he had the means to convince her, talk her into going to visit the old man. Randall left his desk and crossed into the break room, the coffee smell almost making him delirious with desire for it now.

No … talking her into the job wasn't so much the problem, he decided. The bigger problem just now … was how to go about finding her.

———

This morning, she had come to a rundown section of town called Midvale Park, behind the wheel of her Jeep Wrangler, surveilling a tiny white house where she believed the bail skipper to be. She was dressed in boots and jeans and a sleeveless shirt, hanging loose over a taut, trim waistline. The top of her Jeep was furled back, accepting the soft desert breeze.

Andray Moton. She could picture the man.

He had skipped bail on a felony assault charge. Andray had come close to killing one of his several girlfriends who had dared to criticize his lack of hygiene—beating her to within an inch of her life. But it was Andray's wife, Roselle, who had called in the tip that Andray was coming by sometime around nine this morning, saying, *"He wantin' my hard-earned money t'get his ass outta town. Fuck that shit!"* Andray was considered dangerous.

Del first considered the neighborhood itself—a tract of aging prefabs and plastered-up stuccos. Some with pieces of siding missing, others with sagging gutters. All were faded, their paint scaling. In the yards were hulls of rusted-out appliances, rusted-out cars on blocks. The lawns and flowerbeds were all burnt brown. It was an all too familiar scene. This was not the first time she'd come for Andray.

Del collected her weapon from between the seats—her nine-millimeter Baby Eagle handgun. She checked the magazine, then tucked it into her waistband at the small of her back. One last look at the house, she opened the driver's door and slipped out.

She remained there for a time, watching, listening, then crossed around through the yard and up onto the front porch—floorboards squeaking beneath her feet. She hesitated, then knocked softly, once, and waited.

A long moment passed, and then Del heard a slow shuffling inside—the sound of house shoes on worn carpeting. The latch turned, and a shadowy face appeared through a crack in the door. The face belonged to Roselle.

"Where's Andray, Roselle?" Del said.

"How should I know?" Roselle said.

Del let her eyes move past the woman to the darkened room beyond. Her fugitive was here. She could feel it. "I want Andray," she said.

Roselle was looking past Del to the yard below. "You all by yourself? Where yo' SWAT team, whatever?"

"This is my job, Roselle. This is what I do."

"Well, he ain't here. Haven't seen him."

Del placed her palm flat against the door and pushed. The opening widened, and Del could see the woman clearly now. Roselle was no more than five feet tall and pear-shaped, wrapped in a worn terrycloth bath robe and wearing dirty, pink fuzzy slippers on her feet. She peered up at Del through a slit in one good eye. The other eye was swollen completely shut and ringed with a dark purple bruise. Her lip was cut and bleeding.

"What happened?"

The woman said nothing.

"Andray do this to you? Tell me."

"I fell down the basement steps."

"You don't have a basement, Roselle! Your house sits on blocks! Can I come in?"

Roselle hesitated.

Del pushed her way in without further invitation. She reached for the blinds that covered the window and threw them back. Morning light spilled across the room and down the nearby hallway, and Del could see now exactly how Roselle lived.

The place was a shambles. A plate sat atop the television, roaches crawling undisturbed through the dried remains of some distant dinner past. There was a pile of unwashed laundry in the corner, gossip tabloids scattered about. Roselle crossed her arms defiantly and looked back at her through her one good eye.

Del considered the hallway. "Is there anyone else in the house, Roselle?"

Roselle's eyes darted reflexively toward the back.

"You won't mind if I look."

Del moved off without permission, the Baby Eagle poised alongside her leg.

"I wouldn't go in there, I was you," Roselle said.

Del made her way down the hallway, her back to the wall. On her left, she came upon a long, sliding pocket door. She raised her weapon and slid open the door to reveal a pantry—five shelves filled with boxed and canned foods, miscellaneous cleaning supplies. No Andray.

Putting her back to the wall again, she moved on, turning on lights and clearing each room with her weapon—no one under the beds, no one hiding in closets. There was a rear door off the kitchen. It was locked from the inside. No one had gone out. But still no Andray.

Del made her way, still cautious, back up the hallway toward the living area.

When she was once again even with the pantry, its sliding door still open, she hesitated. Something odd in the arrangement of goods. On the lower shelves, food items seemed to be aligned haphazardly. But on the top self, above eye level, cans and boxes were stacked neatly, shoulder to shoulder, in a nice clean display—a solid wall of goods more than a foot high.

Del slipped the Baby Eagle back into her waistband.

Roselle was watching her from the end of the hall.

"So, Andray's not here?" Del said. Then, without hesitation, she drove her hand deep between the stacked boxes of Jell-O pudding and cornbread mix, grabbed a handful of what might have been Dacron sports attire, and jerked hard.

Six-feet-two-inches of Andray Moton, along with boxes of Nesquik and cans of creamed corn, came spilling off the upper shelf. The goods hit the floor in a clattering avalanche. "Oh, shit!" she heard Andray say just before he slammed down hard on the floor, the air punching out of him in a grunt. He had a gun in one hand.

Before Andray could clear the stars from his head, Del stomped her boot down hard on his gun hand, eliciting a yelp as his hand flexed to release the weapon. She kicked it away and rolled Andray over to pin his face to the floor with one knee. Andray was still trying to clear the stars when she snapped the handcuffs on his wrists behind his back.

Now, she stood, dragging him to his feet, saying, "Get up, ass-hole!"

Andray stood to his full height, towering over Del in his Bearcats basketball jersey and baggy shorts. "Shit, bitch! The fuck you doing?" Complaining now.

She pushed him roughly, off down the hallway and out into the living room, where Roselle had retreated to a corner, her arms hugged tightly about her.

Andray was still bitching. "You always on me! Shit! You ain't no cop!"

"No, I'm not. But you remember that, Andray. No matter how many times you try to run, I'm gonna be right on top of you."

Now Andray spotted his wife. "You knew she was coming. You snitched me out, didn't you, Roselle? Shit, bitch! Why you do me like this?"

Del dragged Andray away, shoving him ahead of her now out the front door.

On the porch, Del came alongside him, leading him by the elbow to the edge of the steps. Andray balked, calling over his shoulder, "I'm gonna get you, Roselle. They jails ain't big enough to hold me. You think you in pain now, girl? You wait ...!"

Without forethought, Del jammed one boot into Andray's path and gave him a shove. "No, you won't!" she said.

Andray tripped and pitched forward off the porch—"Hey, shit!"—his hands still cuffed behind his back. He smacked down hard, face first, against the concrete. There was the sickening crunch of bone and a gush of blood from his nose.

Andray lay quiet.

Roselle came out onto the porch, arms still hugged about her. "He dead?" she asked.

Andray groaned a reply.

"Shit!" Roselle said.

Del came down the steps and put one knee hard in the middle of Andray's back. She fished in his pockets and came out with a banded roll of bills—money she knew he had beaten out of Roselle earlier. Turning, she pitched the roll to the woman.

Roselle fumbled the toss, then caught the bills in the folds of her robe. She looked at it, then smiled—a pathetic but genuine smile—and winked with her one good eye. "Yeah, you one tough little sister, huh?"

Del took a handful of Andray's hair from behind. She leaned close to whisper in his ear. "Listen to me, Andray…" She banged his head against the concrete for good measure. "You listening?"

Andray groaned again.

"You ever lay a hand on that woman again, and I find out, I'll come back for you. And I won't stop 'til you're in traction next time. You understand?"

Andray's eyes rolled, then righted dully in their sockets.

In her pocket Del's cell phone began to vibrate.

"Do you understand!" She banged Andray's head again.

Andray managed a feeble nod.

Now she withdrew the phone from her pocket and checked the caller ID.

It was Randall calling.

"What day is it?" she asked Andray.

Andray had to think about it, but said, "Sat … Saturday."

"That's what I thought," she said …

And returned the cell phone to her pocket.

THREE

RANDALL HAD TRIED DEL'S phone several times, no answer. Then
he had driven by her house to check for her, no luck. It left a world
of places she might be. But Randall knew of one place else to look,
that held the greatest probability of her being there—Scotty's
Indoor Shooting Range. It was the last real shot he had at finding her. So Randall drove east, out Tanque Verde Road, across the
wash, and up the gravel drive.

He arrived at Scotty's to find Del's red Jeep Wrangler sitting in
the parking area along with a number of other vehicles. It was mid-
day, and Randall knew she'd be inside punching holes in paper tar-
gets with the nine-millimeter handgun she carried.

Scotty's, Randall knew, was a place of significance to Del, a
place of reverence.

Just two years ago, she had seen a lifelong quest of hers to find
her mother come to a violent end here, at this very range—a violent shootout with a fabled Kentucky evangelist. That, only a week
after losing her father in a fatal car accident. She came here often,
late at night and days off, to exorcize the demons that Randall

believed still haunted her. It was something that both worried Randall and filled him with appreciation for her. But, so often, he wished she could just find something—someone—to help her find closure. What she needed—his opinion—was a man in her life. Someone to watch her back, look after her …

Randall often wished that could be him.

———

There were several shooters at the line when Randall arrived inside. Del was sharing a stall with a good-looking young Hispanic man, mid-thirties maybe. They were both wearing ear protectors, Del looking over his shoulder, as the man popped off shots at a paper silhouette, some thirty yards downrange.

Pop …

Pop …

Pop …

Randall watched and waited.

The target showed a nice arrangement of shots, loosely grouped. Not bad, Randall thought.

But now it was Del's turn.

She stepped forward, drawing her Baby Eagle from her waistband and stepping into a modified police stance, which accentuated the curve of her hip. The man leaned in close—too close, Randall thought—sighting across her shoulder, and down the length of her extended arm.

My God, but she was adorable, Randall thought. Thirty-one years old. Her blonde hair shagged short, tough-sexy.

And, this guy … Randall didn't know him. He felt a slight twinge of jealousy, envying him his apparent youth—Randall overweight these days, and feeling every day of his sixty-plus years.

Randall watched as she quickly capped off rounds at the target.

...pop...pop...pop...pop...pop...pop...pop...

The weapon kicked. Brass shell casings ejected from the chamber and collected at their feet. After fifteen rounds, the gun's slide locked open and smoke curled from the chamber. She ejected the magazine and punched another in place.

When the gun ran empty this time, she let it drop to her side, hit the button that carried the paper silhouette down the wire to them, and examined the results—a tight-fisted grouping, thirty rounds, center-mass, well inside the man's previous pattern. *Jesus!* Randall swallowed.

Now, they were stepping out of the stall, caught up in smiles and comments of appreciation. The man's arm was around her shoulder—too familiar, Randall's opinion. He wanted to slap the guy away, tell him, "Show *some respect.*"

But, then ... that was Del's choice to make. And, should he raise the issue, she would be the first to remind him she was capable of making it.

Randall cleared his voice to let them know he was there.

Del spotted him. "Okay, I know why you're here, Randall."

"Good morning to you too," he said.

"I'm sorry, but you know it's my day off. What is it this time ... kidnapped heiresses, runaway dogs? And, for your information, I've already used up half my morning completing one assignment."

"Andray Moton?"

"Dropped him off at the Midvale Precinct and hour ago. That's when I ran into Mister Wide-Shot," Del said, referring to her male partner with a smile. "We got into a debate about who was the better marksman and decided to come shoot it out to put an end to the discussion. This is Gil Tappa, Detective with TPD. He works homicide on the south side. Gil, this is my boss, Randall."

"Homicide?"

"Past four years. And, she's the better shot."

"Doesn't surprise me," Randall said.

Up close, Randall noticed, the guy was a little older than he'd first assumed. Maybe thirty-nine, forty.

Randall turned his attention to Del. "Well, I'm real sorry to interrupt your day, sweetheart. I wouldn't have if it wasn't something important."

"I'll catch you later Del," Gil said.

"I thought we were going to catch some lunch?"

"We'll do it another time, for sure. Sounds like you've got work to do. I'll head on home. I'm sure Maggie's got a list of things for me to do."

They exchanged a quick hug, and Gil made his exit.

"Maggie? The guy's married?"

"He's a friend, Randall. That's all. A friend at the police department."

"Yeah, you seem to have a lot of male friends," Randall said, not intending the pouty tone his voice.

"I like men," Del said. "So sue me. So, now, what's so important that you had to come looking for me on a Saturday?"

"Why don't I buy you a sandwich at the snack bar. I'll give you all the details."

———

"The client's name is Edgar Egan," Randall told Del. "The girl's name is Lissa Rogers."

They had found a table in the lounge behind the shooting range—Randall with the turkey on wheat, Del the egg salad on rye. There were glasses of iced tea in front of them.

"Where?" she asked, wiping excess mayonnaise from the corner of her mouth with a napkin.

"He's right here in Tucson. Has a place northwest, other side of Pusch Ridge. You won't have to go far; maybe you can still salvage a bit of your day."

"Why didn't he come into the office?"

"He's in a wheelchair... what he told me... asked if I could send you to talk to him."

"And he asked for me personally?"

"Insisted," Randall said.

"Why?"

Randall shrugged, considered his investigator. *God, she was all-over beautiful!* But it was the eyes that always did it for him—ice green, with an intelligent light in them. They were making Randall uncomfortable, just now, the way they were drilling into him. He'd secretly wanted her since that first day she'd walked into his office. Still, he understood it could never be. And, as a result, over time, he had come to care for her more like a daughter. He said, "Personally, I don't think there's really a case here. Two teenage girls, off on a summer adventure? Probably just having fun and letting the time get away from them."

"You said he's the grandfather. What do the parents have to say?"

Randall knew the answer to this but had somewhat been avoiding the question.

Del had grown up with only her father to provide nurturing—and her father hadn't been all that good at playing the tender role. He was distant, aloof, and in the bottle two-thirds of his time. Del was forced to accept being alone and without love at a very young age. Randall knew the circumstances of her life had left their scars. Her emotions ran deep. And, Randall also knew that if Del somehow identified with this missing girl personally, she would challenge heaven and hell to find her. That's why he had wanted to avoid the subject, wanting to avoid triggering that nasty little streak of impulsiveness she had. But now he said, "Both her parents are dead."

That brought her eyes up to look at him again. "Dead?"

There, he'd done it.

Randall nodded. "I don't know all the details," he said. "I only promised you'd come talk to him."

She seemed to think about it. "Egan … why does that name sound familiar?"

"I don't know, but I had thought so too. Just keep me up to speed, let me know what you think. I'm leaving it up to you. It's your decision whether you accept the assignment or not. Okay?"

Del returned the uneaten portion of her sandwich to the plate, took a good long sip of tea, and rose to leave.

"Aren't you going to finish that?" he said.

"I'll leave it for you. I've got work to do."

And, without goodbyes, she made her exit.

Randall watched her go—out through the entrance and into the day. *That was his girl! No time for nothin'!*

Randall studied the half-eaten sandwich she'd left behind. Then with a shrug, he moved it onto his plate.

Why not? he thought. Just because it was no longer her day off … it was certainly his.

FOUR

FOR THE SECOND TIME in two years, Falconet was back in Cincinnati, in the regional offices of the Federal Bureau of Investigation, waiting in the reception area to be called.

He was ATF—Alcohol, Tobacco, Firearms, and Explosives—most recently having been on assignment with Homeland Security, investigating an anti-government group called the Rightmen Militia, who were stockpiling automatic weapons in preparation for the End Days and orchestrating public rants about seizing control of the government. *Nowhere-ville, Wyoming.* The movement ended in a lackluster confrontation that resulted in eleven members of the organization filing out single file with their hands in the air. And Falconet found himself back home in New Jersey, in his one-bedroom apartment, watching episodes of *Burn Notice* and drinking beer.

But now the FBI was asking for him again, reaching across agency lines, as they sometimes did when a particular agent-in-charge wanted someone special.

Falconet was special.

He was second-generation Irish-Italian—growing up in Brooklyn but later moving across the Verrazano Bridge into New Jersey—wearing his leather jacket with the sleeves rolled up, and getting blowjobs in the back seat of his Camaro. Since that time, he'd been married once, was now divorced, and had a teenage daughter who was growing up way beyond her years. He'd been with the Department of Justice for thirteen years. Working some nine of those years undercover. Using his street savvy as his credentials.

Who was asking for him this time? And why?

Falconet had no idea.

"Agent Falconet, you can go in now," the pretty receptionist said.

Falconet drew himself out of the leather sofa and crossed to the large oak door that bore entry into the office of the agent-in-charge.

"Well, well! Frank Falconet!" a voice said from across the room as he entered.

Falconet should have guessed—the man behind the desk was his old friend, Darius Lemon. This afternoon, behind the desk, leaning in on his knuckles like he owned the place.

"I should have known you were behind my being here," Falconet said.

Darius gave him a smile.

Falconet closed the door and crossed to shake his hand across the desk.

"The last time I was here," Falconet said, "the agent-in-charge was George Racine, and you were just a peon getting your assignment given to you like me."

"Haven't you heard? Racine retired last year. I've been given his job."

"I'd say you deserve it. You still sketching those charcoal land-scapes?"

"Deserving, maybe. Sketching, definitely. When there's time. "Have a seat, Frank."

He might have felt somewhat uncomfortable in the austere office surroundings. But Darius Lemon was a man who immediately put you at ease. Gentle. Patient. Polite. Refined. He reminded Falconet a little of the actor Morgan Freeman. Grayer at the temples, now, than Falconet remembered. But still with those same calm, intelligent eyes that took you in and held you, like a pair of loving arms.

They had worked together just two years previously, on an assignment that took them into the hills of Kentucky to investigate the infamous faith healer Silas Rule. That assignment had not ended well. And Falconet had ultimately taken a bullet for it—one he'd survived. But the assignment had also had its upside. It had brought him into contact with a beautiful female investigator from Tucson, Del Shannon. They had fallen in love during their days together in Nazareth Church. He still thought of her often. How was she? What was she doing? He wondered that now…

Darius took his seat behind the desk.

"So…?" Falconet said, slumping into one of the chairs in front of the desk, stretching his legs out. He'd come wearing jeans, a Rutgers sweatshirt, and tennis shoes.

"So," Darius said in return. "You ever hear of a man named Payton Rickey?"

Falconet shook his head. "Should I have?"

"Not necessarily. But he was a part of a hot topic of conversation among several federal agencies for a while. Particularly the Marshals Service."

"Was?" Falconet said.

"He died in a plane crash. Or, so it's been believed. Along with the two U.S. marshals and the pilot who were bringing him to justice."

"That the one where the plane went down in the Gulf of Mexico?" Falconet asked.

"So, you have heard of it?"

"I guess I recall something. So … what? … You want me to go scuba diving to recover the body?"

"In a manner of speaking," Darius said. "We have reason to suspect the man may not be dead after all."

Falconet sat a little higher. "Not dead?"

"It was seven months ago that the plane went down in the Gulf, en route back from Mexico, our fugitive aboard. Coast Guard search teams scoured the waters, no signs of survivors. But last month a body was found washed up in a Louisiana swamp, wedged into the cypress roots along the shoreline. It's believed to have been dredged up by an earlier storm this summer and deposited there. Half-eaten by alligators. But the head and neck and a piece of the torso were still intact, enough to allow us to identify it as one of the U.S. marshals from that flight. And, secondly, enough to determine that the cause of death was not the result of the plane crash."

"Then how?" Falconet asked.

"Strangulation. According to a Terrebonne Parish Sheriff's report, the body … what was left of it … had a belt cinched tightly around its neck."

Falconet considered the idea. "So … the marshal had survived the crash, after all."

Darius nodded. "It would appear so. And, we're thinking, now … so did someone else."

"Payton Rickey," Falconet said.

"You catch on quick. The one person who had a reason to strangle the marshal to death. We have to consider the possibility."

"So, what do you want from me?"

"We want you to find out. Verify our suspicions. And if we're right, find Payton Rickey and bring him to justice."

Falconet rose and crossed to the window to look out. Tugs worked coal barges along the Ohio River. And across the water could be seen the blue-green hills of Kentucky. All of it held both fond and fatal memories of Falconet's past assignment there.

Darius came to stand next to him, eyes on the panorama before them. "This man is dangerous, Frank. He and his brother, Theodore Rickey, crisscrossed the U.S. routinely, committing crimes at their leisure. Both were suspected of hitting liquor stores, kiting checks, whatever money scheme they could conjure up. In Sweethome, Arkansas, they invaded the home of a local bank manager, abducted his wife and two children, and held them for ransom. Once the ransom was paid, Payton shot and killed all three—wife, daughter, son. No conscience, no remorse. A home surveillance camera positively identified Payton to us, but was unable to positively confirm his brother Teddy's involvement... though we suspect he was in on it."

Falconet turned his gaze to Darius. "A bad guy."

"Oh, but it doesn't end there," Darius said. "A nationwide BOLO was issued for Payton Rickey's arrest, and when a Texas highway patrolman pulled him over near Odessa, Payton shot and killed the patrolman on the spot. Once again, the dash cam in the patrol car confirmed Payton as the shooter but never really got a look at the second man involved, believed to likely be the brother, Teddy, once again. That's when Payton fled to Mexico. The marshals went looking for him. Found him. And were in the process of bringing him back to the States."

"When the airplane went down in the Gulf."

Darius nodded.

Falconet left the window and returned to his seat in front of the desk.

Darius settled back behind his desk. "I think you can understand why we want to find this guy. It's just a matter of time before some other innocent gets hurt or dies."

"If he's alive," Falconet said.

"If he's alive," Darius affirmed.

Falconet considered the possibility. "Well, all right … Do we have anything on his whereabouts now?"

"No, that's just the thing," Darius said. "The man hasn't resurfaced, not once, since the plane crash. If he's alive, he's doing an incredible job of pretending to be dead."

"So, no clue?"

"None," Darius said. "That's your challenge, Frank. The man could be anywhere. But we do have one lead to go on."

"What's that?"

"The brother," Darius said.

"This, Teddy? … Yeah, you never said what became of him."

"Well, it seems he went off the radar about the same time as his brother. He too has done a good job of staying lost."

"Until …"

"Until two days ago." Darius leaned back in his chair. "We don't actually have our hands on him yet, but … What do you know about biometrics, Frank?"

"Facial recognition? That kind of thing?"

"In its simplest form, yes. Several major U.S. cities have been involved in a special program with Homeland Security to test the feasibility of biometrics as a means of identifying known terrorists on the streets."

"Big brother watching."

"The way much of the public sees it. They have cameras set up throughout these cities, in high-traffic areas. The cameras scan the faces of pedestrians, passersby, and such, and compare the images to a database of known terrorists. That's the ultimate plan anyway. To test it, however, they filled the database with the photos and information on known federal fugitives. Payton Rickey, along with his brother Teddy, were in that database."

"And the machine got a hit," Falconet said.

"Buying cigarettes at a convenience store," Darius said.

Falconet took time to digest all he'd just learned. Then said, "So, where is this shit town you want to send me to?"

"Why ... Tucson ... Frank," Darius said with a smile.

Falconet felt his heart soar. It all made sense now, why Darius had asked for him. Tucson was the home of the female investigator that Falconet had worked with in Kentucky. Darius had been there with them through the entire ordeal. Darius, this sly old gentleman, was playing Cupid. Giving Falconet work on an assignment there, to spend time in Tucson and possibly seek out his lost love. Falconet couldn't help but love this man to death. A broad smile crossed his face. "You sly old devil," Falconet said.

"Someone's got to get you two kids back together," Darius said. "Since both of you are too proud to initiate it on your own." Darius slid open his lap drawer, withdrew a manila envelope, and slid it across the desk to Falconet. "All the particulars are in there ... biometric photos of Teddy. Screen caps from the surveillance tapes, et cetera. All the personal data. You know how it works."

Falconet collected the envelope but didn't open it. He couldn't seem to wipe the smile off his face.

"Well, that's all I've got for you," Darius said, rocking out of his chair to stand. "Don't forget to say hello to our girl for me ... that is ... if you should happen to see her."

Happen to see her, Falconet thought...

Just try and stop him.

———

In the below-ground parking garage, Falconet took time to inspect the envelope, dumping the contents on the seat to examine biometric images of Teddy Rickey, police photos of Payton Rickey, photos of the crime scene where the hostage family had been murdered, and other official records and reports pertaining to the case. He was hoping Darius had included a photo of Del, eager to see her face once more, those strong, intelligent green eyes looking back at him. But, no. He would have to hold her image in his head for now, until the time came he could see her face to face.

He and Del had had their run at love. And it had been pretty intense, the way he remembered it. They'd survived a lot together, in those short few weeks. And they had been in love, no doubt. But, as summer romances often go, the love affair didn't take. Their time together had ended on a beach in Mexico—both wishing on the stars for time to stand still, freeze-frame their moment in the sun. Both knowing that the likelihood of a lasting relationship was slim. There were just too many barriers. Mostly having to do with their respective careers.

And that's pretty much the way they'd left it. Falconet had moved on to his next assignment; Del had moved on to hers. But not without leaving a million little pieces of his heart—their hearts, he believed—scattered about the sand.

Now, fate—in the form of Darius Lemon—had intervened, and he was getting the chance to return to Tucson, possibly see her again. But... *What if he got there and she wasn't there? What if he got there and she wouldn't see him?* Or, no, no, no...

What if he got there to find she was married?

FIVE

It was just after noon when Del reached the Egan residence in the Pusch Ridge Estates. She followed the drive that led to a circular turnaround in the front of the house, pulling her Jeep Wrangler in behind a late model Mercedes sedan equipped with a rack to accommodate a wheelchair. She killed the engine and stepped out to survey the surroundings.

The place was a sprawling hacienda on a two-acre plot, set against the backdrop of the Santa Catalina Mountains and surrounded by manicured lawns and flowering hedges. Water trickled over artificial rock formations and flowed along a rock-lined canal to empty into a manmade pond. The water was murky. Ducks bobbed for food amid cattails and flotsam. Out a short distance from the main house was a small adobe guest house. A gardener was working his way along a row of oleander shrubs in front of it.

Edgar Egan had money.

The front entrance to the main house was a gated portico leading through to an inner courtyard. Del crossed around the front of her Jeep and was met by a woman coming out to meet her. She was stocky, middle-aged, wearing sturdy white shoes and a starched nurse's uniform.

"Mr. Egan is waiting," the woman said without a bit of pleasantness.

Del reached a hand in greeting. "I'm…"

"Del Shannon. Yes, I know. Come this way."

The woman turned off crisply, leaving Del to follow.

The house was constructed in a rectangle, surrounding a cultivated courtyard. Shaded verandas ran the length of both sides. A flagstone walkway cut a meandering path through the garden, amid sago palms and flowering desert bird-of-paradise. Birds flitted in and out of the foliage, happy with their surroundings. At length, the garden gave way to a swimming pool that drew the eye to the rear of the property where a wide arched opening afforded a magnificent view of the Tucson valley.

"You'll be meeting with Mr. Egan in the study," the woman said, striding briskly ahead of her.

"And who are you?" Del asked pleasantly.

The woman stopped them in their tracks. "I'm Ms. Dengler, Mr. Egan's aide."

"Could I ask… What's your take on Lissa Rogers? You think she's gone missing or just gone off somewhere intentionally?"

"I don't have a take, Ms. Shannon. I'm only here to attend to the master of the house."

"I was only wondering, does she spend a lot of time with a boyfriend? Go on trips out of town? Sleep over?"

The woman observed her coolly and, without reply, turned away.

She led them to the end of the veranda, through a door, and into a large pine-paneled study crowded with books and paraphernalia. She'd gotten nothing from the matron. Let's hope the old man was more amenable, Del thought.

He sat in a wheelchair, hunched over a desk and typewriter. He seemed utterly absorbed in his work, banging away at the keys, oblivious to their arrival.

"Mr. Egan?" Ms. Dengler said, by way of announcement.

When the man didn't respond she called, "EDGAR!"

The man looked around, as if dialing in from another planet. But then his eyes brightened. "Oh, so sorry, Gerda. I'm afraid I was off in my writer head again."

"This is Del Shannon, the investigator, here to talk to you about Lissa."

"Lovely," the man said, rotating his wheelchair in place to face her.

Del extended her hand and got a warm welcome this time, the man clasping her hand in both of his and shaking it generously. "Thank you for coming."

"It's a very nice place you have here."

"Yes, I'm rather fond of it. Did you know it once belonged to the Ronstadts?"

"The singer, Linda?"

"No, but a member of the family. An uncle, a cousin, perhaps. I forget."

"Can I get you anything else, Mr. Egan?" Gerda Dengler interjected somewhat impatiently.

"Only some privacy, dear. Close the door on your way out, will you?"

The woman held Del with what might have been a contemptuous glare, then left the room, closing the door behind her.

"You'll have to forgive my aide," Egan said. "She gets a little overly protective of me when it comes to strangers."

"She's just doing her job," Del said, putting as much matter-of-factness into it as she could muster.

"Yes, well, a little too well at times. I think she thinks she's here to save me from myself."

"Well, she'll make someone a great bodyguard someday." It was a condescending thing to say. But better than telling Egan that Gerda, Ms. Dengler, really needed to take the stick out of her ass.

"You've come at my request. Please, won't you sit down?"

Egan motioned her toward a leather office chair that looked well-worn but comfortable.

"That was my chair before I had the requirement of this wheeled contraption. It needs to be replaced, but I'm afraid I maintain a ridiculous sentimentality about it."

Del thought she understood. The chair reminded her of her father's recliner at home. He'd been gone for two years, but she was still reluctant to dispose of it. "No, it's great," she said, testing it for comfort. "I like it."

"So you've come to help us find Lissa?"

"I've come to hear what you have to say," Del said. "You're the grandfather, I understand?"

"Actually, I'm not the biological grandfather. Lissa's mother was my adoptive daughter."

"I see," Del said.

She took a moment to look around, consider her surroundings.

The office-study seemed more like an Old West museum. Besides stacks and stacks of books, every square inch of space was filled with Western memorabilia. There were hackamores and bridles hanging from pegs on the wall. In the corner, a saddle sat astride what might have once been an actual hitching post. A bone-handled six-shooter was slung in its leather holster across the saddle horn. Next to the hitching post was a hat stand with different styles of Western hats. There was a wagon wheel leaning against the wall. Above the bookshelf, a sign read: *Butterfield Stage*

Line. Another read: *Buffalo Bill's Wild West Show*. Wanted posters were tacked to the pine paneling. Indian artifacts—feather headdresses, arrow quivers, tomahawks, pottery, and the like. And there were yellowing, tintype photos—dozens of them, here and there—offering glimpses into the past, faces that were mostly stoic or just tired, reflecting the sobering, harsh realities of life in the Old West. They were lined precisely across a wooden shelf. Del noticed an empty, dust-free space on the shelf where it appeared a photo was missing. She didn't comment. Instead she inquired, "What is all this stuff?"

"It's inspiration, my dear."

"For what?"

"You don't know me, do you?" Egan gave her an impish little smile that cheered the space around them. His body may have been withered, but the man within was alive and well. His blue eyes twinkled when he spoke.

"Should I?" Del asked.

Egan rotated his chair to a nearby bookshelf, then rotated back, bringing a book with him to present its cover.

"*Showdown at Wade Gulch*," Del read aloud. "Wait! You're *that* Edgar Egan? You write Westerns."

"I am. And I do!" he said, his eyes flashing brightly, pleased with the secret he'd now revealed. "A few of my novels have even been made into movies, I'm proud to say."

"I'm sorry. I thought your name sounded familiar," Del said.

"Don't be sorry. It's refreshing, actually, to find someone who doesn't find the need to fawn over me."

"So, tell me about your granddaughter, Mr. Egan. I was told you are concerned about her."

Egan gave her a shrug. "Well, I don't know what to think, really. It's unlike Lissa to not call, stay in touch. On the other hand she's … well … she's an adventuresome young woman. Always taking off on one fanciful discovery mission or another."

"Does she live here with you?"

"Yes, one of the spare bedrooms is hers. But within the past year she's taken to living in what I call the bunkhouse. The guest quarters, you see. You must have seen it when you came in?"

"Yes, I did," Del said, repicturing the small adobe unit that sat off from the main house.

"A young friend of hers, Kendra Kozak, lives there with her. The girl comes from a rather troubled background. She and Lissa became fast friends."

"How long have they been gone?"

"Hmmm … a little over three weeks, I believe. Lissa said they were going to take a little road trip. A summer outing, if you will, before school starts. Classes actually started this week, without her. That's why I'm concerned. She would never miss school. She's a good student and never fails to check in with me when she has something going on. I heard from her every other day, until a week ago Thursday. Would have expected her back by Sunday. She doesn't answer her cell phone. Doesn't respond to my messages."

"The last time you spoke to her, did she give you any indication where she was, what she was doing?"

Egan shook his head sadly. "Only that things were going well, and that they were having fun."

"Hmmm," Del said, considering. "And what about the friend, Kendra? What do her parents have to say?"

"Not in the picture," Egan said. "They wouldn't even know she's gone."

"Well, pardon me, but I guess I have to ask then … you said your granddaughter is independent, adventurous … why do you feel reason to be concerned? Couldn't it be she's just off having fun with her friend, forgetting to call?"

Egan shook his head. "She's a very responsible young woman."

"What about a boyfriend?"

"No. No one significant. I think it's important that you understand something about my granddaughter, Ms. Shannon." Egan rotated in place and retrieved a framed photo from the desk behind him. Rotating back, he handed it to her. "As I told your Mr. Willingham, Lissa is a very motivated young woman. Always been driven to succeed. An incredible swimmer. Someone the other teens want to follow."

Del considered the photo. The girl in the photo was carrying a full backpack, a ponytail poking out from the back of a ball cap. "She's pretty. Where was this taken?"

"The Moab, I believe. Another one of her explorations. I think she had it in her head to find meteor samples that trip."

"And did she?"

Egan shook his head. "I don't know. It doesn't matter, really. It's the quest that's important to her."

Del couldn't seem to take her eyes off the girl in the photo. Bright and cheerful, fit and tanned. But something familiar about her. Something in the eyes, or maybe the cut of her mouth. Egan was offering the photo as evidence of the girl's wholesomeness. But Del saw it as further evidence of a girl—young woman—who was simply into having fun. She considered the photo a moment longer, then said, "Tell me about Lissa's parents? I understand they are both deceased."

Egan seemed to wither. His gleeful countenance dropped, and he sagged farther into the webbing of his wheelchair. "It's a long, depressing story," he said. "Her father was killed in Iraq. A Marine. An incredibly good man and good father to Lissa. She was eight at the time of his death. She was devastated. As were we all. Then, two years later, her mother was killed by a drunk driver in a violent car accident. That was on Lissa's eleventh birthday. My daughter had left work early in order to celebrate the occasion with her."

The story left Del feeling sad for the girl. Sad for herself. She understood the pain of loneliness, all too well. The pain of loss. And she also understood the need to fill the emptiness with cheap, sometimes gratuitous, thrills. Whether Lissa Rogers was missing or not, she was a *lost girl*, the way Del saw her. Someone searching—as she herself had searched—for something to fill the void. She said, "And, so, you've been caring for your granddaughter ever since?"

Egan nodded, staring into his cupped hands, a sad, strained look on his face. "Perhaps, not so well."

"And have the authorities been notified?"

"I made a report. But they're not inclined to believe there's anything to worry about at this point. I'm so hoping you will help us."

Del considered the man's plea. She felt sorrow for the elder Egan. And, while she could certainly identify with Lissa—the *lost girl*—her need for adventure, her need for thrills, she wasn't altogether convinced there was a reason to consider her missing.

Del said, "Mr. Egan, I must confess I don't see much in the way of foul play involved. I can't help feeling that Lissa and her friend will find their way home in a few days and all will be forgotten. I really don't know how I can help."

"Well," Egan said, clearing his throat, "I did so hope."

"I'm sorry," Del said, rising to offer her hand. "Perhaps we could give it a couple of days, and if you haven't heard from her still, you can give me a call."

Egan brought his sad eyes up to meet hers, but extended his hand to say goodbye. "Would you like Gerda to show you out?"

"I believe I can find my way," Del said. She turned to leave, then turned back to Egan. "I suppose there is one other question I could ask..."

"Yes?"

"You said your daughter... Lissa's mother... is your adoptive daughter... Is the biological mother in the picture anywhere?"

"I can see why you might ask," Egan said. "But it's not an issue. My daughter's real mother... Lissa's biological grandmother is also deceased. She died a few years ago."

"Then you did know her?"

"Yes," Egan said, casting his eyes downward for a moment, then bringing them to look at her again. "As so many young mothers do, who've given a child up for adoption, she came looking years ago for the daughter she felt she'd abandoned. She didn't want to interfere with her daughter's adoptive life, mind you, but was only seeking to be allowed to follow her daughter's progress from a distance. I must confess, I took pity on her. I met with her privately, shared photos and the like. Even my wife and daughter didn't know. It's been my guarded little secret all these years. I've never so much as uttered the woman's name aloud. But I suppose I can share with you. Her name was... Louise Lassiter."

The name struck Del like a sharp slap across the face. *Louise.*

She knew this woman. More than knew, really. Louise Lassiter had been Del's teen probation officer—her savior. She had taken Del on as her special project, mentoring her through her difficult teen years. And, for years, even after her probation had run out, she had continued to be a friend. Serving as something of a surrogate mother. Providing advice. Nurturing her to adulthood. Replacing the vacuum left by the absence of Del's own mother, Ella. Louise was—in Del's mind—single-handedly responsible for everything positive Del had become. It caused a wellspring of memories to

45

come rushing in. Louise in her flowered muumuu. Louise with the rings on every finger. Louise with the big laugh, and bigger handbag. Her straight-talking advice. Her timely catch phrases for every difficult situation. "*The thing about the devil, Del,*" Louise used to say, "*is the devil knows how to wait.*" Well, the devil had waited a long time to spring this news on her.

Louise was gone, it was true, having died several years past, after a long struggle with ovarian cancer. But her memory still burned hot in Del's heart.

"*Louise,*" Del said, unaware she had spoken the name aloud.

"What was that, my dear?" Egan was asking.

Del didn't respond immediately. She was still thinking of the woman who had meant so much to her. The news explained a lot. A lot that Del had always wondered about. Louise had never married. She never seemed to have many friends. She'd led a solitary life. But she had all but *adopted* Del as her own. Del, perhaps, doing as much to fill the hole in Louise's life as the other way around, it would seem now. Del felt a stab of regret for the woman who had given her so much, and a pang of sympathy for the kind old gentleman, Edgar Egan, who had taken time throughout the years to help ease Louise's pain and carry her secret honorably.

Del came back into the moment long enough to say, "Nothing...I was just thinking."

She turned to go, then paused again, her hand on the doorknob this time. Without looking back, she said, "I'll see what I can do to find Lissa."

That's all that was left spoken between them.

Del pushed out into the courtyard. And into a day that had suddenly turned overcast.

SIX

PAYTON RICKEY DIDN'T LIKE Terrebonne Key. Didn't like the solitude. Didn't like the quiet. Quiet was for slugs. Quiet was for grandpas in their rocking chairs. Quiet was for graveyards.

Payton wasn't ready for the graveyard.

He'd been hiding out on Terrebonne Key for seven months. And—to his way of thinking—it was time to get the fuck on down the road. There was just one thing holding him back: lack of money.

Just that, and being under the thumb of the island's matron—Ivess.

The way it had come to be was something of a fluke—both a godsend and a bitch of bad luck. There had been that family back in Sweethome, outside of Little Rock. It had started as a simple home invasion—knock once, push your way inside, terrorize the family members and take what you could find, leave them shaking in their house slippers. Only the fine-looking house he and Teddy had chosen turned out to be the home of a bank manager, Sweethome Bank and Trust, Main Street, USA.

The call, the ransom demand … it hadn't all gone the way they had figured. The teenage daughter had bitten Teddy on the ear, when Teddy had tried feeling her up. Teddy had slapped hell out of the girl, bringing the young boy and hellcat mother to her defense. All hell had broken loose. At that moment, Payton was on the phone trying to negotiate the deal. And when the bank manager—cooperating at the time—heard the cries of his loved ones in jeopardy, he panicked and alerted bank security, who called the cops. Payton had to pull Teddy off the teenage girl, and the two made a run for it. But not until after laying waste to all three of the family members, eliminating the possibility that anyone could later ID them.

And that would have very possibly been the end of it. But for the home security system and the surveillance camera that caught him, full face, on the way out the door. Teddy's face had not been identifiable, Payton dragging him backward out the door. And so it was Payton alone the Arkansas State Police issued a felony arrest warrant for.

They'd gone on the run—he and Teddy. And it had looked like they might have actually been able to put some distance between themselves and Sweethome, were it not for the Texas state trooper who pulled them over for a busted taillight. *A fucking taillight!* Well, they left the trooper at the side of the road next to his cruise, two bullets in his chest.

That became the deciding factor—head south of the border for a time, let things cool down.

They'd had three good months in Cancun—paradise, man—before U.S. marshals showed up. Payton would have been facing death or at very minimum hard time. And he would be serving that time right now, if it hadn't been for the plane crash.

On the way back across the Gulf of Mexico, the twin-engine Cessna carrying Payton, the pilot, and the two U.S. marshals went down in the Gulf near the mainland of Louisiana. Helicopters, Coast Guard cutters—they were all out there searching. Payton had seen their lights scanning the waters from where he bobbed among the wreckage, with the one surviving marshal. No sign of the aircraft or any of its human cargo was ever spotted. And no sign of Payton was ever found either. All members were presumed dead. Payton included. And later legally declared so by a judge.

Dead! Payton had seen to it that the surviving marshal had become so, in fact, by looping his belt around the man's neck, drawing it tight, and watching his limp, lifeless body slip quietly beneath the waves. The man had been near death anyway, Payton concluded.

Payton himself had washed up—waterlogged and with a broken leg—a morning later, onto the private beach at Terrebonne Key. Ivess had found him—her and the little Cajun—and nursed him back to health.

All that—from the plane crash to his blessed landfall on Terrebonne, to being declared dead and out of the eye of authorities? ... Godsend.

Having Ivess be the one to find him? ... *Bitch of Bad Luck.*

Now, he was here, bored to the brink of suicide and not thinking of himself so much in paradise anymore, but rather *hell.* Or more appropriately, *purgatory,* stuck between heaven and hell—Ivess and her ways on one side; the authorities and a prison term on the other.

But now ... *another godsend* ... the teens had shown up.

———

Payton took the path down to the bungalows. There were two of them, set down among the trees away from the main house. Guest quarters, the way Ivess considered them. Payton had taken residence in one—Ivess claiming "*she would have no man sleeping under her roof.*" Though it didn't keep her from having him between her legs from time to time. The other bungalow became reserved for Teddy, once he'd come to the island to join Payton. Now it served as the holding cell for the teens. At least until he got the money. Then … well, who knows what would happen then.

Payton went first to check on the teens, feeling antsy not having talked to Teddy in the more than three days since he'd left for Arizona. He arrived at the bungalow to find the big male cat, Java, secured by a long chain just outside the door to the girl's bungalow. The chain was just long enough for the cat to move about, having reach to the door exit as well as the one window, preventing the girls from making a break for it.

Leave it to the little Cajun—Payton thought. It allowed Leggett to go about his business while ensuring that the teens were damn well secured. *The man was resourceful.*

Payton thought of the teens now, inside. He would like to have a peek through the window, see what the two were up to. Maybe catch them entwined together, naked on the bed, giving each other comfort… *What he liked to imagine!* … But not only had the Cajun saw to it that the girls couldn't leave, he'd made sure to fix it so no one else could get inside. He was crafty that way, the little bastard. Payton gave the tiger a look; the tiger gave Payton a look back—a hungry gleam in its eye. Payton decided it could wait until another time. *Java!* The big male was unpredictable without Leggett around to control it.

Payton gave a last look at the bungalow, then turned away and headed back up the path—early afternoon, time for a drink. He stopped off at the cabana, which sat about halfway down the path between the main house and the bungalows. It was a thatch-roofed affair, with wicker stools snugged up to a fully stocked rectangular bar. There were party lights strung around the overhead and hung throughout the nearby trees. Reminiscent of some Jamaican island getaway. Ivess called the cabana her "common area." But Payton wasn't sure whether she meant a place for the common people, or just a place common to the rest of the facilities. Either way it didn't matter, he guessed. A bar—any bar—was safe haven as far as he was concerned. A place to be free of Ivess for a time.

Payton poured himself a drink from behind the bar and pulled up a stool on the other side, laying his cell phone on the bar next to him. He was still anxious to hear from Teddy, see if he'd made it to Arizona, see if he'd made contact with their mark. He was tired of waiting. Tired of anticipating. And wanting to call Teddy directly see how things were going. But, at the same time, he didn't want to interrupt Teddy's work in progress.

So, Payton sipped and waited.

From where Payton sat, he could see Ivess off through the palms, down there on the artificial beach she'd created. Sitting in one of two lounge chairs, afternoon drink in hand, facing off across the waters of the Gulf. *Peaceful. Fucking quiet.* A large red-and green beach umbrella flapped above her in the breeze. She was wearing her customary old fashioned, one-piece swim suit, a billowy wrap about her legs to hide the varicose veins. She had a scarf about her neck and Wayfarer sunglasses covering her eyes, a large floppy hat for additional shade. And on her feet, high heels. *High heels! On the beach, for God's sake!* Something Payton had trouble wrapping his mind around. *Pretentious bitch!*

Alonda was back on duty, Payton saw. The housekeeper. But currently attending to Ivess's needs, bussing the small table next to her and serving up madam's second mint julep of the day. The female tiger, Gigi—more peaceful and better trained—lay in the sand beside her chair, head high, nobly surveying the Gulf of Mexico and whatever it imagined lay beyond.

That was all good, for now, Payton thought. Ivess was occupied. Off his back.

Payton took another sip from his drink and checked his watch. It was going on three o'clock, that would make it—what?—almost one o'clock in Arizona? Was Teddy in Arizona? Had he made contact? How far away was Arizona anyway?

Shit!

Payton sipped his drink, growing more anxious by the second.

When his nerves could hold the strain no more, he picked up the cell phone, found Teddy's number, and clicked *Call.*

He waited ... waited ...

The phone rang once ... twice ...

Come on! Answer, damn it!

A hand suddenly clapped down on Payton's shoulder, giving him a start and causing him to slip partially off the stool. He flipped the cell phone shut and turned, expecting to see Ivess standing there.

It was Leggett.

"Jesus Christ! Don't you ever announce yourself!"

"Gar ici!" the Cajun said, his way of saying, *Look here!* "Ivess for to tell you she's waiting?"

"Now?" Payton said, throwing a quick look back toward the beach. Sure enough, Ivess had left her lounge chair.

Leggett shrugged. "The time be," Leggett said.

Jesus! Payton thought. *Second time this week?*

It was customary—Ivess's custom—that whenever she wanted him, she called. And it was routine—Payton's routine—that he would go to her. *Lovingly! Dutifully! Penitently,* for being such a bad man. It was payment, really. Favors for her allowing him to stay, hid-out, on Terrebonne Key.

God! he thought. *What a price to have to pay!*

But his staying here had served its purpose, he had to admit. While he wasn't exactly free, he was out of prison, out of the public eye, away from authorities. Going nose to nose, toe to toe, with Ivess—never the other way around—had bought him time at the very least. Time for his name in the world to die down, lose importance. Time for him to find a way around it all. Though, serving Ivess was maybe only slightly more appealing than rotting away in some jail cell, guarding his ass from other inmates.

But only slightly.

Payton nodded his understanding to Leggett.

And the little Cajun turned off up the path toward the bunga-lows, his assignment complete.

Payton knocked back the last of his drink, slid off the stool, and slowly made his way up the path toward the main house. All his hopes, so far today, had been tied up in Teddy calling with an update. But, now, duty called. And, his favorite hope of the moment was...

That Ivess could get off quickly.

———

She was already in position when Payton reached the bedroom—naked, face up on the bed. Like a corpse in a coffin, he thought. Her arms stiff at her side, a sleep mask over her eyes so as not to see him coming. *My God, she was strange*, Payton thought. He studied her lying there for a moment, her pasty white thighs, spreading torso, small pointy breasts. A triangle of gray-and-black pubic hair between her thighs. *Jesus, God!*

The female tiger, Gigi, lay on the floor at the foot of the bed, glaring at him. There were times he'd think … *I'd rather mount the cat than this hag of Terrebonne.* But, then, the cat could take his head off in one sure bite; Ivess only bit off little pieces at a time.

Payton told himself, *Suck it up! You'll be getting off the island soon!*

Payton took a deep breath, and said, "I'm here. Anything special you want this afternoon?"

"Don't get inventive," Ivess said, her superior tone. "Be quick. But be thorough. I have things to do."

Romantic.

Payton thought of Teddy, again. Of the money. Of everlasting freedom. He fixed his mind on those thoughts, trying not to think about what came next. Then, slowly … dutifully … he began to undress.

SEVEN

CLOUDS HAD FORMED IN the afternoon sky—a monsoon build-up that would soon bring wind and rain. Del had left the Egan hacienda and had driven directly to the cemetery where Louise was buried. The same cemetery where her own mother and father were both interred. Her head was filled with thoughts—thoughts of Edgar Egan, Louise Lassiter, of Lissa Rogers and her friend.

The news that Lissa was Louise's biological granddaughter had left her feeling down and awash in guilt. It had been months since she'd last visited the gravesite. And, now, looking down on the inscription on the stone—*Loving Friend, Loyal Servant*—Del couldn't help but feel that she'd somehow abandoned her former mentor, left her to deal with the tribulations of life alone. An irrational thought, she knew. Still ... *There's no mention of Hurting Mother.*

Del had thought she knew Louise. Yet in all the time they'd spent together, throughout all their mother-daughter-like talks, Louise had not once mentioned a daughter that she'd given up for adoption. Not once had she ever burdened Del with her pain—pain Del now understood she had carried deeply.

But that was Louise.

"*No good deed goes unpunished,*" Del remembered Louise once saying. "*When it comes to the devil, it's either pay him now or pay him later,*" Del said now aloud.

Had the devil returned to collect on Louise for all the kindness she'd given?

As if as a response from above, a male voice said, "If it makes you feel any better, I agree."

It was Randall's voice.

He had been standing behind her on the lawn, a Stetson hat in hand. One that Del had never seen him with before. She wasn't sure how long he'd been standing there, or how much he'd heard. But Randall had a way of reading her, seeing into her darkest corners, and recognizing her pain.

She said, "How did you know to find me here?"

"Edgar Egan called," he said. "First to further implore me to send you to look for his granddaughter. Then to say he was concerned about you, a name he revealed that seemed to come as a shock to you. This is where you come when you're upset … well … here or the shooting range … I took a shot and came here."

"He doesn't need to implore you any further, Randall. I've decided to take the assignment."

"Well, that's good, because I told Egan you would. He's sending over a retainer this afternoon."

Del nodded.

"Maybe someday you can fill me in on the details. But for now I'll just be happy knowing you're all right … Are you all right?"

"I will be."

Randall nodded, then turned his gaze to the gravestone. "I guess she was a pretty good old broad, wasn't she?"

"I wish you had met her," Del said. "You would have liked her."

Randall nodded. "Say, you like my new hat?"

"I don't know, let me see it on?"

Randall donned the Stetson, squaring it away on his head.

"Tip it down over one eye."

Randall tipped the brim.

"Yeah ... some guys can't wear hats, but I think you pull it off."

"Really?"

"Yeah."

Randall gave her a smile.

Del understood that Randall was simply trying to lighten her mood with small talk. But now her gaze went back to Louise's grave, her mind on Lissa Rogers and her friend.

"You have any plans?" Randall asked.

"Not really. I'll do some checking. Hope that something comes up."

Randall said nothing more. He studied her for a moment longer. Then said, "Well ... Let me know if you need anything." He tipped his hat a little lower over his eye and moved off down the hill.

Del remained over the grave, a swell of regret filling her heart. A pre-storm gust of wind lifted her hair from her forehead. "If your granddaughter is missing, Louise, I'll find her," Del said. "I promise!"

———

It took Payton close to forty minutes on top of Ivess to finally get her over the top. She finished with a slight gasp—nothing more—then pushed Payton off, to stand and climb back into her gown that had been draped across the nightstand at the ready. "I'll let you know when I feel like it again," she said, leaving Payton alone to dress and leave her house.

Payton didn't have to be told twice. He dressed quickly and went out through the kitchen, through the backyard to the path leading back down to the cabana. He needed a drink—first!—then he needed to call Teddy, maybe scream into the phone, "*Get me the hell out of here!*"

At the cabana, behind the bar, Payton poured himself a stiff shot of bourbon, banged it back hard, then refilled his glass and took it around to find a stool to just sit and sip for a time—wanting the booze to burn all recent images of naked Ivess from his brain.

The witch of Terrebonne—as Payton had come to think of her.

Ivess had once been a Vassar girl, Payton had learned. She'd been raised in relative wealth, the granddaughter of the billionaire fashion mogul Remy DeMarco. By all rights—Payton had initially believed—Ivess should have been wealthy. Money tucked into every nook and cranny of the house, dripping from her fingers like ice cream from a cone on the Forth of July.

But that was not the case.

Ivess—he'd discovered—had been the middle granddaughter of three. Inwardly directed. More interested in nature and spiritual solitude, the utopian way of life, than in following the family into the fashion and high-finance world, as her two sisters apparently had. Old man DeMarco—*Granddad*, as Ivess referred to him—had tried his best to cultivate Ivess's interest in the family empire. Something that came natural to her two siblings. He'd fostered her through the finest schools, assured her of a brilliant future, brought her into his plush penthouse offices in the Manhattan Fashion District.

But—middle child and ever the oddball that she was—Ivess had not taken the injection of high-rolling acumen or come to embrace societal parlance. She wanted nothing to do with it.

So, upon Granddad DeMarco's death, the bulk of the fortune had gone to the other two sisters—heirs willing to continue the

DeMarco name. But, still being at least loyal to the middle, awkward granddaughter, Granddad had willed Terrebonne Key to Ivess. *Her pleasure.* It had been an island acquired as one of hundreds of speculative land holdings of the DeMarco estate—a place remote from the societal doctrine that Ivess scorned, a place replete with coastal wildlife. A place with a history.

And what about money? What about bills?

Well, as Payton had learned during one of the sessions where he was required to sit and share cocktails at sunset—beloved Granddad had established a trust fund with a bank in Houma to manage the needs of Ivess and Terrebonne Key. Give her the lifestyle she so desired, without putting money directly into her hands.

With trust approval, Ivess remodeled the then-rundown plantation-style mansion—built by the island's previous owner—and made it well and new. She'd brought in exotic birds and rare animals. Employed a minimal house staff of two, to see to her needs. Brought on Leggett—the cat whisperer—to manage and train her beloved white tigers. And slipped into the reclusive life she'd so long desired. Rich by all accounts, eccentric without question—but without money ever crossing her palm, except for a pittance of petty cash, used to tip delivery men and such, which she kept in a jar in one of the kitchen cabinets. The occasional boat would arrive with supplies, or something new that the trust may have allowed her to order. All that was required of Ivess DeMarco was a simple, monthly notarized signature on the account ledger, arranged for by an agent of the Houma Banking and Trust Company.

Yes, many were the nights when Payton would lie awake in his bungalow and dream of strangling the bitch to death. But without Ivess there to sign the invoices, life on Terrebonne Key could grind to a halt. The food would get eaten up. The supplies would dwindle.

And the island and its buildings would, eventually, be taken over by Mother Nature.

Payton had also considered, many times, just leaving the island, taking off. He'd actually threatened such. Take the boat and be gone, him and Teddy. Only, those times, Ivess would remind him that he owed his life to her and … well, also … one call to authorities to inform them that a certain believed-dead fugitive was very much alive and well … well, then, Payton would be on his way back to Sweethome to face a very clannish Arkansas jury. He also considered that life on the run without money in his pocket would be certain to lead to his demise. All it took—as he had learned—was a broken taillight or such, and he'd be facing hard time again.

And, so, feeling trapped, he had come to understand that his choices were either to remain his entire life on the island as Ivess's puppet—*her boy*—or scheme a way to score enough money to get him and Teddy far enough away that neither Ivess's threats nor the threat of the law itself could affect him. Preferably some South American country. Brazil sounded nice.

It was something that he and Teddy had discussed many times. But not until the teens showed up had they actually conceived a good way to accomplish it. Now, Teddy was in Arizona, looking to make the dream a reality. And all Payton needed to worry about was that Teddy didn't somehow fuck it up.

Payton knocked back another strong shot of whiskey, then dialed Teddy's number.

This time his brother came on the line.

"Where the fuck are you!" Payton said, not giving Teddy a chance to say hello.

"Nice greeting, brother," Teddy said.

"You should have called me! I'm going crazy here! The teenage girls … Ivess … Where are you? Did you get the money yet?"

"Jesus, Payton! Ease up! We're looking good. We got into Arizona last night. Found the one girl's rich grandfather. Scouted a location for the ransom delivery. Now all we have to do is make the call."

"We? Who is *we*?"

"Filo ... I told you about him. I needed someone to help drive. You know I don't own a car! I needed transportation, someone to help with the driving."

Filo. Payton had to think. *Oh, yeah!* A guy Teddy knew from Houma. Met him at the strip club. He said, "I don't like you bringing someone else into it."

"Filo's cool. We drove his pickup out. He even fronted a few bucks for gas. I told him he'd get it back when we got the money."

"You're not cutting him in as a partner. Let's get that straight!"

"Naw, give him a few bucks for whiskey, that's all. He'll be happy."

Filo, Payton thought again, feeling the concern rise in him.

But, then, the knowledge that things were moving along overrode his concerns and he decided to let it go. "You know what to ask for?"

"Fifty thousand ... enough to make our move, but not so much that the mark can't come up with it without getting authorities involved ... just like we planned."

"All right," Payton said, taking another sip of whiskey and feeling a little better now.

"This is gonna work out fine, brother," Teddy said. "Then me and you will be on our way. All those little brown-skinned girls with their Brazilian bikini waxes ... Rio de Janeiro—look out!"

There was a long pause.

"Anything else?" Teddy finally asked.

"No ..." Payton said, then recanted. "Yeah!"

"What?"

"Just make sure you come straight back with the money. No stopping off at any of the strip clubs. You'll have it all spent before you get here, and I want—the fuck!—off this island."

"No problem . . . Hey! . . . How are our little girls doing?"

"Don't worry about them," Payton said. "Just get back here with the money."

"Just save the redhead one for me," Teddy said.

Payton ended the call.

———

Teddy folded his flip-phone closed, but held onto it, anticipating his next move. He and Filo had found what he thought to be an ideal location—an abandoned mining camp on the northern slopes of the Catalina Mountains, high above the town of Oracle. The name of the camp—according to a map Teddy picked up in a convenience store—was *Peppermint*. Dumb-ass name for a camp, much less the mine that gave the camp its name—but a good location. It was isolated and quiet. And from the ridge he could see down onto Oracle Junction and a good portion of Oro Valley, monitor all roads leading into and out of the mountains.

It was a good plan. And Teddy had seen the old man's house . . . *Luck be a lady!* . . . He appeared to have money.

Teddy turned his attention now to his accomplice, Filo, sitting down near the stream that ran parallel to the gravel road. The man seemed oblivious to what was about to go down. Which caused Teddy to consider that maybe his brother's concerns were valid. Filo was a drunk. And not all that bright . . . But maybe that was good, he reasoned now. And he came cheap. He hadn't offered him much to get them there. And all that was required of the old sot was for him to keep his mouth shut afterward.

So ... it was time.

Teddy put his thoughts of Filo aside now ... rehearsed in his head for a moment what he was going to say ... then flipped open his phone and dialed the grandfather's number.

EIGHT

DEL WASN'T SURE WHERE to start. There was little to go on and no signs that anything tragic had even happened. She was still holding out hope that Lissa Rogers and her friend would simply show up, filled with the excitement from their summer adventure, innocent of the fact that people were becoming concerned. It very often turned out to be that simple.

But, then, sometimes it didn't.

Del said her goodbyes to Louise, paid homage to her parents' graves, and made her way across the lawn to the road where her Wrangler was parked. She was just slipping behind the wheel when her phone rang.

It was Edgar Egan, his voice plaintive on the verge of hysteria. "My granddaughter! She's in trouble!" he said.

"Slow down, Mr. Egan. What kind of trouble?"

"She's been kidnapped. I just got a call."

Del thought of Louise again. "What did the caller say?"

"They said they wanted fifty thousand dollars. They said they'd give me one hour to put it together, and they would call back with instructions. They said, 'No police' or they will kill the girls ... he said 'the girls' ... they have both of them."

"Have you called authorities?"

"No! They said 'no police,'" Egan said again.

"All right! Just hang on. I'm on my way."

Del pocketed her phone and slid behind the wheel. In minutes she was on Oracle Road again, heading back to the Egan residence.

She reached the hacienda-style home within twenty minutes. It was going on three p.m. The clouds, which had been building since noon, had now turned dark and ominous, lending to the mood of the moment. She had barely gotten the Wrangler parked in the turnaround in front when Gerda came hurriedly out through the portico to meet her.

"Come quickly! Quickly! They're on the phone again!"

The kidnappers weren't wasting any time. Gerda led Del hurriedly back through the courtyard and down the covered veranda to the study.

Edgar Egan was on the phone when they arrived, his face pale, and there were deep lines of concern creasing his brow. He was speaking into the receiver in a high-pitched voice, sounding on the verge of hysteria. "Don't hurt her! Please! Please! Whatever you do! Don't hurt her!"

Egan spotted Del and waved her over. Gerda remained in the doorway, a hand to her mouth in obvious distress.

"Who is it? What do they want?" Del inquired.

Egan was back to concentrating on the caller. "I understand! Yes! Completely! I'll do whatever you say! Fifty thousand ... I have it ... No police, like you said."

"Ask to speak to your granddaughter," Del advised.

"Is my granddaughter with you? Can I speak to her?"

Egan listened into the phone. The pained expression on his face told Del that there would be no cooperation. *Their way or the highway.*

Egan was shaking his head defiantly now. "No. I'm sorry. That's not possible. I'm confined to a wheelchair. I can't bring the money to you." He listened some more. "Yes ... I understand, but ... I do have a young woman here," he said, glancing up at Del, hope replacing the defeated look in his eyes.

Del nodded. "Find out where and how."

"The woman can bring the money to you. Please just tell me where, when? ... Yes! ... Yes! ... Hold on! ..." Egan extended the phone to Del. "He wants to talk to you."

The turn of events had come out of the blue—a sudden, jarring confirmation that Lissa and her friend were being held against their will and that their lives were in jeopardy. Del took the phone from Egan and placed it to her ear. "You have the girls?"

"Who's this?" a male voice said into the phone.

"A friend of the family."

"You're not a cop?"

"No," Del said honestly.

"What kind of car do you drive?"

"A Jeep Wrangler. Red with a black canvas top."

"All right. Give me your cell number. Take the money and drive to the town of Oracle. You know where that is?"

"Yes," Del said, picturing just north of where she was now and around the back side of the mountain range.

"Good. At Oracle, take the road leading up the backside of the mountain toward Mount Lemon. No weapons and nothing cute."

Del related her cell number to the man on the phone, then asked, "How will I know you've really got the girl?"

"I'll have proof when you get here."

"And where is that, exactly?"

"Don't worry about it. Just start driving. You'll hear from me again."

The caller hung up.

Del handed the phone back to Egan.

He listened into the receiver for a moment, and hearing the dial tone, hung up. "They've got Lissa. They'll hurt her if we don't give them the money."

"We should get the authorities involved," Del said.

"No! No cops!" Egan pleaded. "The caller said they would kill her if we didn't do exactly as we are told! I don't care about the money. Just give it to them and bring her back."

"These men are desperate. And desperate men are dangerous."

"The man said to come alone," Egan said, almost inconsolable now. "I kept telling myself she's just somewhere with friends, every-thing would be fine, everything would somehow be..." he stopped, not knowing how to finish the thought.

Her doubts about there being any cause for concern were no longer an issue. And, for the first time since meeting with Egan, Del was glad she had come. The old man, the writer of Western sagas, was on the verge of a meltdown. Things were moving fast. Too fast. Whether the kidnappers had planned to take the girls, or whether Lissa and her friend had haplessly stumbled into trouble, was un-clear. Either way, the bad guys were making the most of it. And they had allowed no time to think, no time to prepare—only time to comply. "All right," she said to Egan. "Do you have that kind of cash available?"

"Yes, I have a safe. I was able to put it together. Gerda will pre-pare it for you. Just promise me you'll do as they say and bring my granddaughter home unharmed."

"I'll do all I can."

Del turned to Gerda, who had remained in the doorway. She was studying Del, now, perhaps gauging her fitness for duty. But, then, satisfied, or simply resigned, she turned out the doorway to do Egan's bidding.

"I have to tell you, Mr. Egan. The authorities should be brought in on this. But you're the client, and I'll comply with your wishes."

"I trust you. I do. Just bring her back. Please!"

Del gave a reluctant nod and said her goodbyes.

At the Wrangler, at the front of the house, Gerda met up with her, carrying a small athletic bag stuffed with cash.

"It's all there?" Del asked.

"As Mr. Egan wishes," Gerda said.

Del took the bag and tossed it onto the passenger seat inside the Wrangler. She felt between the seats and found her nine-millimeter Baby Eagle, checked the magazine, and tucked it into her boot beneath the leg of her jeans.

Gerda was watching, giving her a somewhat disapproving look, as if believing such work was better left to a man. Then she turned away and disappeared back through the arched portico.

Del thought of Louise again. "I'll do my best," she said. And with a deep breath, slid behind the wheel and headed out.

———

She drove north on Oracle Highway as the caller had instructed. Overhead, dark clouds roiled and churned. The air had turned startlingly cool—what the weather people called a *sinking air mass*. At the forefront of the storm would be gusting winds, blowing dust. Behind it torrential downpours. Not uncommon in the desert during the late-summer monsoon season. It was something to stay ahead of if she could, something to pray would not complicate the money drop. But with the caller running the show, and Edgar Egan insisting that she go it alone, there was no choice. Del kept a steady pace and tried not to think too hard about Lissa and her friend

———

In Oracle, she found the turnoff onto the road leading up the back side of Mount Lemon—a rutted gravel road, marked for four-wheel-drive vehicles only. Eyes on the road, thoughts on what was to come, Del called Randall. "The girls are being held for ransom."

"Ah, Christ!" Randall said. "I really didn't see that coming. What do they want?"

"What they always want. Money and no cops. I'm on my way now."

"You're not going alone?"

It was a rhetorical question, Del knew. Randall knew her well enough to know she wouldn't be waiting around for someone else to handle it. And she wasn't going to make excuses. These things you had to act on, not discuss. Still, the situation had *disaster* written all over it. She understood that, and so did Randall. He was simply expressing his concern.

"I'm in Oracle," she said. "I'm not sure where they're leading me."

"What can I do?" Randall asked.

"You can contact the Pinal County sheriff deputies and have them put a team together at Oracle Junction. Tell them, no choppers, the caller has threatened to kill Lissa Rogers and her friend if he sees any sign of cops. I'm afraid they'll kill the whole deal. This may be the only chance we have to bring these girls home. I don't want to screw it up."

"You think they're serious?"

"Dead serious. Just tell them I'll call back when I find out where I'm supposed to make the drop."

"You should wait for authorities."

"There's no time, Randall. Have you seen the skies?"

There was a momentary pause. Del imagined Randall crossing to the window to look out.

"It's cloudy overhead," he said. "I can't see beyond the buildings."

"Well, there's no sun here, and the clouds are … Oh, hell!" Del said, suddenly, catching a glimpse in her rearview mirror.

"What? What is it?" Randall's anxious tone mirrored her own.

Del swerved her Wrangler off onto the shoulder of the road and stepped out of the vehicle. The skies over Oro Valley had gone from gray to pitch-black. A massive dust storm, a *haboob,* as they were called, had formed to the west and had begun to march east, churning the desert floor into a giant wall of sand and debris. Flashes of heat lightning lit the inner core of the clouds, giving warning that a violent monsoon was building behind the dust front.

"It doesn't look good," she said into the phone. "I don't think I've ever seen a storm like this."

"Then turn your sweet ass around and get out of there, fast!"

"It's too late, Randall. The ransom is going down."

"They'll wait for the money!" Randall said.

Del was still studying the storm. The front had already grown to a whopping twenty miles wide, she estimated. And had roiled to a height of some eight to ten thousand feet, judging by the surrounding mountains. It had already engulfed the towns of Red Rock and Marana, and, seeming to hunger for more, now had its sights set on the higher, northwestern slopes of the Catalinas. Right where Del was headed.

Del considered Randall's advice.

She had no living relatives of her own that she knew of. And, since Louise had been like a mother to her, the daughter Louise had given up for adoption was like a sister she'd never known.

That made Lissa something of a niece to her. *Aunt Del,* she thought now, liking the sound of it. She had to go through with it. Del said, "If Lissa is with the caller, she could be in the way of the storm, too, Randall. I can't abandon her."

"Del! Listen to me—"

"Sorry, boss," Del said. And ended the call.

She had no more than closed her phone when it rang again. The caller ID was blocked. This would be the caller calling back, she believed. "I'm here!" she said, answering quickly, before it had time to ring again.

"Why did you stop?"

The caller could see her, Del realized. He was looking at her this very moment.

It caused her skin to crawl—the thought of invisible eyes running over her. *Touching her,* the way it seemed.

"There's a storm coming," she said.

"You afraid of getting wet?"

"It's a dust storm. A bad one. It could be dangerous."

"Do you want the girl alive or not?"

"Yes! Is she there with you?"

"Just do as I say and drive."

Del climbed back behind the wheel and pulled out onto the roadway once again.

"All right," she said. "I'm coming."

"Good."

"There was a long pause, and then the man said, "You're pretty. I hadn't expected that."

There it was. Something she had expected.

"Where do you want me to go?" she said, ignoring the caller's attempt at foreplay.

"All business? All right, it can wait! Keep going until you get to the rock that looks like a bird sitting on a nest. About a half-mile farther."

"Pigeon Rock?"

"If that's what it's called. You'll come to a service road on the left. Take it."

"You're leading me to Peppermint."

"You know it?"

"I've been there a couple of times."

"Good. Then take your cell phone and toss it out the window."

"But…"

"Let me see you do it! I'll be watching you all the way. One hint of law enforcement—anyone!—game over. There will be no second chance. The girls will die."

It was a clever plan, Del had to admit. She knew Peppermint was an old abandoned mining camp, where she and her teenage pals, Angel Padilla and Jimmy Samone, often went to escape the world, drink, and hang out. It was a real-life ghost town, set against the side of the cliff—elevated and remote. Reluctantly, she held the cell phone out the window, gave the caller a chance to see it, then chucked it off the side of the road.

In the valley behind her, the massive storm was continuing her way. Sheriff's deputies would be reconnoitering in a parking lot somewhere near Oracle Junction, getting suited up and waiting for her call. But soon the storm would engulf them, making it impossible for them to respond, impossible for helicopters to take to the air. And Del now realized the very real possibility that the kidnappers were actually counting on the fairly predictable monsoons for help. *Could they have envisioned a storm of this magnitude?*

The old ad slogan, *You've come a long way, baby!* suddenly came to mind. Del hoped she'd come far enough. She found the service road leading up into the canyon, took it as she'd been instructed, and tried to remain calm.

She was in this all alone.

———

Teddy was able to follow the woman's progress through high-powered binoculars, watching her all the way from where she first appeared on Mount Lemon Road, to the turnoff at Pigeon Rock, and on into the hills, through snakes and turns, heading his way. She was alone. *Good.* The coast looked clear behind her. And she had ditched her cell phone as he'd instructed. Playing along nicely. Even the weather—as the weatherman had predicted—was cooperating. It was all coming together as planned.

Teddy scanned his binoculars west, checking on the storm. He could see into the valley below, but only so far—his full view blocked by a bluff that projected into his field of vision. All he could determine was that there were some pretty nasty-looking clouds moving in. Still, he knew it was coming. The day had turned freakishly cool and quiet, and the wind had picked up considerably.

That's good, he thought. Besides, there was no turning back now. He'd broken communications with the woman—broken her communications with the world. With a little luck, the woman would be here before the storm. He would collect the money and ... well ... who knows ... the woman in the Wrangler wasn't bad-looking, not bad-looking at all ... maybe get something more on the side.

Teddy watched the Wrangler, still progressing, until it entered the tree line, a quarter-mile or so below the camp. Then he lowered the binoculars.

Now, he placed a call to Payton on Terrebonne Key. "The gravy train is on its way!" he said when Payton answered.

"Good! Another reminder! Make sure you don't spend it all on whores before you get back here with it! Remember that's our ticket off this fucking island."

"Come on, Payton! What do you think?"

"I think you can't keep it in your pants long enough to get a single, simple job done. But okay, enough of that. Filo's there with you?"

Teddy turned his gaze down the hillside to where his accomplice was sitting on a large round rock, plunking pebbles into the creek that followed the draw. The man reminded Teddy of the actor Steve Buscemi—bug-eyed and wiry, anemically pale. A shrimper who lived in a house trailer off the Little Caillou Bayou. A drunkard who had trouble getting work and even more trouble keeping it once he found it. "He's sitting on a rock," Teddy said.

"Somehow, that doesn't make me feel better," Payton said.

Teddy reminded himself that perhaps Payton was right. It would be wise to keep an eye on Filo. Especially after this was all over. The man could let his mouth run away with him—especially when he was in the bag. He said into the phone, "I'll call you when I've got the money."

Teddy ended the call.

"Time to get ready," Teddy said, calling down the hillside to Filo.

Filo plunked a last stone into the water, then clambered down off the rock.

Teddy came down off the hillside, stepping into the rutted roadway that ran alongside the gulch.

Filo came up from the creek to meet him.

"Why don't you move your pickup over behind the rocks and hide yourself? Our visitor will be here soon."

Filo said nothing but went off as instructed.

Teddy watched him go, shaking his head. If his instincts were right, he considered now, he would have to do something about Filo...

Once this job was done.

NINE

THE ABANDONED MINING CAMP of Peppermint sat in a gap between two hillsides. A rocky creek bed ran the length of the gap, paralleled by the gravel road that had brought Del there. The camp—a ghost of its former self—stretched up the hillside. Ramshackle wooden structures were set into the rocks. There were other half-structures of adobe, mud and stone, which had been reduced to crumbling ruins by wind and rain and time. Hand-chiseled recesses in the rock formed steps that led up the steep incline to a boarded-up hole in the cliff face—the mine itself. Above the entrance to the mine was a faded sign: *Peppermint Mining Company*. Rusted mining implements were scattered about.

Del pulled the Wrangler to a stop and killed the engine.

She had arrived ahead of the storm, but the skies in the canyon behind her roiled with dark and thunderous activity. The camp lay eerily quiet—no one to be seen—a foreboding stillness to the air. Del studied the landscape for a moment, then opened the door. The wind had picked up, ruffling Del's hair as she stepped out into the open doorway of her Wrangler. Looking back across the canvas top, she scanned the rocks and buildings for movement. She saw no one but could feel eyes upon her—watching, waiting.

"I'm here!" she called into the wind, which was gathering force by the minute. "Are you there?"

A sudden gust dislodged a tumbleweed from beneath one of cantilevered structures and sent it bounding off down into the creek bed, as if in a hurry to remove itself from danger.

The camp lay quiet, but for the hush of the wind.

"Show yourself!" she called.

Again, there was no reply.

"I came alone as you asked!"

Nothing moved.

Del felt suddenly vulnerable, naked to the eyes that she knew were on her. Normally, she would have carried her Baby Eagle, her nine-millimeter handgun, tucked into her waistband at the small of her back, beneath the denim shirt. But the caller had said 'no weapons,' so she'd concealed the gun in her boot, beneath her pant leg. Now she wished it was closer at hand.

The storm front was reaching the canyon.

"There's a bad storm headed this way!" Del called into the hush of wind. "We need to finish this quickly!"

Nothing.

Del reached inside the Wrangler and withdrew the canvas athletic bag, lifted it in view. "I have the money!" she said.

"It's all there?" a voice finally said. It came from somewhere on the hillside above her.

"Just as you asked!"

Some forty feet away, up the hill, a man stepped out from one of the buildings onto a small porch. He was tall, muscular. Wore a white, short-sleeved dress shirt, casual slacks. His hair was blond, short on the sides, spiked on top. He had a smooth face, light-complected. But he carried in his demeanor a certain dull, dark formidability that made him seem dangerous at first glance, possibly quick-tempered. He appeared to be holding a gun of some type alongside his right leg. "You're alone?" he asked.

Del nodded.

"All right, then. Step out where I can see you."

The wind was beginning to blow harder, billowing her shirt and whipping her hair, first one way across her forehead, then the other. "Not until I see the girl!" she said.

"You want to do it the hard way?"

"The straight-up way. The money for the girl. That's the deal."

"Seems to me the deal's whatever I want it to be."

"Not as long as I have the money," Del said.

"But as long as I have the girl," he countered.

"What about Kendra Kozak, the other girl?"

"They both send their love," the man said, his voice dripping with sarcasm. "Now step away from the vehicle and let me see your hands."

"Produce the girls!" Del said, stubbornly.

The man gave a weary glance away, as if tired of this game they were playing—*I'll show you mine if you show me yours*—then he brought his eyes back to her, narrowed and full of menace. "Here's how it will work," he said. "You do exactly as I say, without discussion. We get the money. And as soon as we're clear of the canyon, I'll make a call to my partner, who is elsewhere, and the girls—both girls!—will be released unharmed. Got it!"

The man kept referring to *we*, Del noticed. And to a partner elsewhere. From that, she could infer that there were a minimum of two men involved, possibly more. So far, she'd only seen this one. Where was the other?

She said, "That wasn't the deal!"

She was stalling for time—that's all—time to think, time to consider options. Sooner or later she would have to do as he said. And that would involve stepping out from behind the relative safety of her vehicle, placing herself in the open where she was far more vulnerable.

"The deal has changed," the man said.

"Then we are done!"

Del tossed the money bag back onto the front seat of the Jeep, making a show of it. Then started to slip back behind the wheel.

"Leave and you'll never see the girls again," he said, calling to her over the rising wind.

Del stepped back out to face the man again. "How do I even know you have them?"

The man changed hands with the weapon and withdrew something from his shirt pocket—a card of some sort. He sailed it her direction. It caught the wind and ricocheted off the hood of her Jeep. She batted it to the ground, then stooped to pick it up. It was Lissa Rogers' driver's license.

Del turned back to the man on the hillside. "It proves nothing!"

"It proves enough. Now, I've given you something, you give me something. Step out into the open where I can see you."

"Not on your life," Del said.

"Then on yours!" his reply.

Del felt a sharp prod at the small of her back and knew it for what it was—the point of a knife blade. A second man—one more piece of *we*—had appeared behind her, unheard, in the whistle of wind through her ears.

"Keep your face forward," the man at her back said, his voice crusty, a smoker's rasp. His face was unshaven and bristly against the back of her neck. His hands were rough—a workman's hands—and he smelled of fish. He prodded her a little harder with the point of the knife. "Now do as he says."

Del turned her eyes up to the man on the hill once more and reluctantly stepped away from the safety of her Wrangler and out into the open.

"What now?" Del said, directing her question to the man on the hill.

"Lift your shirt."

Here we go, Del thought. She'd been in dangerous situations like this before, and it always came down to this … *Lift your shirt … drop your pants … while we're here, sweetheart, why don't you and I …* If she were a man standing there, she knew, they would have already gotten down to business. Maybe he'd have killed her right off. Or maybe he would have just taken the money and vehicle and left her stranded. There would have been no small talk. No sexual innuendos. But she was a woman, wasn't she? And this job, this dangerous way of life, it was one she had chosen.

So deal with it! she told herself.

Hesitantly, Del lifted her shirttail with one hand, revealing first a taut bare midriff, then the lower swell of her breasts.

"Higher," the man on the porch said.

It occurred to Del to make a move for her weapon, the Baby Eagle strapped to her ankle. But she had the sense that the little man, off behind her, could be agile and quick with the knife. He would be upon her before she even got her pant leg up. And the man on the hillside had his gun in hand. She wouldn't stand a chance. All that it would accomplish would be to reveal that she had a weapon, and further jeopardize the lives of Lissa and Kendra. For now, all she had in her favor was false bravado and stubborn defiance. She dropped her shirttail. "That's all you get! Now, where's the girl?"

The wind had continued to pick up, coming in gusts that carried bits of sand and grit that stung her face and flapped the tail of her denim shirt.

The man stepped down off the porch and began making his way down the hillside toward her. She could see, now, that the gun in his hand was a Smith & Wesson .38-caliber revolver. She wondered if he knew how to use it. It was a question to ponder, but not one to test. The man reached the bottom of the hill, bounding off the slope with surprising agility for his size. He approached to within arm's length of her. Up close now, Del could see a small teardrop-shaped scar in the soft flesh beneath one eye. His lips were thin, like a razor's edge. His revolver was pointed directly at her midsection.

Del thought of her cell phone now, lying on the roadside somewhere down the canyon. And thought of Randall. If Randall had tried to call and had gotten no response, would he be on the phone with the Maricopa County Sheriff, sending them on their way to look for her? Could they find her? Could they get here in time? Or, down there in the valley, had the storm already begun raging too hard for them to respond? Whatever the case, she knew she couldn't count on anyone or anything. She was in this alone. Something she had stubbornly insisted upon, and now regretted. She had no planned moves. No secret weapon. No ace in the hole. All she could do was let things play out, search for a window of opportunity, and take it. Del put as much steel into her backbone as she could muster, showed him the defiant set of her chin. "So what now?" she said, all but shouting over the coursing wind. "We gonna dance?"

The man reached out and used one thick finger to part the lapel of her shirt, lay hungry eyes on the soft flesh beneath. "I wasn't thinking about dancing," he said.

Del pushed the hand away. "There's no time for games. We need to get this done and get out of here! That storm is bad. It's coming this way!"

"I'm not worried about the storm," he said.

"You should be. There's a monstrous cloud of dust. Then will come the rain. This entire canyon could flood."

Still near her Wrangler, where he had confronted her with the knife, the little man said, "I think the woman is right. We should just take the money and go, Teddy!"

Teddy! Del thought. The big man with the gun, his name was *Teddy*—a name to remember.

Del ventured a look in the little man's direction. He was looking off down the canyon, where the clouds were sparking off flashes of lightning, gathering in intensity. When he turned back, she could see the worry in his thin, drawn face.

"You go on, little buddy!" Teddy said. "I'll catch up to you at the motel."

From out of town, Del thought. *Something else to remember.*

"I think we should just go! Leave her! We've got the money."

"Filo, Filo, Filo," he said, as if to say, *Tsk, tsk, tsk.* "And have me miss the best part? You go on. And don't worry. You'll get what's coming to you."

So, the second man's name was *Filo.*

It suddenly occurred to Del that she was likely dealing with one pro and one amateur. The little man, Filo, was uncomfortable. The one with the gun, Teddy, was way too comfortable. He'd done this kind of thing before.

"It's looking real bad," Filo said.

"Get the hell out of here! Go!" Teddy said, raising his hand in a mocking gesture, as if to strike Filo, though the man was several yards away.

Filo hesitated for only a moment, studying the bigger man carefully. Then, without further protest, he turned down off into the gulch and disappeared behind a ridge of rocks. Moments later, the sound of an engine could be heard starting up, and a dark blue, older model pickup emerged from hiding and headed out of the camp.

She was hoping to catch a glimpse of the license plate, but now Teddy had her chin between two fingers and was turning her gaze toward him. The pickup drove away without identification. She was with Teddy, alone now.

"That's your bus!" she said. "You missed it!"

"There's still the Wrangler!"

He had confirmed what she'd come to realize. That the man had never really had any intension of letting her leave the camp alive. He would rape her, kill her, and stuff her body down the Peppermint mineshaft. Or simply leave it lying in the road. And consistent with that as his motive, Teddy's eyes did a slow slide down the length of her. A guttural sound emitted from his throat. His tongue snaked out to wet his lips. The wind continued to blow.

"I think you should just take my Jeep, the money, and, go," Del said. "Just like your friend suggested. The storm is on its way."

The man continued to hunger over her. "There's time," he said, his voice low now, only a whisper beneath the wind.

"You don't plan on letting me leave here, do you?"

Without warning, Teddy's free hand shot out to grab the bodice of her shirt and tear it away. Buttons popped, fabric ripped, one bare breast fell free. Now he grabbed her in a forward headlock, buried his face in the opening of her shirt, and bit down hard on one breast.

Pain tore through her.

Now, his mouth was seeking new flesh.

The muzzle of the gun still pressed into her ribcage. Del struggled against the arm holding her. She twisted, kicked, bucked against him. But the man was strong, easily as powerful as she'd imagined.

"Don't fight it! You shouldn't have come alone is all," he said, making his unwanted advances her fault.

Del continued to struggle.

The wind was buffeting hard against them now, the storm front surging. Del was the first to see the wall of dust that appeared at the entrance to the canyon—the enormity and power of it astounding. "Let me go!" she cried, more fearful now of the imminent storm than of the man with the arm locked about her neck.

Teddy ignored her protests. He drew his hand back and slapped her hard across the face. Del felt her lip split, tasted blood inside her mouth. Stars spun inside her head. And for a moment she thought she might lose consciousness. She fought against the temptation to just go with the feeling, slip off into some other worldly peace, let it all just happen.

But now he was grabbing her by the hair to begin dragging her up the slope, toward the wooden structure she'd first seen him emerge from.

"Stop! Bastard!" Del cried. She was forced to grab on with both hands to prevent her hair from being ripped from her scalp.

Randall's warning *Don't go alone!* rang in her ears.

"*The storm!*" Del cried.

They had made it only halfway up the slope when the gust front arrived. Wind driven dust and debris slammed into them with blinding force. The world around them went instantly dark.

With the impact, Teddy lost his grip on her hair. She tipped backward and fell, tumbling feet over elbows, down the hillside— half pulled by gravity, half blown by the force of the wind.

Teddy himself was driven to his knees by blasting sand and grit. He used one arm to cover his eyes, the other to steady himself against the hillside.

Del rolled to a stop at the base of the slope, just in front of her Wrangler. The vehicle served as a partial windbreak, giving her time to wipe dust from her eyes and scramble to reach for the Baby Eagle beneath her pant leg.

Teddy let out a howl of defiance against the storm. He rose to his full height against it, letting his size stand in resistance. And through squinted eyes, he turned his sights back on Del. His mouth formed a silent, inaudible threat as he stormed back down the slope toward her.

Del drew the Baby Eagle, thumbed the safety in one clean motion, and pulled off one shot...

Pop!

The shot was barely heard through the roar of the storm. But the slug struck Teddy, center-mass, and staggered him backward into the wind.

She gave it a one-count and fired again.

This time the bullet struck the right side of his chest at the heart. The fight went instantly out of him, and with a final push from the wind, he pitched forward and rolled the remaining distance down the slope, to land at her feet, face down.

It was over, all but the storm.

Sitting flat on her backside, the middle of the dirt road, Del let her head fall against the front bumper of the Wrangler and rest there. The wind whistled around her.

She thought of Lissa Rogers and her friend Kendra Kozak now. Two men had come to collect the ransom. Now one was dead and the other was gone. And there had been no indication whatsoever where the girls were being held. Would the remaining, unnamed, third man attempt another contact? Or would he panic, dispose of the hostages, and make tracks for parts unknown?

She had screwed up! Del realized now. In her anxiousness— *impulsiveness*—to do good, she had left the teens in a more vulnerable position than before.

A voice told her, *It's not your fault! You did what you could!* but she ignored it, more comforted by self-pity and regret.

Minutes passed with Del sitting there, her head against the bumper of her Jeep, the wind and dust blustering around her. The dust front eventually passed, and the wind subsided. Now the sounds of thunder could be heard echoing through the canyon. The first drops of rain plunked against her face—the beginning of the second act, as monsoons usually went.

Del dragged herself to her knees—her exposed, damaged breast throbbing with pain—and crawled her way to the man Teddy, lying on the ground.

She considered the revolver, lying on the side of the hill, where it had fallen, but left it there as evidence. Then she began to search the man's pockets, seeking identification.

There was no wallet, no driver's license. She found his cell phone and checked it. It was one of the prepaid variety. There were no saved contacts in the registry. Only six calls in the "Recent" call registry—two calls to the Egan residence, two calls to her own cell phone, and two more to a restricted, *blocked*, number. It was no immediate help. It was more crime-scene evidence, but Del decided to hold on to it anyway, see what, if any, future calls might come in. She slipped it into her pocket.

Now, she emptied the remaining contents of the man's pockets. All he had on him, besides the phone and a small amount of cash, were two items. One was a keychain with a single key—perhaps to a car or some other type of vehicle. The second item was a book of matches. The matchbook cover read: *Houma Lace—The Little Caillou's Finest Gentleman's Club.*

Del wasn't sure where Houma might be—if in fact it was a place. And she sure didn't know what a *Little Caillou* might be. But Lissa Rogers and Kendra Kozak were still out there, their whereabouts unknown. And the responsibility for their fate was squarely on her shoulders now. These items, only, were all she had to go on.

"I'm so sorry, Louise," she said, her voice feeling tiny. Del stuffed the matchbook and keychain into her pocket next to the man's cell phone, and tucked the Baby Eagle behind her back where it belonged. She did the best she could to secure the open front of her shirt, and then stumbled her way back behind the wheel of her vehicle.

The monsoon rain reached the canyon and began pelting down upon the canvas top of her Wrangler. It was late into the afternoon. The last light of day could no longer be seen through the dense, dark clouds overhead.

Del's heart weighed heavy.

It was Saturday. A date night. A night for wine and camaraderie and slow sex.

And all she really felt like doing ... was *crying*.

TEN

LEGGETT DENOUX WASN'T SURE he liked the idea of helping Payton with whatever scheme he had going. The two teenage girls, *Oo ye yi!* They had stumbled onto the island in some foolish adventure, and now Payton had them. What was he planning to do to them, this man who had washed up on Terrebonne Key? Leggett didn't know for sure. But he did know better than to cross him.

Leggett made his way from the big house—a brown shopping bag under his arm—down the path toward the bungalow that Teddy usually occupied but that was now being used as a place to hold the girls. Ma'am Ivess had finished with him for the day, and it was getting dark. Time for his beauties to hunt, be free again. *Like s'posed to be, dem!* He had Gigi, the female tiger, with him on a leash. It was time to collect Java.

Leggett found the big male right where he'd left him, at the end of his chain, outside the bungalow, maintaining his post by the door. He didn't like having to chain the big tiger, restrict his freedom. He loved his beauties equally. But Java was still in the early stages of training, his male aggressiveness more difficult to control. Java came to his feet at the sight of Leggett. He gave off a growl and arched his back—a reminder that he was ultimately the master of his domain. Leggett hooked Gigi's leash to that of Java's and turned to the front door of the bungalow.

He had come bearing some items of comfort for the girls—the shopping bag stuffed full—things he had begged and borrowed from the house staff. All without Ivess being aware. Wanting to make the girls as comfortable as possible. He rapped once on the door and entered.

The teens were inside, moving about aimlessly, nothing to do. Leggett felt a stab of sympathy for what he thought of as *mal pris*—a bad situation. The girls turned their eyes on him, uncertain of his role in their captivity.

"I brought some t'ings, each a one," Leggett said, setting the shopping bag on the bed for them to consider on their own time.

"Thank you," one of the girls said, the sweeter one.

"Jis some' t'ings," he reiterated.

"We appreciate it," the same girl said, seeming not to know what to say to him.

Leggett nodded. Their presence here made him uncomfortable. The room was small, the girls young and pretty. "*Mais…*" he said, looking to excuse himself and go.

"Mr. Leggett?" the girl said.

Leggett turned backed to her.

"The other two men, they're not very nice? You don't seem like one of them."

Leggett wasn't sure what to say.

"Can you help us? Maybe just let us go? We won't tell anyone, we promise."

"I make for the wish I could," Leggett said.

The second girl spoke up for the first time, crossing her arms in defiance. "You take the tigers away every night! What's to prevent us from just leaving?"

Leggett turned to them. " "Ahhhhh, naw, naw, naw!" he said. "Mes pischouettes, you have to stay here, youse. My beauties are on the loose, see. And, also … Ooo ye yi! … you don't want to run into the Rougarou, him!"

"Rougarou?"

"The monster! You don't know? Half wolf, half man, half demon. It stalks the bayous, this very island, nigh'time, looking for pischouettes just like you!"

Neither girl said anything for a moment, then the first one said, "That's just a legend, right?"

Leggett gave them both a grave look of concern. He wasn't sure the first girl bought it. But the second girl was peering off into the dusk that was now turning into darkness. Leggett felt it would be just enough to keep them put for a while. He let his grave expression linger on them for a moment longer, then turned without further word and left the bungalow.

Happy to be outside, back with his beauties where he was more comfortable, Leggett went about unhooking both cats' leashes. "Aw, righ', *mes chéris*! Go be tigers, youse!" he said.

And without being told twice, the tigers bolted off into the mangrove together.

The finest pair of killing machines Leggett believed he'd ever seen.

ELEVEN

THE ENCOUNTER ON THE mountain had taken its toll on Del, both physically and mentally. Her lip was sore, her muscles ached. Her breast still throbbed from where the man had bitten her. And the guilt she now felt, over losing the chance to recover the teens, was weighing heavy on her.

"*I'm sorry, Louise,*" Del said, tossing back a shot and chasing it with beer. "*I've let you down! I screwed up! And, now, your grand-daughter and her friend may never be found!*"

She'd come to McGuff's—a cop bar, down the block from her offices. The place was mostly empty. A television above the bar was on—some news channel, working, sound muted, to inform them. The bartender, Jimmy, milled about behind the bar, washing glasses and rearranging alcohol on the shelves, keeping himself quietly busy. A pair of Tucson cops, who Del knew from the street, sat at a table, across the way, drinking and talking quietly to each other. She had nodded her hello as she'd entered but had found a seat alone at the bar where she could brood privately. The only other patron was a man at the far end of the bar from her, drinking alone and casting expectant looks her way.

The atmosphere was custom-made for self-pity.

It was times like these—times of strife—that Del's mind ran to introspection, looking deep into the mirror of despair, to see herself, levy judgment from without, as some other observer might.

She was alone in her life. Her parents were gone. Louise was gone. And—as Randall had so often pointed out—there were no regular women friends to rely on for consolation. There was no man in her life, either, to lean on. Ed Jeski, the cop who had taught her all that she knew, had possibly been the closest thing to such a person. But Ed was gone, too—murdered last year in a motel across town. There had been the resistance fighter she'd fallen in love with only a short time later, Francisco Estrada. He was gone. Only the rodeo bull rider, Alan May, with his calm demeanor and dry cowboy humor, would be someone to take her in his arms and whisper reason in her ear. But this time of year he would be somewhere up north, possibly Canada, following the rodeo circuit, wherever it would take him. None of them … no one … was here now, when she most desperately needed someone.

Where was *her* knight in shining armor, as movies insisted there be?

Randall had been supportive—*well, sure.*

She'd called him once she was off the mountain.

"You'll have to contact Edgar Egan," he'd said.

"I already have. And I've talked to the Pinal County investigators and given them my statement," Del had told him.

"So, then, you can't blame yourself. You had to take the bastard down."

His supportive tone had made her feel somewhat better, but only for a time. Randall could only do so much. And his role as her boss—no matter how much he felt for her—only allowed him to go so far toward commiseration, without his offering bossly, *fatherly*, advice.

"I do care about you," he'd said. But, then, countering his consolations with, "But you've got a nasty little streak of impulsiveness in you that I worry about sometimes. I'm afraid it's going to get you killed one day."

Had she been impulsive in her decision to make the ransom drop alone?

Maybe! But the storm…

It was Del's attempt to rationalize her actions, defend them.

It was a lame attempt. She was in no way ready to accept reason—only pity.

Del ordered another shot and a beer.

The man down the bar from her was still watching, sizing her up. *Who was the blonde drinking alone? What was her story? What would it take to get her out of here and back to the hotel room?* She knew what he was thinking. *Would she go if he asked?*

The bartender delivered her drinks without comment and went off to ring the tab. Now, the man was sliding off his stool with his drink and coming her way, as she knew he eventually would.

He was dressed in a suit and tie—suit rumpled, tie loosened. His hair was neat on the sides but falling casually across his forehead in an all-too-intentional way—the *smarmy nice-guy* look. She pegged him for an out-of-town salesman. Wife and two-point-five kids, somewhere back in Shaker Heights maybe. A BMW, station wagon in the two-car garage. Voted Republican.

Del knew the type.

He could give a rat's ass about what was troubling her, but he would offer his sympathy, say all the things he believed she wanted to hear. His sales training would guide the conversation. He would wager all his hope, all his confidence, on the idea that his cool charm and gentlemanly behavior would ease her off her stool and back to his hotel room.

He approached, already working the Robert Redford smile for all it was worth.

"Can I buy that last shot and beer for you?"

"Thanks," Del said, turning her head to look at him across her shoulder. "But I think I've got it covered."

"You look like you could use some company. Maybe a shoulder to cry on?" He slid one cheek onto the stool next to her—half-sitting, half-standing, only half-committed to winning her, the way she saw it.

Del turned on her stool to face him now. "What's your name?"

"Ken."

Of course it was, she thought.

"Well, Ken, I think what you should do is go back to your hotel room, turn on *SportsCenter*, and only pretend we got to know each other."

She turned back to the bar, leaving Ken with his sheepish look.

"Come on," he said, reaching to put a hand on her shoulder. "I'm just trying to be friendly."

"You should take you hand off me, Ken."

"Oh? Why?" he said, using his fingers to massage the muscle there.

Del leveled her gaze on him. "'Cause I've already killed one man today, and I feel like it just wasn't really enough." She held his eyes with hers, letting him see the very real possibility for himself.

The hand stopped massaging and dropped to his side.

He stood there for a long moment trying to think of something clever to say. When nothing came to him, he turned for the exit, tossing down some cash on the bar to cover his tab. "*Bitch!*" she thought she heard him say, as he pushed out the door and into the night.

Del took up her shot and downed it, then chased it with a slug of beer.

On any other night, she thought, she might have considered taking Ken up on his offer. Or, at very least, let him down easy, leave him with his manhood intact.

But not tonight.

Tonight it would take more than a *Ken* to get her out of this bar. Tonight it would take a champion. A defender of good over evil. Handsome and strong...

A knight in shining armor maybe.

Del remained at the bar no more than fifteen minutes longer, then paid her tab and pushed out the exit and into the night. She collided briefly with a man entering the bar, and strode off, without apologies and without looking at him. She made her way briskly along the sidewalk toward Church Street, where her Wrangler was parked at the curb. She half-expected to find Ken sulking outside the bar someplace, maybe leaning against the building, waiting for a second chance to redeem his manhood.

She didn't see him.

But halfway to the corner, she heard hurried footsteps closing fast on her from behind. A hand reached to grab her shoulder.

Del spun sharply, driving the heel of her palm up hard beneath the man's chin, taking him backward off his feet. She heard the wind punch out of him as he slammed down hard against the pavement. Watched his head bounce once. Watched his eyes roll upward, then close.

Del stepped back, prepared to finish the job if necessary with a boot to face. When, suddenly, she realized she knew this man.

And it wasn't Ken from the bar.

"Frank?" she said, not believing her own eyes.

The man she'd just taken down was federal agent Frank Falconet. A man from her past she had tried hard to forget about. A man from two years back, who she had thought she once loved but believed she would never see again. Her heart skipped a beat at the sight of him.

"Goddamn, Del," Falconet said, his eyes reopening, working to find focus.

"Oh, God!" she said, a hand to her mouth now. "I'm sorry! Are you okay?"

He was still dazed but starting to get it collected. "I... I'm..." he said, dragging himself up onto his elbows.

Her initial surprise and elation subsided, and a stab of annoyance struck her. "Jesus, Frank! You know better than to sneak up on me like that! I could have killed you! What the hell are you doing here anyway?"

"I talked to your boss, Randall. He said I'd find you here," Falconet said, checking carefully to make sure all his body parts were still attached.

"Here, let me help you up," Del said, reaching a hand to him.

He took it, and she helped drag him heavily to his feet.

"You blew past me coming out of the bar. I couldn't believe it was really you," he said. "I've been shot six times in the line of duty, but I can tell you it's a little embarrassing getting my ass kicked by a girl."

"Well, it's a good way to get killed. I thought you were this other jerk from the bar."

Falconet tested his jaw; it was apparently still working.

Now they took time to stand and look at each other—two long-lost lovers, reunited—warmth in both of their eyes.

Falconet reached for her, and Del wrapped her arms around his neck and hugged him tight. "It's good to see you, Frank."

"I wasn't sure you'd want to after our last conversation. When was that, a year ago?"

"I've missed you," she said, tucking her head shyly to his chest.

Falconet stepped her back to get a good look at her. "Fuck! You're as beautiful as ever."

And so was he. Del took time to appreciate the man before her.

He was still lean and hard at thirty-nine years old, still exuding that raw masculinity that she knew him for. He was dressed in casual street attire—slacks with a short sleeved pullover hanging loose over his belt, Skechers over dark socks. He was sporting a good deal of five o'clock shadow that she knew came easily for him, giving him a sensual, animal appeal—the Italian gene of his Irish-Italian DNA.

"I can't believe it," she said.

"I've thought a lot about you lately," Falconet said. "You're probably wondering what I'm doing here."

Del slipped back into Falconet's embrace. "Do you have a room somewhere?"

"Just up the street," Falconet said, his voice suddenly taking on a husky quality. "Would you like to come back with me?"

Del nodded into the crook of his neck and let Falconet fold her under his arm and lead her away.

Things could only get better now, Del believed.

See … Frank *was* a knight in shining armor.

TWELVE

"I still can't believe I'm looking at you," Falconet said, tracing a finger along the soft inner flesh of Del's thigh.

They had made love slowly, tentatively at first, gaining momentum to finish in a heated rush—Del seeming to let go of something deep and anguish-filled, something with teeth, wild and pulling at restraints. Now they lay together—Del on her back, one knee raised, moonlight caressing her soft skin. Falconet was propped on one elbow looking down at her, feeling wonderment at the reality of actually being with her again.

"Your timing couldn't have been better," she said.

"You've got bruises," he said. "A cut on your lip. What happened?"

"It's a long story." She rolled to face him.

He could see wetness rimming her eyes. He put his arm around her to hug her close. "I've got time," he said.

Del clung to him more tightly, volunteering nothing for a while. "I've missed you, Frank," she said. "I've tried to put you out of my mind."

"It's been too long since we last talked," he said. "I recall you were in a pretty dark mood that time. You'd just lost an old friend, Ed Jeski, the cop. He'd been found murdered in a motel."

"You told me you and Jolana were going to give your marriage another try," she said, taking the conversation in an uncomfortable direction.

"I hurt you," Falconet said. "Does it still bother you?"

"That was a year ago, Frank," Del said, rolling away from him, to lie looking up at the ceiling. "I've come to terms with it."

"Well, for what it's worth, we did try ... Jolana and me. For all of about thirty seconds. It was never going to work out. We divorced in January. I have a one-bedroom efficiency in Elmwood Park, when I'm actually there to enjoy it." He studied her. "I've thought about you almost every day since."

"Me too," she said. "Mostly about our time back in the hills of Kentucky. At least the good parts of that time. Sometimes I think about going back there, taking over my mother and father's old house and just getting away from it all."

"The job?"

"Everything."

Falconet gave that some thought. "So, are you currently seeing anyone?" He hadn't really meant to go there but couldn't help himself. Now he was fearful of the answer.

"There are guys," she said.

"Guys!" It struck Falconet with a sharp punch to the gut. "There's more than one?"

"I don't live in a convent, Frank. So ... okay ... there's this one guy I've been seeing a bit."

"Another cop?"

"No, actually, he's a daredevil."

"What's that supposed to mean?"

"Well, for starters, he gets himself shot out of a cannon at the Tucson Raceway on Friday nights. But he also skydives, climbs mountains…"

"How old is this guy?" Falconet said, feeling a stab of jealously.

"Twenty-eight. A couple of years younger than me."

Falconet grimaced in the dark. "Well … is he like good-looking or something?"

"You see things in a very one-dimensional way, Frank."

"I guess I just want to know what you see in the guy."

"Well, since you're asking, he's got a body that's out of this world, and a face like a movie star. He's easygoing and fun to be with. Is that good enough for you?"

Falconet lay back on his pillow. Crazy, but he realized, now, in all the memories, all the thoughts he'd had of her over time, he'd never really pictured her with anyone else but him. The revelation formed a rock that settled in his stomach and lay there.

Del moved to lay her head on his shoulder, apparently sensing his change in mood. "Aww, Frank!" she said. "You can't really be upset. We haven't seen each other in almost two years. Haven't talked in more than one. You didn't think I was just sitting home Friday nights. If it makes you feel any better, I don't see it going anywhere."

Falconet realized he was working up a pout and warned himself against it. Del was not like other women. She was strong and independent and hated weakness—in herself and in the men she chose to be with. So, of course she hadn't been sitting alone at night. But he guessed he'd hoped that she'd been too busy to fall in love. He said, "It's just really good to be here."

Del lifted her head to look at him. "Yeah, so why exactly are you here, Frank? I asked earlier and you didn't answer. What brings you to Tucson? Are you still with ATF?"

Falconet sat up against the headboard, letting go of the funk he'd fallen into. "Well, it's a funny thing," he said. "I'm back working for Darius Lemon again."

"How is Darius anyway? Still sketching charcoal landscapes?"

"Getting promoted is more like it."

"So what's it this time? Bank fraud? Homeland security?... No more religious zealots, I hope."

"No ... this time I'm hunting a dead man," Falconet said.

———

Lying there in the dark, in the hotel on Congress, Falconet went on to tell Del about his meeting with Darius Lemon—a man she knew from their previous adventure together. He explained about the fugitive who had been presumed dead, the result of the plane crash that was transporting him back to the states for trial. About the body of the U.S. marshal, washing up in the swamp in Louisiana after a summer storm. How the marshal had been strangled with a belt as opposed to being killed in the crash. And how this, and that, related, was why they suspected the fugitive might still be alive.

"And you think your fugitive might be hiding out in Arizona?"

"Actually, it's the fugitive's brother I'm here for," Falconet said. "We got a hit on a biometric camera—"

"Biometric?"

"Face recognition, that kind of thing ... anyway, it's believed that where the brother is, our fugitive can't be far away. We want to question him. A man named Theodore Warren Rickey. Better known as Teddy."

Del sat up to look down at him, amazement in her expression. "Teddy?" she said. "Teddy Rickey?"

"Why? You know of him?"

"Oh, I know of him, all right!"

"Yeah? How?" Falconet asked.

"Well, for starters," Del said, "I shot and killed him just a few hours ago."

———

It was Del's turn to tell her story. To relate her meeting with the elderly Western writer and his concern for his missing granddaughter and her friend, their summer adventure to who-knows-where. She filed him in on the subsequent ransom demand that confirmed the girls had fallen into trouble. And told him about the events that led to her putting a bullet in Teddy Rickey—an action she now regretted because it left her without a single clue to the girl's whereabouts or who might be holding them.

"Hence the cut lip and bruises," Falconet said.

"It got pretty rough."

"Well, it sounds to me like you had no choice but to put him down," Falconet said. "But I think I've got a suspicion who's holding the teens."

"The brother?"

"Payton Rickey ... You're quick," Falconet said. "He's wanted for a triple murder: three family members, a mother and two children. Kidnapping, theft, extortion. The additional murder of a Texas highway patrolman."

"He sounds like he could be Teddy's brother, all right."

"Oh, he's a bad dude, sure enough. It doesn't bode well for your missing teens."

Del sat back against the headboard. She seemed to have slipped into a dark, thoughtful mood again.

"You're processing," Falconet said.

"Yeah, well ... you remember me telling you about Louise Lassiter, my teen probation officer?"

"She was like a mentor to you or something?"

"More like the mother I never had. I learned today that Lissa Rogers, one of the missing teens, is Louise's biological granddaughter. Louise had a daughter she never told me about. One she'd given up for adoption at a young age."

"That explains your mood," Falconet said, realizing he was drawing attention to the very thing he wanted to avoid.

"It explains why I feel like I'd like to kill someone...someone else," she added.

"So, we go get this guy, together," Falconet said. "You think he's somewhere in Tucson?"

Del shook her head. "No. I got the impression the teens were being held elsewhere. But I do have one clue," Del said, slipping off the bed to retrieve her jeans that were bunched on the floor near the entrance. She returned with the matchbook from Teddy's pocket. "It's not much to go on. I've also got a keychain with a key to something on it. And his cell phone, which doesn't reveal much, either, other than blocked calls...unless you've got a way to decipher where the calls originated."

"We can hook it up to a flash box," Falconet said. "Most police departments have them these days. If the phone's memory card is intact, they can scan it to get the call history. Know anyone with the local PD?"

"I have a friend," Del said.

"A friend?" Falconet asked, feeling an instant pang of irrational jealousy.

"Just a friend," Del said, offering the matchbook for him to consider.

Falconet took it—still feeling a bit of jealous pain—and read the inscription, reciting it aloud. "*Houma Lace...The Little Caillou's Finest Gentleman's Club.*"

"So much for gentlemen," Del said. "You ever hear of these places?"

"As I recall," Falconet said, "Houma is a town in southern Louisiana, and the Little Caillou is one of their bayous."

"On the Gulf of Mexico!" Del said, putting Teddy together with his believed-dead brother.

"You got it. Exactly where the plane went down … where the marshal's body was found … where my fugitive, Payton Rickey, was last seen alive."

"So, how are you with Cajun cooking, Frank?"

"Probably beats the buffet here at the hotel," he said.

"Good! Then, what do you say to a little road trip together?"

"Exactly what I was thinking," Falconet said. Actually thinking … *together!*

He liked the sound of that.

THIRTEEN

FROM THE WINDOW OF the bungalow, Lissa Rogers stood peering out into the night. The island's inhabitants—Payton, Leggett, the woman called Ivess, and the servants she'd heard of—had long since retired to their beds. The birds—the mix of indigenous gulf land waterfowl and their imported tropical sisters—had ceased their daytime chatter and had hunkered down for the night. And the moon and stars—as had been the case each night since their arrival—were in slumber behind a blanket of clouds. Even Kendra lay sleeping. Lissa could hear the soft rise and fall of her breathing. Despite their circumstances, she appeared at peace for a time—the night outside quiet and dark as pitch.

Only Lissa was restless.

She had tried to weigh her motives for being here against the situation they'd found themselves in. They were being held, true. But this place, the bungalow, wasn't all that bad. *Was it?* They weren't tied down or bound or anything. They'd been fed. And the Cajun, Leggett, had been caring for them, providing them with amenities to make their stay easier.

Their *stay.*

That was the way she'd come to think of it. Temporary at best.

So, maybe things would work out. Their captors would demand money from her grandfather ... her grandfather would pay it ... and their captors would let them go. Wasn't that the way it would all work out?

No.

Lissa had come to understand the seriousness of their situation. They were being held for ransom ... that much was simple enough. But what would happen once the ransom was paid? Or if it wasn't paid? Would Payton and his brother just let them go, let them get in their kayak and leave?

Lissa knew that wasn't likely.

They had stumbled on a man who was in hiding. A fugitive of some kind. That much she'd deduced from the conversations she'd overheard and from the comments made when they were first taken captive. Teddy saying, *"You can't let them go, Payton! They've seen you, gotten a good look at you. Describe you to authorities right down to ..."*

So, no!

Whether the ransom was paid or not, the brothers had no intention of releasing them. They would likely kill them, keep the money, and go on with their lives as fugitives, one way or another. No one knew they were here; no one would be able to find them. They were in this alone, with no way to gain freedom. The brothers were armed. They were on an island, surrounded by water. The male tiger stood guard outside their door by day, and both tigers roamed the mangrove by night. The very mangrove where their kayak was stashed—the kayak their only means of transport off the island. And the nights, thus far, had remained overcast, the island pitch-black, unnavigable in the dark. Even if they managed to elude the tigers, how in devil's name would they find their way through the mangrove in total darkness, to the exact spot where they had left the kayak? All this troubled her. And, at the same time ... broke Lissa's heart.

"Lissa?" Kendra said from the bed, awaking to find her there at the window studying the night.

Lissa said nothing.

Kendra sat up in bed. "What is it? What are you looking at?"

"Nothing. Just thinking," Lissa said.

"Are you worried about your grandfather?"

"I suppose," Lissa said.

In truth—she had to concede—she'd been thinking about more than just their freedom. She had been considering her original reason for coming to Terrebonne Key. Remembering her initial enthusiasm over the grand adventure, recalling her excitement at just finding the island. Proving that it simply existed had been a rush. Her fascination hadn't faded—not because of their immediate circumstances, and not because of her fear of what was still likely to come. The Jacob Worley tintype was still in her possession, in the nightstand next to her bed. And the secret, that she believed she knew about the photo and the island itself, was still with her, alive within her head. Nothing had changed in that regard. The only thing that had changed ... *was her opportunity to prove it.*

Kendra slid out of bed and came to stand by her at the window, look out into the night. "We're in trouble, aren't we?" she said.

"Yes, I think we are this time."

Kendra turned her eyes to Lissa now. "You've never even told me why we came."

Lissa considered her friend. She looked pale, tired, and run-down. She could see the strain that their incarceration had put on her in the dark circles beneath her eyes. "All right," she said, "I guess it's only fair." She considered her words a moment, then said, "I know about this island. I've been reading and studying about it for months. I planned this trip as an adventure. Just the two of us. A summer quest."

"I don't understand."

"There's treasure on Terrebonne Key, Kendra. Hidden treasure! And I think I've figured out where it is."

Kendra was staring at her in the darkness. "You're crazy, you know it!"

"Not really. It's got to do with the photo I showed you."

"The one of the old man?"

Lissa crossed to the nightstand and withdrew from the drawer the tintype photo she had brought with her. She couldn't see the image in the dark, but she could remember it precisely from memory—the old man, dressed in his Sunday best, a three-piece suit of the time. A derby. His pocket watch dangling from a fob on his vest. He was posed, looking into the camera. His hands gripped the lapels of his coat, one index finger extended, as if pointing to the watch. The watch read two o'clock. The photo was nearly a hundred years old, mounted in a silver frame. The frame, decoratively engraved with little arrowheads, symmetrically strung around the entire perimeter of the photo, pointing this way and that.

"This is why we came," she said. "The man in the photo is named Jacob Worley, the original inhabitant of this island."

"So?"

Lissa crossed with the tintype and collected an unlit lamp from the nightstand and sat down on the floor with both, next to the bed. "Sit!" she said. "And pull the blanket over us. I want to turn the light on, and I don't want anyone to see."

Kendra remained reluctant, but sat, dragging the blanket over them like a tent. "What are we—ten years old?" Kendra complained.

"Pretend we are," Lissa said.

"You're a lot of trouble."

"I know," Lissa said.

Secreted beneath the blanket, she turned the lamp on. Its bright glow filled the tiny secluded space inside. "There!" she said, her eyes adjusting to the light. "Now let's take a look at the photo together."

She handed the tintype to Kendra. And Kendra turned it against the glare to look at it closely for the first time.

"Okay…first…" Lissa said, "the photo was taken in a garden that is supposed to exist on this island. The things I've read refer to it as the 'sculpture garden.'"

"I don't get it? What's the big deal?"

"Well, here's the thing…there's this legend, see. The legend of Jacob Worley…that's the old man in the photo…'Jacob Worley and the legend of the sculpture garden treasure'…Gold…silver…maybe jewels…A fortune worth millions, it's believed."

"You're kidding! That's what you dragged us out here for! A treasure hunt!"

"Shhhh! Keep your voice down," Lissa said. "We don't want anyone to hear."

"There's no one to hear! We're in the room alone, under a blanket, in the middle of an island."

"Just listen, okay. This is for real, I promise."

"Why not?" Kendra said, layering on the sarcasm. "Given that I've got nothing better to do…*since we're both friggin' prisoners here!*"

Lissa leaned in and gave her friend a peck on the cheek. "You're cute when you're mad. You know it?"

Kendra released a long sigh. "Okay! Lay it on me! What's this big funky legend all about?"

Lissa said, with a smile, "It's going to blow your mind!"

Speaking in whispered tones, beneath their makeshift hiding place, Lissa began to tell her friend the story. In the late eighteen hundreds and into the early nineteen hundreds, a man named Jacob Worley had prospered as a jeweler and silversmith—selling and trading precious metals and crafting and importing fine jewelry for sale in and around New Orleans to Louisiana's social elite. Worley was a superb businessman, investing and reinvesting his profits, until he was reputed to be one of the richest people in the state. Being well-to-do, he also gained a reputation for being something of a gadabout, showing up at posh social gatherings, lavishing contrivances on the ladies, and rubbing elbows with reputed gangsters of the time. Worley also had a taste for the opiates. So much so, that in time the drugs' long-term residual effects became deleterious to his mental health. He became paranoid, darkly suspicious of business partners and people around him. He even began refusing sexual favors from women out of fear that they were involved in some vast conspiracy to steal his money.

Delirious from the effects of the drugs, one day Worley pulled up stakes in New Orleans. He converted the bulk of his holdings into silver and gold and took up residence on a remote and reclusive patch of land at the far reaches of East Bayou—Terrebonne Key—putting alligators and snakes and miles of swamp between him and his detractors. With that, Worley embarked on a new and solitary lifestyle. He had portions of the land cleared, a fine Southern mansion built, servants brought in to care for him. And, consistent with his eccentricities, he commissioned a garden to be built: a garden surrounded by marble sculptures. Sculptures, many believed, Worley envisioned were there to protect him.

He was in his late fifties at this point in time, and his mind was already far beyond repair. His addiction grew, as did his paranoia. So deeply so, that at one point he was said to have expelled all his servants from the island, choosing an isolated existence over fear of losing his wealth.

Years passed; Worley's dementia progressed; and his life and estate fell into decline. Still fearful that intruders would invade Terrebonne and rob him, Worley set about burying his cache of gold and silver. Then—as it came to be said—in order to identify the spot where he hid his fortune, he commissioned a photograph to be taken—a photo of himself, at the center of his sculpture garden, amid his protective stone guardians. A photo staged as a reminder to himself where he'd stashed his loot. A tintype, set for all time in a silver frame, engraved with style, at the hand of the old silversmith himself.

Worley passed in 1921—as alone in his final days and hours as he had been in the last years of his life. His decayed remains only came to be found much, much later, by curious adventurers to the island. Who reported finding his remains in bed, a needle still protruding from the decayed skin of his arm, the tintype photo still clutched in his bony grasp.

Back in New Orleans and throughout the towns along the bayou, gossip surrounded Worley's death. From gossip grew speculation about the whereabouts and ultimate worth of Worley's fortune. From speculation grew fable. From fable grew legend. But, all agreed, the tintype held the secret to the location of Worley's fortune. The photo taken in his sculpture garden, surrounded by twelve marble statues. His one extended index finger, pointing to his watch, at precisely two p.m. A reminder to himself, and now to the world, that his cache could be found beneath the marble sculpture that sat at the two o'clock position in his garden.

It all sounded so simple …

However.

Early fortune seekers had come to the sculpture garden, removed the statue at the two o'clock position, and unearthed the massive base upon which it set … *to find nothing.*

In years to come, the tintype and the supposed secrets that it held became widely debated.

Had Worley really created the photo for his personal benefit—fearing the failure of his own memory, a means of reminding himself where he'd buried his gold? Or, in a more benevolent view, had he created the photo out of some deathbed need to extend his legacy of wealth to a future generation? Or had he created the photo as some sad, demented joke? *"Worry yourselves over the photo. But never mind, you'll never find what's mine!"*

Whatever the truth, the whereabouts of Jacob Worley's long-hoarded cache was never recovered, and in time, folks quit coming and the photo became lost to history.

"So, the guy was on drugs," Kendra finally said.

"You're missing the point."

"You said, people tried but never found it."

"Right."

"So, what are we doing here?" Kendra had brought the discussion full circle.

"We're here because I've figured something out that no one else has noticed."

"You're kidding me, right?"

"No … see … are you ready for this … look at the photo again."

Kendra studied the photo once more.

"What everybody rightly assumed was that Worley was pointing to his watch to indicate position. But what they didn't take into account … and perhaps Worley himself, in his demented state, didn't realize … is that tintypes are actually negative images."

"Meaning?"

"Meaning that his watch is actually reading ten o'clock … and that he's pointing with his right hand, not his left."

"You're kidding, right? You figured this out?" Kendra said, still skeptical.

"I'm sure of it!"

"Okay, so why didn't they just look under all the sculptures, if they believed the sculpture garden is the place?"

"They're big, I'm guessing! It apparently takes a lot of work to unearth the stone bases they sit on. At any rate, when no treasure was found, people came to believe the photo held no significance to the location of the treasure at all. Just an old man, in his old suit and hat. His hands on his lapels."

"Okay … and this is the last question I'm going to ask … if the treasure is there, as you say, under the ten o'clock statue, how do you figure us two little girls are going to be able to get to it?"

"I don't, I guess," Lissa said. "I suppose I really just wanted to see the garden for myself, see if the possibilities for my theory could be right. Wouldn't it be great to be the ones, out of all people in history, to make the discovery!"

Kendra seemed to think about it. "I don't know," she said.

Lissa killed the lamp and threw the covers back. Then rose and crossed back to the window to look out into the darkness again. "All I wanted was to find the garden, see it for myself. But now …"

Kendra came to join her at the window again. "What are we going to do, Lissa?"

"I guess we're going to try to get out of here somehow. We just can't do it tonight. It's too dark. But if we get a clear night and a good moon, well …" She shrugged.

"There's still the cats and the Rougarou. Even if the monster is an old wives' tale, are you prepared to go out with tigers roaming free?"

"I think we have to."

"It's all too crazy," Kendra said.

"Yeah. Crazy."

Lissa turned her gaze back out into the night. She wished she'd remembered to bring along the folder with the Internet printouts and aerial Google map of the island. With those they might be able to plot an alternative route back to the kayak, one that didn't take them off into the mangrove. But no matter. One way or the other they would have to get there.

But first … they would need a night that was clear.

FOURTEEN

"I GUESS I'M JUST wondering if you've lost your mind?" Randall said on the other end of the phone line.

They were on their way to Houma—Del driving, Falconet in the passenger seat, the rag top of her Wrangler furled to let the wind blow through.

She had already told Randall about the matchbook and Falconet's connection to Teddy Rickey. About the fugitive brother, who was believed now to be alive. And his background as a felon. She didn't tell him about his propensity to murder hostages when things went south. Now she said, "There's one other thing, and this should convince you ... We met with my friend at TPD this morning ... Gil Tappa ... you remember him?"

"Your 'friend,'" Randal said, layering on the sarcasm.

Del could almost see him forming little quotation marks with his fingers. "Yes, my friend," she said. "At any rate, he was able run the memory card from Teddy's cell phone through some kind of program they have and pull the call history. The calls to Teddy's phone ... just before the ransom went down ... were made from

115

Louisiana. The calls pinged off a cell tower located between Houma and another little town down the road, called Cocodrie."

"Does it pinpoint the calls?"

"No, that's the thing," Del said. "It can only give us the location of the tower, not the actual location of the caller. Gil says the calls could have been made anywhere within a twenty-five to maybe thirty-five-mile radius of that location. Depending on the height of the tower, strength of the signal, and some other factors. But if the caller is calling from where the girls are being held, we know they're somewhere within that radius."

"That's still a pretty big area to cover," Randall said, holding on to at least a bit of his skepticism.

"Well, it's something to go on. It ties together with the investigation the Feds are working on. I've got Frank in the car with me now."

"Good!" Randall said. "Maybe he can keep you from shooting anybody else this week."

The remark stung just a bit—Del remembering that killing Teddy had possibly put the teens in further jeopardy. But she took it for what it was—Randall's way of reminding her that her headstrong ways could get her into trouble. It was something she'd just learned the hard way.

"What we need to do," Del said, "is find the second man who was on the mountain with Teddy. The man named Filo. He's the key to everything. If, in fact, he returned to the Houma area."

"Okay," Randall said, relenting. "I guess that does sound promising ... But assure me you'll stay in touch and keep me informed. I want to know every little bit of progress, understand!"

"Of course," she said, in all innocence. "Don't I always?"

Randall appeared to be ready to hang up, when he said, "Oh ... before I go ... one other thing I thought you'd want to know ... I got a call from the prosecutor's office this morning. He tells me Andray Moton looked like he'd been beaten with a stick. Sent over a photo of the man. Looked more to me like he'd kiss-smacked a Greyhound out on I-10. What the hell happened out there in Midvale anyway?"

"He fell down the steps," Del said.

"Really? How many times?"

"I'll talk to you later, Randall."

"You do that," Randall said.

Del ended the call.

"Randall doing okay?" Falconet asked.

"I think he's going through menopause."

"Right?" Falconet said. Then after a pause, "This guy, Filo, I've got some of the folks back in Cincinnati trying to come up with a full name. I'm not expecting much to come of it. But I think he's still our best shot at finding Payton Rickey. We'll need to put in some legwork when we get to Houma."

Del took her eyes from the road long enough to look at Frank. His own gaze was turned away out the passenger side, watching the desert and mountains of the Southwest passing by. He was unaware of her studying him—his rugged profile, now smoothly shaved, the hint of Old Spice, mixing with the wind through the sides of the Jeep.

He had saved her, she thought now. *Her knight.* Plucking her out of the depths of despair to stand on her feet again. And he had brought along vital information—a name, Payton Rickey; a face; the confirmation that the matchbook was significant in its connection to the Gulf.

Did she need a man to be with? A man to back her up? Randall had always been insistent so. But she had never recognized before now just how vulnerable she could be—a woman alone in difficult and dangerous times.

117

Why had she been so resistant to Falconet's two-year-ago proposal of working together?

She wasn't sure. But the close call at the Peppermint Mine had taught her just how vulnerable she was without backup. Perhaps without Frank, himself.

So, now, they were together … on the road to somewhere … A team. A pair. A partnership. And her heart felt light at the thought of it. She said, "I think Houma Lace should be the first place *we* start … What do you think?"

FIFTEEN

PAYTON WAS GETTING ANTSY. Morning had come, and he hadn't heard anything from Teddy since just before the ransom was about to go down. His instructions had been simple. Hadn't they? *"Get the money and call him when the job was done."* How hard could it be?

He had called Teddy's cell phone a couple of times earlier and got no answer. Had something gone wrong? Then, again, had Teddy decided to make a stop at a strip club in Tucson, blow the money in a VIP room before he could get back with it? Or ... *Oh, Christ, say it wasn't so! ...* Was it possible Teddy had decided to take off with the money without him?

No! Strike that shit from your mind, Payton thought.

He and Teddy were way too close for anything like that. They were brothers. Tight since childhood. There was a sacred, maybe secret, bond between them—familial—that was born of dark deeds and mutual dependency. Those days ... oh, those days of growing up together ...

Fucking childhood! Payton thought. Clay Rickey, their father ...
what a piece of work he was.

Payton and Teddy had often been made to stand by and watch as their father beat their mother mercilessly—leaving her bloodied, bruised, and sobbing in some corner of the house.

That crumbling farmhouse on the outskirts of Bakersfield.

He recalled how he had sometimes tried to comfort his mother after such violence, only to be pushed away by her.

Why was that?

He had wondered such as a child—and now even as an adult— *Were he and his brother the reasons behind the beatings? Did their father take out his hatred of them on their mother? Did she then blame them for the conflict?*

Well, but, then ... he and Teddy had endured their own share of domestic violence at their father's hand. It was most often Teddy who bore the brunt of it. Payton wasn't sure why that was. But wondered, at times, if perhaps their father never really accepted Teddy as his own—perhaps believing Teddy a bastard, conceived outside the marriage.

There was no real evidence of that, not that Payton could see. He and Teddy looked enough alike to dispel any notion that they were unrelated, even in part. So ... did that mean that both Payton and his brother were not the offspring of the man they called father?

Fuck! What did it matter!

The sonofabitch was stone-cold dead and lying in a shallow grave back behind the barn. Teddy had helped him dig the hole after Payton showed him what he'd done—blown the man away with his own goddamn gun, after one particular beating Clay had given Teddy. The last *fucking* beating he'd give either of them or anyone.

Their mother had died seven months later. That was the year Payton turned eighteen, Teddy just sixteen. And the two of them had hit the road, taking off for parts unknown. How could they have ever known or predicted that very road would one day lead them to Terrebonne Key?

No, they were still together. *Brothers.* Teddy would be back with the money.

Those were the things Payton was thinking as he left his bungalow this morning.

He checked first on his two hostages, inside the opposite bungalow. The male tiger was already stationed outside the door at the end of its long chain. The teens were both inside—he could see them, past the window, moving around, doing girly things he supposed—getting dressed, brushing their hair. He wished he could get a closer look inside. But ... there was Teddy to be found.

From there, he headed to the cabana bar, thinking on a drink before he tried calling again. He seemed to be drinking earlier and earlier these days—a sign he was growing desperately dissatisfied with his situation, anxious to make his move.

He was worried about Teddy. Growing more nervous about the two girls. What if one or both of them managed to escape? What if Ivess discovered them—two cute young girls, here on the island? In Teddy's bungalow! *Jesus!* She'd have his balls! Likely feed them to one of the damn cats!

Ivess seemed to be getting more and more suspicious of him, day by day—something else to worry about, bring anxiety to the situation. She was checking up on him more frequently, calling him to her earlier in the day. Sometimes having Leggett do it for her. Always with the questions... *What was he doing? What happened* to the money in the cookie jar? Didn't he have something he was sup-posed to be doing?... And criticizing his drinking, his... "lack of initiative."

Oh, he had initiative! He was about to *initiate* his release from Terrebonne Key.

So, where the hell was Teddy?

Payton understood he couldn't hold the two teens forever. Sooner or later he would have to get rid of them. But he still told himself that he should hang on to them for a bit longer. Maybe keep them as insurance, in case something went wrong.

Like Teddy not coming back!

Use them for hostages if Ivess ever had a change of heart and called authorities on him.

Once he was free, of course, he could drop their bodies in the swamp or whatever—feed them to the tigers. But maybe not until after he had a go at one or both of them. *They were cute young things.*

At the cabana now, Payton poured himself a drink and pulled out a stool to sit on. He sat sipping, letting the liquor work to calm his feelings of anxiety. Ivess was nowhere to be seen. *Good.* She wasn't yet on the beach—the beach chairs sat empty, the umbrellas tied closed against the wind. Leggett was nowhere to be seen either. They were possibly together this morning, Payton considered. Leggett working with Ivess and her Gigi. Maybe down in the garden—giving the fe-male cat its remedial training, reinforcing its managed behavior, keep-ing it domestic. Reinforcing Ivess's handling of the cat, as well, making sure she knew just what to do, how to keep the cat in line if it sud-denly reverted to its ingrained wild nature. Tigers could, and would, do that, if left to their own devices. Payton had witnessed it a number of times, requiring Leggett's intervention to calm them down.

Payton sat and sipped, not particularly wanting to do anything but think and feel. Let the morning breeze stroke his face. But, still, there was Teddy to contact. He had last tried Teddy's phone the night before, lying in bed, in the dark. Like the attempted calls earlier, there had been no answer. He had left messages. The first message he'd left said simply, "Call me." The second said, "Where the fuck are you?" Neither call had been returned.

Okay ... so ...

Find out why.

With the alcohol not quite doing the job of settling his nerves, Payton set his drink aside, withdrew his cell phone, and dialed Teddy's number once more. He took his drink up as he waited for it to ring.

"Hello?"

Shit! Payton almost said aloud. Someone had answered, but it wasn't Teddy.

A woman.

Payton hung up quickly.

Why was a woman answering Teddy's phone?

Payton checked his phone, to make sure he'd called the right number. Then tried again. This time the call was answered, but the person on the other end didn't say anything. They just held the phone and waited.

"Teddy?" Payton ventured.

"Who is this?" the woman's voice said again.

Damn it!

Payton silently cursed his brother. A woman was answering his cell phone. If Teddy had stopped to pick up a woman, hire a prostitute or anything of the like, he was going to have to fucking kill him—regardless of him being his beloved brother.

Goddamn it! Where was Teddy? And why was a woman answering his phone?

Payton hung up a second time.

Payton knocked back the remainder of his drink and went around to the other side of the bar and poured himself another. He stood sipping, thinking. Had he punched in the number wrong? Not once, but twice? *No way!* Was there something wrong with the phone service, crossed signals, maybe? *Not likely!*

Payton took a seat with his fresh drink and dialed again.

This time the woman's voice said, "Who is this?"

"Let me speak to Teddy," Payton said.

"Teddy's not here. You want to tell me who's calling? I'll give him a message."

Was she kidding?

Payton considered his response carefully. He could tell the woman to have Teddy call Payton immediately, but he didn't like giving out his name. *Payton Rickey was supposed to be dead, remember?* He could say, *Have Teddy call his brother.* The same thing. Giving away too much information. Have Teddy call the island—a little less informative, but did he really want to mention the island? It was his sanctuary.

What to do? What to do?

Payton sat considering just how to respond to the woman, when she offered, "Teddy won't be coming back, if that's what you're wondering." Like she could read his mind.

Who was this woman?

"Why would you say that?" Payton asked.

"Just a premonition."

"Who is this?" Payton said, his voice rising unnaturally.

"Someone who knows about the teens you're holding hostage! If I were you, I'd let them go while you still have a chance to get out of this thing in one piece."

The woman's warnings hit Payton like a fast-moving train. His foot slipped off the bar rest, nearly toppling him off his stool.

His drink spilled down the front of his shirt. *Shit!* Who was this woman, and how did she know about the hostages?

"You're ... mistaken," was all he could think to say.

"Am I?"

"Who are you? What do you want?"

"I want you to let Lissa Rogers and her friend Kendra go."

Payton took a solid hit off what was left of his drink. *Jesus!* The woman, whoever she was, knew far more than she needed to about the teens. *Goddamn! Who was she?* A cop? Some kind of federal agent? What had happened to Teddy?

"Where's Teddy?" he said again. "Why can't I talk to him?"

"That's not important. What's important is that you tell me where the teens are being held. Let's get this over with."

"You a cop?" Payton asked.

"Does it matter?"

Christ! she had balls. And she was smart, this woman—not giving anything up but coming across like she had all the answers.

How much did this woman really know? Was she just bluffing, trying to drag information out of him?

Just then, Payton heard someone calling to him. "*Oh, Payton! ... Pay-ton, darling!*"

Christ! Not now! Not now! A knack for bad timing, it was Ivess, coming down the path from the main house.

Payton had more questions he wanted to ask—more things he needed to know about this woman. But Ivess was coming, as always, to poke her nose into his business. He flipped the phone closed, dropped it quickly into his shirt pocket, and leaned on the bar casually with his drink.

Ivess appeared wearing a frilly beach wrap of some kind, the sheer material trailing after her in the morning breeze. "Oh, there you are. Having a drink so early, dear?" she said in a disparaging tone. "You've got entirely too much time on your hands. Come with me to the beach. I want you to rub tanning lotion on me. I've decided to take some sun. I'm too pale, don't you think?"

Like Moby-fucking-Dick, Payton thought. *The woman was born without blood in her veins.*

Ivess took the drink from his hand and set it on the bar. Then she took him by the wrist and dragged him off his stool, urging him, *please* follow her, and *please* do her bidding.

Payton went along, as she required—the woman with Teddy's cell phone on hold for now.

He allowed himself to be led, all the way to the beach.

Overhead, gulls soared and squawked noisily. Ivess stripped from her wrap and stretched naked on one of the lounge chairs. "Use the lotion, dear," she said.

Payton found the tube of Coppertone and squeezed a dollop into the palm of his hand. He fought back the urge to be sick, the idea of once more touching that pasty white skin. Then, slowly, he began applying the lotion to her body. His own skin had gone clammy.

The day from there seemed to slow, like time through an hourglass. Egrets scuttled in and out of the waves. From along the path, Leggett came with the female tiger, Gigi, bringing Ivess's pet to join them. He was back to being Ivess's *boy* again. Back to living out his hell.

Payton thought about the woman on the phone. His dream of freedom had just gone up in smoke, evaporated into thin air—or so it seemed. Was there going to be any money? Any fifty thousand dollars? Any airfare to Rio de Janeiro? And where the fuck was Teddy? What had happened to him? Who was this very ballsy woman who somehow knew he was holding the teens? What else did the woman know?

These were the questions that haunted Payton's day. And he had no answers. What he was sure of was ...

He had to find Teddy and find him fast!

———

Del flipped Teddy's cell phone closed and dropped it into the seat next to her. "He hung up. Sounded like someone in the background," she said.

"What do you think? Could that have been Payton?" Falconet asked.

"I don't know. We can't be sure. But whoever was calling was calling for Teddy, and he sounded rattled that Teddy hadn't answered."

"That was a smart thing you did," Falconet said, "challenging him like that."

"I was a little afraid that if I pushed him too far, he would harm the girls, maybe leave them for dead and go on the run."

"I think you played it just right," Falconet said. "If that is Payton, if he's still alive, wherever he's been hiding out, he's pretty well secluded. I don't think he'll be going anywhere just yet. My guess is he'll try to use them to effect his escape or maybe try another ransom attempt. It was also smart not to tell him Teddy is dead. That might cause him to feel all hope is lost."

"I want to find this guy, Frank. I want to find Lissa and Kendra and bring them back."

"I know you do. And we're going to do it, too. You'll see. I'm betting on Houma."

"Let's just hope the bet is right, Frank."

Del looked to Falconet, there on the seat across from her. A dark shadow had crossed his face. He said, "Payton is a dangerous man. We both need to be careful."

"Nothing's changed, Frank. We get to Houma, we find Filo, Filo leads us to the teens before it's too late. That's the way it's got to work."

"I just feel the need to warn you, we get there, be sure to watch your ass."

"Why, I thought it was your job to watch it for me, Frank," Del said, lightening the mood that had become way too serious.

"It's a good job to have," he said, going with it, a smile breaking through on his face. "I'm just saying ... if it is Payton Rickey we're dealing with ... don't underestimate him, okay?"

Del turned her attention back to the road and gave the Wrangler a little more gas. It was good to be working with Frank again. Good to have him back in her life. And she wondered: if Falconet had been there on the mountain with her, when she went to pay the ransom ... would things have turned out differently? Would Teddy still be alive to lead them to the girls? *Maybe. Maybe not.* Still, life was hard when you go it alone. It caused her to think of how heartbroken Frank had been—that time in Mexico—when she had turned down his offer for the two of them to stay together, work together. Had it been the idea of commitment she'd been afraid of? Afraid of getting too close? Afraid of the change it would bring into her life? Or had she just gotten cold feet?

Del wasn't sure. That had been two years ago. Maybe she could say she'd grown since then. Maybe she could say, life and the lonely hours had changed her. Perhaps, having a man in her life wouldn't be such a bad thing. And she could surely do worse than Frank. By a long shot. Jeez! She could be married to, say, Donnie Ray Ewing, the Human Cannonball ...

No! Frank, if there was one ... was a keeper.

SIXTEEN

THEY ARRIVED IN HOUMA on Monday, late afternoon, after driving straight through, twenty-two hours, with only gas stops and a few hours' sleep in the car along the way. They had received no more calls on Teddy Rickey's cell phone, and Del was starting to question if they were even dealing with Payton Rickey at all. Or, if coming to Houma wasn't just as crazy as Randall had said it to be. She was tired. And despite all they knew about the origin of the calls to Teddy's phone ... despite the matchbook identifying Houma Lace as a place of interest ... their one hope was resting on the prospect of finding the man, Filo ... in belief that he could lead them to where the teens were being held.

It was still a long shot—as Randall had warned.

"We'll need to find Houma Lace," Del said.

"I'm already on it." Falconet said, consulting his iPhone, punching letters into the search engine. "Looks like you can keep going on Main Street to Little Caillou Road, then head south."

Del followed Falconet's directions, on through the downtown business district, passing storefronts and government buildings.

Houma—the seat of Terrebonne Parish. Then took Little Caillou Road south. The highway meandered, mirroring the snakes and turns of the Little Caillou Bayou itself—the tag line on the book of matches, *Little Caillou's Finest!*

The waterway was somewhat unimpressive, at least at this point. A narrow channel of water, giving off the stench of dead fish and rotting vegetation. A *Filo* smell. That thought alone buoyed her confidence some. They were in the wetlands, fisherman's paradise.

Small commercial fishing boats lined the banks of the bayou, along with private pleasure crafts—some big, some small. The bayou stretched on—twisting and turning—snaking its way to the Gulf of Mexico, as Del recalled from the maps they pulled up on Falconet's phone.

She drove on.

Soon, office buildings gave way to more rural settings. Open grazing land spread off in all directions—the landscape entirely flat. On the off-bayou side of the highway, the road was lined with fish canneries and warehouses, low-end commercial businesses. There was a diner, a liquor store, a truck repair shop, a pawn shop, a bait shop … another bait shop … She continued on, seeing more of the same, until a large billboard, with rather suggestive advertising, appeared, reading: *Houma Lace, Girls-Nude-Girls, Happy Hour Prices, Drink Specials, The Little Caillou's Finest—Half Mile on Right.*

Soon Houma Lace itself appeared, looking more like a roadhouse than the gentlemen's clubs Del was used to seeing around Tucson. It was a long, low frame building, sporting flashing tawdry neon outlines of well endowed feminine forms. At this time of day, a little after four o'clock, the parking lot was mostly empty, only a handful of cars in the parking lot, a couple of Harley Davidson motorcycles near the entrance. Not much action going on, on either side of its doors, it seemed.

Del pulled the Wrangler into the parking area and slipped the gearshift into neutral, letting the engine idle. "Not that impressive, is it?" she said.

Falconet had been studying the club with a pained expression on his face. "I had hoped this might at least be fun."

"You think we're crazy for coming here?"

Falconet turned to look at her. "As long as we're together, what's the difference?" Then he turned back to his door and stepped out.

Del realized he was probably right. If it hadn't come to be that they were in this together, she wasn't so sure she'd have taken the chance on a book of matches and driven all the way to Houma alone. But together ... well ... it somehow felt right. And, once again, Del was struck by just how much she'd been missing in life without someone to share it with.

She killed the engine and stepped out to join him.

The area had a cheap, tawdry feel to it. Across the exceptionally wide parking area was a low-rent motel. On the bayou side of the road, at the water's edge, was a seafood restaurant called *The Shack*. It was mostly that—a shack, sitting right at the end of a long dock where more fishing and pleasure boats were tied off. Up and down the strip were more bait shops, more commercial and industrial businesses.

"At least we've got a place to stay," Del said.

"Right? My kind of place," Falconet said. "I know now we've come to the right place."

"How's that?"

Falconet smacked at a mosquito that had been buzzing about his neck. "Because Darius never sends me anyplace decent. Why's it have to be so fucking humid?"

"I think you just answered your own question, Frank. Come on, let's see if they've got a room. And then buy me something to eat. A girl gets hungry you know."

———

At the registration desk, Del studied Houma Lace through the window—the deskman eyeing her—as Falconet filled out the registration form.

"You come to work the titty bar?" the deskman said, addressing his comment across the lobby to her.

"What kind of question is that to ask a lady?" Falconet said.

The deskman shrugged. "It's about the only reason women stay here."

"Just give me the damn key!" Falconet said.

The deskman handed Falconet the key without further comment, and Falconet collected Del by the elbow and led her out of the lobby. "You believe that guy?"

Del had to smile. It was a side of Frank she'd never seen before— the jealous boyfriend side. She decided she kind of liked it.

Their room was on the second floor, off the landing that ran the length of the building. Falconet gathered his bag; Del gathered her duffle; and together they climbed the stairs to their room.

The place was small, but surprisingly cleaner than she'd expected. She dropped her bag on the chair and plopped down on the bed, testing it for comfort. "It'll do, I guess."

"We need to get some air conditioning going," Falconet said, crossing to the small unit beneath the window. "I feel like I need a snorkel to breathe in this place."

While Falconet set about making the room livable, Del perused the room, her eye landing on the telephone directory inside the base of the nightstand. She retrieved it and thumbed to the "R" section of white pages, looking for *Rickey*. There was no Theodore Warren Rickey listed. No Payton Rickey either—no surprise. No Rickeys whatsoever, as it turned out.

A nagging seed of doubt had settled into her thinking, maybe brought about by the overwhelming enormity of their task ahead. How did they find one man … one stinky, smelly fishermen … in an area populated by stinky, smelly fishermen? *Don't think that way*, she scolded herself. You're tired. You'll find Filo … you will … you and Frank together.

You and Frank together, she repeated to herself, and laid the directory aside to cross and put her arms around Falconet from behind. "I'm glad you're here, Frank," she whispered.

It was all it took to get a kiss that lasted long and hard.

She took it all in, feeling the heat in him rise, and driving her own excitement, up, up, to the brink of the abyss before pulling away to catch her breath to calm her heart. "Save that thought, Frank," she said, thinking of Lissa now and of Kendra Kozak. The two of them, possibly somewhere nearby, within some thirty-five-mile radius. "Let's get a bite to eat. Then let's check out the strip club."

It elicited a frown. But Falconet gave in to reason. "Right," he said, clearing his throat. "I recall a diner up the road."

Poor guy. He looked all twisted up inside. Del gave him a pat on the shoulder, feeling just a bit sorry for him. "Maybe we should leave the Wrangler parked," she said. "You can walk it off."

SEVENTEEN

FILO WAS JUST COMING out of the liquor store when he spotted a man and a good-looking blonde coming along the sidewalk up Little Caillou Road. Goddamn, if she didn't look familiar!

He could swear that this was the woman who had come to the mining camp to deliver the money. But ... *how the hell could that be?*

It seemed too impossible.

He watched as they crossed the parking area to the entrance of the diner, hand and hand, like any other local couple, maybe. But, no—goddamn it!—short blonde hair! Slim figure! Good-looking!

It was her! He was sure of it now.

He remained watching from inside the doorway to the liquor store until they had disappeared inside.

How the ...? How was it possible? Was she looking for him? How in hell did she trace him back to Houma? What kind of woman could do that?

All Teddy's fault! Filo thought. Just had to go and let his urges get the better of him. Now he was dead and that woman was here in Houma, fourteen hundred miles away. *Oh, this could not be good!*

Teddy had been shot and killed, or so he had learned. The incident had been reported on the news. Filo had seen it while he was still back in the motel room in Tucson, waiting for Teddy to return with the money. Shot and killed with a gun in his hand. *With his dick in his hand, more like it!* Filo had wanted to finish the report for them. He had been shot by a woman investigator, as they'd stated, who had been commissioned to deliver the ransom. Filo had packed his bags that very night, not bothering even to check out. And had gotten back into his pickup and hightailed it down the highway for home.

It had never been his intention in the first place, really, to get mixed up in a kidnapping scheme. He had only gone along as Teddy's driver, his transportation to and from—given the man didn't even own a car. He had questioned the advisability of it, even from the very beginning. And again, there, on the mountain, as the transaction was going down. What kinds of shit could go wrong, end you up in prison?

That had been his contention all along.

And now he was back in Houma, and so was the woman. An investigator, as the news had stated. And smart by all accounts. Looking for him perhaps, but more importantly, probably, looking for the two teenage girls that were at the root of all his problems.

His first thought was maybe he could just go to the woman, cut a deal. But he'd been on the mountain, complicit in the kidnapping. And what if it turned out that Teddy's brother had—hearing the news—killed the two girls? Would he be facing murder charges as well?

Filo had heard stories of Teddy's brother. Things Teddy himself had told him of their past. The wild and crazy-ass adventures. The two of them. Cross-country crime sprees. He remembered something about a family up north someplace, Arkansas maybe, that had been at the cause of them winding up in Houma. A long story about U.S. marshals and downed airplanes.

Payton was hiding out, so, of course, he was the one who had stayed behind to hold the teens. Payton—a wanted fugitive. *Ohhhh*... Filo didn't want to think where this was headed.

Get back into your pickup and head straight back out of town. Don't even bother going back to the little silver-bullet house trailer by the water he called home ... forget about a change of clothes ... belongings and such ... just hightail it! That's what Filo told himself.

But, now, he considered Payton, out there on Terrebonne Key.

To his understanding, that was where the hostages were being held. A private island, secretive and remote. Had Payton actually heard the news? Did he even know that his brother was dead? Filo hadn't before thought of that. Should he have tried to contact the man?

He supposed he had figured Payton would have simply learned of the outcome from the television news, the way he had. And he considered himself under no real obligation to inform him. He didn't even know the man, really. They'd never even met. And, besides ... it was possible that Payton didn't even know that he had gone with Teddy to do the job. If that was the case, why even admit—to anyone—unnecessarily, that he was complicit in a crime?

These things, and so much more, were going through Filo's mind as he waited and watched from the doorway of the liquor store.

Leaving town was maybe not really an option, he decided. He'd barely had enough money in his pocket to get back home from Arizona. And, now ... hell ... only the change left over from the liquor he'd just purchased. It would be another week before his unemployment check arrived.

So ... *ride it out,* he thought. *Take your fishing pole down the bayou. Stay off the streets and out of the trailer as much as possible. Let things blow over.*

From the doorway, Filo pondered his risks a moment longer. Then, in an impulsive rush, he pushed out the door and made a quick dash to his pickup. He cranked the engine, backed around in a quick arc, them floored it, casting furtive glances at the diner, as his tires took hold and the pickup lurched off through the parking area.

Five-fifteen, he noticed. He could be down on the water by quarter to six.

"I need to hit the restroom," Falconet said, pushing out of the booth they'd taken along the window.

Del sent him off with an absent nod. Her thoughts were off out the window, thinking of Lissa Rogers and her friend Kendra. Thinking of Louise and the old Western writer Edgar Egan. They were depending on her—all of them—to bring the girls home alive. It was a big task. And it all seemed to hang on whether she could find the man named Filo.

As she sat with her gaze beyond the window, she thought at first she might be seeing things. *Stress-induced hallucinations.* But the vehicle pulling out of the parking lot of the liquor store next door looked a lot like the pickup that Filo had been driving that day at the Peppermint mining camp. An older model, dark blue with primered gray patches in places. She was too far away to be sure, and the glare on the window obscured her vision, but damn if the man behind the wheel didn't look like Filo.

Del slid from her seat and quickly headed for the door, blowing past Falconet, who was returning from the men's room.

"Del?" he called after her.

But she was already at the door and out, into a dead run into the parking lot. The pickup had already made it onto the highway and was rapidly accelerating, heading south, back in the direction of the motel and Houma Lace. Del gave chase for close to forty yards down the sidewalk and into the roadway before giving up, breathless, her hands on her knees.

Falconet caught up to her, breathing hard as well. "What the hell, Del?"

"The pickup truck, Frank..." she said between gasps of air. "That was it!... That was Filo!... He's in Houma!... He's here!"

Falconet threw a glance down the road. "I don't see anything. Are you sure?"

Del nodded. "I got a glimpse of him, just before he sped off."

"What about the license plate?"

"Only a partial," she said, straightening now. "But that's enough. We know he's here."

Falconet threw another glance in the direction of the vanished pickup, then took Del by the arm. "Come on. There's nothing we can do now. Let's finish our meal before it gets cold."

Del nodded and let him lead her back to the diner.

She still wasn't sure how they would go about finding Filo, but they were one step closer...

And that was enough for now.

———

It was well after dusk—the night air muggier than ever—when Del and Falconet left the motel and crossed the parking lot to visit Houma Lace. The neon female outlines were glowing brightly—

calling all men. The parking area was filled to capacity. And where earlier there had been only a couple of motorcycles at the entrance, now there were more than a dozen.

"It would be nice if we found Filo sitting at one of the tables," Falconet said, as they passed between the rows of cars.

"I think that would be too much to ask. I may have spooked him this afternoon, chasing after him. If he recognized me, he may have gone underground."

"Well, if he's a regular, maybe the strippers can tell us where that Teddy fella hangs out. He had to have lived somewhere."

"We'll see," Del said, as she reached the entrance ahead of Frank.

"Wait," Falconet said. "You're not going inside are you?"

"What were you expecting, Frank? That I'd sit out here and wait for you?"

"Well, yeah, I guess ... I don't know what I was thinking ... I mean ... you're a girl and all."

Del crossed her arms and gave him a look. "I think the deskman called it a titty bar, Frank. I've got a pair of qualifiers."

"I guess I was just thinking the dancers would give me more information if I was alone ... you know."

"You afraid I'll spoil your fun, Frank. Or you afraid I'll attract too much attention myself?"

"All right! Have it your way! But I'll be watching your back!"

"Please! I know what you'll be watching, Frank!"

Del turned and pushed her way inside; Falconet remained behind, spacing their entry so as not to appear together.

———

Beyond the entrance, heavy blackout curtains separated the entryway from the main club. A scantily attired young woman, positioned beyond a ticket window, waited to collect a cover charge. A burly bouncer, African American, stood nearby, smoking a cigarette and looking bored. Del reached for the pocket of her jeans to pay the cover.

"Huh-uh! Ladies' night!" the bouncer said, in a deep, Barry White voice, and parted the curtain for her to enter.

"Thanks," Del said. *Now was that so difficult?*

Inside the club itself, music blared. Bright spotlights highlighted a runway, where a tall stripper with short dark hair was stalking back and forth, liquid-hipped, in time with the beat. She was naked down to a sequined G-string, small breasts thrust forward. She showed off her athletic ability by lifting one leg straight up over her head, parallel to her torso, holding it there to snake her tongue along the smooth flesh of her thigh, then continued her parade down the runway.

Male patrons lined both sides of the stage. They watched with exaggerated indifference. From time to time, one of them would reach a dollar bill up to the young woman, and she would come forward to let him tuck it into her G-string, let him reach for flesh, only to slip away, strut on, to the next patron with money to give.

As the raspy voice of Bob Seger told the crowd about what life was like *down on Mainstreet* in another city, Del found her way through the shadows to a table in the back. She took a seat at a small table and let her eyes adjust to the darkness of the room. All around her were male patrons, some watching the dancer on the stage, others watching the myriad of scantily clad strippers who prowled the club soliciting lap dances. Others were keeping a few of the dancers busy, sitting back, legs stretched, while the girls ground their bare backsides against them or leaned in to press their breasts close, smothering the male patrons with cheap perfume and silky flesh.

Del could feel eyes upon her as well—thirty or more nearly naked young women there to look at, and it wasn't enough for some men, she guessed. They wanted to know *Who is the blonde in the boots and jeans?* A waitress came by, and Del ordered a beer.

She was told there was a two-drink minimum. She agreed with a nod, and the waitress went off toward the bar. Minutes later she was back with two bottles of Corona. Del paid and generously tipped the girl, a gesture of sisterhood, then sat back to sip and study the scene. Nearly all the patrons were men. Most were in work clothes and caps with various fishing emblems above the bills. These mostly, she believed, belonged to the fishing boats lined along the bayou across the road—shrimpers and the like. Some were likely workers from the canneries—seeking entertainment at the end of a long day's work. A few were dressed in biker wear, elaborate embroidered patches adorning the backs of their denim vests. These were clustered mostly together, in the far dark corner of the club, as though they'd arrived in pack formation. A single dark-haired Asian girl was attempting to entertain the lot of them, allowing herself to be pushed playfully, like a doll, from one biker to other, around the circle.

There was one couple—man and woman—sitting at a table against the back wall. They were both in office attire, as though they'd come straight from work to be there. The man was maybe in his fifties or early sixties, his suit rumpled, his tie looking like it had belonged to his father before him. The woman, bleached blonde— only slightly younger—wore a too-short skirt and blouse, rings on nearly every finger. She had one hand draped around the man's shoulder; the other hand lightly stroked his thigh. It was Monday night in Houma—life finding its way—there on the Little Caillou.

Del spotted Falconet entering the club, putting his wallet away after paying the cover. He passed by her with more of a grimace

141

than a glance and found a seat farther back amid the shadows and ordered a beer.

Del scanned the faces of the men in the room. As might have been expected, none were Filo—they couldn't be that lucky. As one of the dancers passed by, Del waved her to the table. She was ebony in color. Tall and made taller by six-inch heels. "You want a lap dance, sugar?" the girl asked.

"What's your name?" Del asked.

"Everybody call me Silk."

Del could see why. Her skin was shiny, flawlessly smooth. "I just want to know, has Teddy been in lately?"

"Teddy?"

"Teddy Rickey."

"Oh, you mean 'Albino'? I call him that cause he so *white*. Know what I mean? Yeah, he sometimes come in. But I haven't seen him tonight."

Or in the past three nights, Del thought, picturing the man dead with her bullets in his chest.

It had always been Del's philosophy that there are no coincidences, only incidents that coincide—something Louise had taught her. That things that seem to add up, usually do. She and Frank had come to Houma on not much more than a hunch, but within only hours of arriving had spotted Filo and had now confirmed that Teddy Rickey had, in fact, frequented Houma Lace. It was a small town for the most part. People in small towns tended to know each other. She said, "Does Teddy live nearby?"

"He live right here, sugar. In all the time. Was wondering where he got off to."

"What about a guy named Filo?"

"What do I look like, directory assistance! You ain't some kind of cop, is you?"

"I'm just a girl looking for some answers," Del said.

"Well, this is bullshit!" Silk said, and turned to go.

"Wait!"

The girl paused.

"It's really important, maybe life or death. One working girl to another?" Del said. "I really need to find the guy named Filo."

Silk scanned her up and down. "Yeah, you could pass for one of us."

She leaned in conspiratorially, giving a cautious glace about the room. "Won't say where he lives, but Filo ... his real name is Filbert Lohman. Only locals call him Filo is all."

Bingo! Del thought. She gave Silk a nod and produced a twenty and tucked it into the girl's garter. It got her a smile.

"Say hello to the little man for me. And you take care," Silk said and moved off to solicit her next dance.

Just like that, Del thought. She believed that Silk possibly knew where Filo lived, but that was okay. With his full name, she could run that down from there.

Del turned her attention to Falconet, who was getting a lap dance from the tall brunette with the short hair who'd come off the runway to work the floor. She'd always thought of Frank as a pretty straight shooter, someone who could be loyal to the right woman. Right then, however, his mind and hands were full of tall brunette, seeming preoccupied, maybe overjoyed. He was a man, after all.

But that was okay ...

She'd just have to wait to lay the big news on Frank.

———

Del chugged a bit of her beer, then rose and left the club. Outside, in the parking lot, Del withdrew her cell phone, scrolled to Randall's number, and waited as the call connected.

When he came on the line, Del said, "What time is it there?"

"Oh, roughly six-thirty. You in Houma?"

"Yes, and I've got a name for the second man who was on the mountain with Teddy. Is Patti still in the office?"

"Just left. Was about to leave myself, but what can I do for you?"

"I need an address in Houma for a Filbert Lohman."

"That your Filo?"

"That's him. He drives a vehicle, so the Louisiana DMV must have a record of him. I'd like you to get in touch with Gil Tappa again at TPD."

"The married guy who puts his hands on you?" Randall said.

"Just call him. Tell him it's for me and that it's urgent. He's a good guy. He's helped us already, and he'll help out again. I need to know where Filbert Lohman lives."

Del supposed that she could have waited for Falconet, have him draw on the vast resources of the FBI. But she wanted to go all the way with this, counter Falconet's machismo by dumping Filo in his very lap and showing him she wasn't just the girl he thought her to be. Call it feminine pride, or call it setting the record straight, but either way she'd show him.

"Just what are you up against?" Randall was now asking in his somber, fatherly tone he used whenever he was concerned for her.

"I don't know yet," Del said. "We just need to find Filo."

"Your Fed fella still with you?"

"Falconet?"

Del felt a hand on her shoulder and spun quickly. Falconet was able to stop her this time, before she put him down again.

"Jesus, Frank!" she said, covering the phone receiver with one hand. "You really have to stop sneaking up on me like that!"

"Sorry! I didn't want to say your name! I thought it might be the caller again."

Del gave him a grimace, but returned the phone to her ear.

"What's going on?" Randall asked, more boss than father now.

"Nothing. Just a little governmental oversight. You got what you need?"

"I'm on it," Randall said.

"Good, call me as soon as you hear something."

Del ended the call.

"Who was that?" Falconet asked.

"Randall," Del said. "So … did the leggy brunette offer any information?"

"You know, they're not as forthcoming as you might expect," Falconet said, sounding genuinely surprised that the girl hadn't fallen in love and offered everything she knew. "I guess we'll have to try another approach."

"I guess we will," Del said, unable to stifle the smug grin that had crossed her face.

"Wait! You got something?" Falconet said, looking as though he half-wished she hadn't.

"Just Filo's real name, Filbert Lohman. But I'll have to wait until Randall calls me back with an address."

"How is it they spilled their guts for you and not for me?"

Del gave him a shrug. "Sisters, doing it for themselves, I guess," Del said. "But I think some guy should buy me a drink and tell me how totally awesome I am."

"What? You don't have a sister for that, too?" Falconet said, peeved and showing it.

"Some things are better left to men, Frank." She gave him a smile that settled the score between them.

"Let's see if The Shack, across the road, is still open," he said, putting an arm around her shoulder.

Del let herself be manhandled.

After all ... a little machismo was maybe a good thing.

EIGHTEEN

IVESS HAD KEPT PAYTON busy applying baby oil to her back until she was beet-red from the sun. Then she had called him to her bed, and afterward insisted he share brandy with her on the beach and watch the sun go down together—every minute of which was spent catering to her whims, right up through dinnertime.

Payton believed the constant demand on him was the result of Ivess's growing suspicions, growing jealousy. Her wanting to occupy every minute of his time with attention to her—only her—so there would never be any doubt about what he might be up to otherwise.

Now that it was nighttime and Ivess was finally ready to let him retire to his bungalow, he was just about too worn out to think about Teddy... and ransom money... and...

Still, he had to find out what had happened.

The calls he had made to Teddy's cell phone that morning, and the prodding questioning from the woman who answered, had left no doubt in his mind that Teddy had run into trouble. But what kind of trouble exactly? Where was he? What had happened to him?

The woman had known about the teens he was holding, so Teddy must have made contact, made his ransom demand. But had he ever received the money? Or had something gone awry with the handoff? Payton had to find out. *But how?*

He wasn't sure exactly how he was going to go about finding Teddy. He had no contacts in the outside world. No one was even supposed to know he was alive. The only person he could maybe look to for information was the man who had gone with Teddy to Arizona. The man named Filo. But Payton had never actually met the man himself, and knew very little about him. Only what Teddy had told him, off and on, from time to time—that he was an out-of-work shrimper Teddy had met at Houma Lace, a strip club on the mainland. How the hell was he to go about making contact, go about finding this man?

Payton wasn't quite sure.

He also questioned what Filo might know of him, of his dead-fugitive status, of his being alive on Terrebonne Key. Twenty-some-odd hours in the car together, the drive from Houma to Arizona, he could imagine would lead to a lot of talk. Did Teddy tell Filo about him? Did he fill Filo in about the teens, as hostages, being held out there on the island? If so, it raised the questions *Where was Filo in all of this? And where was the money?*

All these questions, Payton thought, and only one way to actually find out. He would have to leave the island.

Not good! Not good at all! Payton thought now. *Not good*, also, was the issue of the teens—what to do with them if he left the island for a time? What should he do with them? Should he just get rid of them, dump them in the swamp? Or should he hang on to them, hold on to the idea of the ransom until he could see if it still needed to be collected? And who could he trust to manage them while he was gone? Could Leggett be trusted to keep them out of sight, away from Ivess? Or would he go running to the Island Queen as soon as his back was turned?

So many questions.

But Payton could see no other recourse. He'd have to go to Houma, try to pick up some kind of trail. That left one other consideration. *How to get there?*

The only reasonable transportation on and off the island was Ivess's pleasure craft, the *Sand Castle*—stupid fucking name for a boat, he believed—and Teddy had used it to get to the mainland. Now it was sitting somewhere along the Little Caillou Bayou waiting for someone to retrieve it. Something else he'd have to explain to Ivess, anyway, if she noticed it was gone. The only way he could figure getting there was he'd have to take the dinghy—a small craft that usually stayed shelved inside the boat grotto.

Then—*Oh, boy, then!*—there was Ivess herself. How the devil was he going to be able to get away long enough to go to Houma, find out what happened to Teddy, and get back without her knowing it?

Payton's woes seemed to be multiplying.

Well, he would have to just suck it up, that was all there was to it. Do it and be done with it. And, do it tonight, he believed, before Ivess's suspicions took her on a stroll down to the boat grotto to find the *Sand Castle* gone. Or, worse yet, to the bungalow to discover the teens.

So, he had stayed with her until after dark, until she was already tipsy from drink. Then he had slipped a sedative into her glass, and toasted her with a smile.

The sedative hadn't taken long to work; she had gone under with her drink glass still in her hand. Payton had carried her to bed.

Confident she'd be under for a while, he raided the kitchen money jar—the only place on the entire fucking island where there was cash of any kind. He saw there wasn't all that much left after Teddy had raided it for enough cash to get to Arizona. So, he took two twenties, then considered—fuck it!—and took the rest. Eighty-four dollars altogether.

Payton left the mansion and went off to find Leggett.

He hoped still to find him on the beach, where Leggett liked to work with the cats, late in the day, put them both through their paces, before releasing them to the mangrove for the night. But it was getting late and he had missed him there. So, he moved on to the bungalows to see if Leggett was there to give the teens their dinner.

There was a light on in the teens' bungalow. No Java guarding the door.

Payton stole a peek through the window and... *My, oh my!* ... The two teens were in there, barely dressed. Their recently rinsed shorts and tops were hanging on a line above the sink. The prettier of the two, Lissa Rogers, was sitting on the edge of the bed, brushing her hair, dressed in a gown Leggett had supplied her. The other girl was parading around in nothing but her bra and panties, attending to their undie-things.

Ohhhhh ... how Payton wished he had time to pay the girls a visit. He got a rise, despite already having serviced Ivess. But there was no time. There were empty dishes stacked on the small table. Leggett had already come and gone.

Payton had to get to Houma. Do it now, before his world—his free world!—came crashing in on itself. He mustered all his resolve and, with a sigh, pulled himself away from the window. Now, he considered Leggett again. There was only one other place he could be—down in the sculpture garden, preparing to release the tigers. Payton left the bungalows and followed the path back past the cabana, back past the house, then down the path that led to the garden.

He had just reached the wrought-iron arched entrance when he spotted Leggett out there in the middle of the garden, working by lantern light, surrounded by all those staring stone sculptures. The tigers were milling restlessly at the ends of their leashes. Payton called to him, wanting to reach him before the tigers were off the leash. "Hey, hold on there, little buddy!" He hurried on into the garden, step-dragging his gimpy leg behind him.

The cats snarled as he approached.

"Java! Gigi!" Leggett commanded, jerking hard on their leashes. The cats settled and dropped down on their haunches. "D'lady and gent, dey gettin' anxious," Leggett said.

"Yeah, I guess so," Payton said, eyeing the cats warily.

"What for you want?" Leggett asked.

Payton considered the tigers for a second longer, imagining them stalking the bush at night. There was an abundance of wild pigs—peccaries—that roamed the island. More of the nonindigenous wild-life that Ivess had collected for her animal kingdom. Payton imagined there were fewer of them since the cats had arrived. He said, "Yeah, listen. I have to go into Houma for the night."

"You gonna leave da island?"

"I don't want to, but I have to. I need to retrieve the boat. And I need you to keep an eye on the two girls until I get back."

"Teddy's naw coming back, him?"

"I don't know. I need to check on him. He may have ... had an accident or something. I don't know, we'll see."

"What about ma'am Ivess?"

"She's sleeping," Payton said. "You just make sure you don't wake her. All I need is for her to come snooping around the bungalows. You understand?"

Leggett's expression knitted with concern.

"Don't worry, little man," Payton said. "I'll be back by daybreak. Just make sure to keep Ivess occupied when she wakes up. I'll be taking the dinghy, so it'll be slow going."

Just then, the brush at the far perimeter of the garden rustled, and a trio of pigs came into view. They made their way along—a father, mother, and one piglet—rooting at the earth with their snouts and making grunting sounds, searching for food. The tigers sprang to their feet with a snarl, lunging against their leashes, nearly dragging Leggett off his feet. "Java! Gigi!" Leggett commanded. The cats continued their tug-of-war.

The pigs eventually moved off into the bush, grunting and squealing.

"Just hang onto those two until I'm out of the way, okay? I'll see you in the morning." Payton moved off quickly toward the arched entrance.

When he had reached the path behind the house once more, Payton turned to give Leggett a wave. Leggett waved back, then squatted down next to the cats to unhook their chains. "Time for my beauties to hunt," Payton heard Leggett call. He wasn't sure whether the little Cajun was talking to him, the cats, or just talking to himself. At any rate, the tigers sprang free of their restraints and tore off into the nearby mangrove. *Jesus!* Payton thought, swallowing hard at the images he was conjuring in his head now. *Either one of those could tear a man apart. Together…?* Payton didn't want to think about it.

Payton stood watching the mangrove until the cats were no longer in sight. Then, remembering his mission, he headed on down the path to the boat grotto.

NINETEEN

THE SHACK—JUST THAT—WAS A sad little wooden shanty that sat at the end of the boat dock, on stilts. An outdoor deck off the side jutted out over the water's edge. They walked past boats, bobbing against their moorings. Some fishing boats, some meant for shrimping, other pleasure boats, built for speed.

Falconet led the way inside. The place was small. A handful of other diners at the tables. A number of good ol' boys bellied up to the bar. The din of conversation seemed to carry.

"It would be nice to have a quiet place to talk," Del said.

Falconet caught the barmaid as she passed. "There's no one on the deck outside. Can you serve us out there?"

"Sure," she said, with an *it's-up to-you* shrug. "If the mosquitoes don't run you off."

"We'll take our chances," he said.

The barmaid ushered them out the door and to a seat overlooking the water. The bayou lay peaceful, the water moving lazily, quietly, below.

"Two beers," Falconet said. "Whatever you've got on tap."

The barmaid went off, letting the door close behind her.

With the noise of the restaurant muffled, Frank reached for Del across the table. She gave him her hands, and the two stared into each other's eyes.

"You did good tonight," Falconet said. "I was being a dick back there earlier."

"You've just forgotten what it's like to work with me," Del said.

"I haven't forgotten how great it is. I still can't believe we're back together." Falconet squeezed both her hands in his. "Are we together?"

"I think we came to this point once before, on a beach in Mexico."

"I never could understand why you wouldn't commit. I think we're perfect together."

Del shrugged. "I don't know. I was in a pretty dark place. I'd just lost my mother, my father. It was hard to picture a future of any kind."

"And what about now?" Falconet asked.

Del turned her gaze to the bayou. It seemed she still didn't have an answer for him.

"It was the main reason I went running back to Jolana," Falconet said. "That was a mistake. I really didn't want to pick up with her again. I just wanted to have someone to be with while I licked my wounds. Estranged wives are good for that."

"I guess ex-wives are good for that, too," Del said, bringing her eyes back to meet his.

Falconet said nothing.

"We're spending time together," Del said, still unable to completely ease Falconet's pain. "That's a good thing, isn't it?"

Falconet forced a smile. There were things he wanted to say. Things he wanted her to know. He wanted to tell her that he hadn't stopped thinking of her, not even for a second, since their time in

Kentucky together, two years ago. He wanted to tell her that lying in bed next to Jolana, those times, he couldn't stop picturing her as the one beside him. He wanted her to realize that many times he had felt like he was losing his mind that they weren't together. He wanted to confess it and have her confess the same.

But now, rehearsing it in his head, he realized how desperate and pathetic it all would sound. How weak it would make him seem. And Del was not a woman to be attracted to weak men. She didn't have room for weakness in her life.

So, okay, he thought. Ride it out. Enjoy this time together and hope for the best. He only hoped he wasn't leaving his own heart unguarded...

Available to be broken once again.

The barmaid came with their beers and went off inside to do her job. Del studied Falconet, his eyes on the waters of the bayou. In the span of ten minutes, he had gone from being joyous at the reality of being with her, to being dark and brooding over the uncertainty of their future. She guessed she could understand. She was slow to offer love, slow to commit. The opposite of what she was in her job. *Impulsive.*

Frank, on the other hand, rushed to love, like a thirsty man rushing to water. Oddly, this seemed to be opposite of his approach to the job. Falconet was more thoughtful, more deliberate in his approach. There was probably an explanation for it all, something for psychologists to write papers about. But it left the two of them at odds sometimes. Both on the job and in their relationships. Maybe that's why it was they gravitated toward each other. Another truth in life... *Opposites attract.*

Still, they weren't all that opposite—Frank and she. Frank—like she believed herself to be—was competent in his work. He was tough and smart, shrewd and insightful when it came to the minds of others. He was sensitive and good, down deep. A fine and decent person. And, he was handsome! *Oh my God!* That Irish-Italian mix that gave him his swarthy sex appeal.

The only thing that held her back, prevented her from going the distance with Frank—that time in Kentucky, and later on the beach in Mexico, perhaps even now—was his constant need to have her love confirmed. As though he felt the winds of love could change at any minute and he had to get constant weather updates to know just how to dress.

Still, it wasn't just him. She understood she came with her own cautious predisposition. The need to have the future known before embarking on it. The need for a road map, disaster preparedness...

Why couldn't she just say yes? Say it and let the chips fall where they may? What would it take to come to terms with love?

Looking at him now, in the context of all she was feeling, Del felt a sudden need to reach for him, gather his hands in hers, and this time speak the words of comfort, of love, he so desperately wanted to hear.

Instead, she said, "Can I tell you something about me, Frank?"

Falconet drew his eyes from the window to look at her.

She said, "Maybe something I've never told another living soul."

———

Falconet listened as Del poured her soul onto the table in front of him. She told him of what it was like growing up with her bitter and verbally abusive father. Of the nights she went to bed crying as a little girl. Of the wall she had built around herself to protect herself from people and the pain they could inflict. A wall that had not been entirely torn down as an adult.

"There was this abandoned property out near Helmet Peak," she told him. "The house was mostly gone. The slab remained and a portion of two adobe walls were standing. But there was this old watertower, sitting up on stilts. The wooden tank was mostly intact, except for a rotted hole in its side near the bottom, which made it a dry tank. I would go there sometimes, you know, after getting into it with Roy, my father. I'd climb this rickety old ladder, and crawl through that hole to the inside." Del shook her head, despairingly. "Sometimes I would just sit in there all alone. The smell of dry rot all around me."

"How old were you at the time?" Falconet asked, seeing the pain she could draw on at just the thought.

"Maybe twelve when I first started going. But my visits there lasted all the way into my teens. I would see scorpions crawling in and out of the rotten planks, but I didn't care. I would think some-times ... What if one of them stung me and I died, right here in this old rotting watertower ... would anybody bother to come looking for me?"

"Sounds pretty bad," Falconet said.

"I think sometimes I was actually daring the things to sting me. You know, like testing fate. But they never did. And I'm still here."

"You don't seem to think that way now. I mean, fatalistic."

"Don't I? Look at the job I've chosen."

Falconet said nothing. He believed she could be right. He had known her to take wild chances.

"I don't want to sound morbid," Del said. "It was Louise who helped me through those years."

"You miss her, don't you?"

Del nodded.

"I remember one time I was feeling particularly resentful of my father. I ran out in the middle of one of Louise's counseling sessions. I was about sixteen then. Just bolted and ran. Louise found me at the tower. I refused to come down. And, so, she climbed that rickety old ladder and squeezed through that hole to sit inside with me. She was a big woman. I could tell she was scared to death. A fall from that height could have killed her." Del looked down at her hands, clasped now atop the table. "She always went all the way for me. That's why…"

Falconet saw tears welling in Del's eyes. A single tear had broken free to stream down her cheek. He reached across the table and wiped it away, gently, with the back of one finger.

"That's why I have to find Lissa Rogers, you see. I was the daughter Louise wasn't able to enjoy. Lissa is her true granddaughter—a granddaughter Louise never got to meet. She went all the way for me; now I have to go all the way for her. I have to bring Lissa back safe; that's all there is to it." Now she took time to wipe her own tears from her face, dab at the moistness in her eyes.

Falconet wasn't sure what to say. He'd learned something of her background during their time together in Kentucky. Learned something of Louise's role in Del's life. But now he thought he understood. The walls Del had built in childhood were mostly still standing. And perhaps that's what made it so difficult for her to commit to love. Everyone—every thing—she'd ever known had abandoned her, in one way or another. Her father was gone, her mother was gone, Louise was gone. Even the former boyfriend, Ed Jeski was gone, found murdered in a motel room, as he recalled. It caused Falconet's heart to break for her, made him feel sheepish and selfish for expecting so much, so soon. He said, "We'll find Lissa. We'll bring her home safe. I promise."

They ordered another round of beers and sat quietly for a time, each dealing privately with their respective demons—Del herself content with the silence that had overtaken them. Falconet was a good guy. It had been therapeutic, the chance to unburden herself to him. She guessed that was what real couples did. They served as gym mats to each other, wraparound padding to absorb some of the blows of life on the other's behalf. Accepting the bruises, the scars, that came double for conjoined hearts. Falconet promised they would find Lissa and bring her back safe. And she believed him now, the confidence in him, transferring across lines of love to her, making her more confident in the process. That's what being a couple was all about. That's what having a mate did for you. It gave you strength. It allowed you hope.

Del sipped her beer and studied Falconet, his gaze beyond the window. His thoughts off beyond the bayou. She could love this man, she thought. Did love him, perhaps. But could she ever fully commit?

They continued to sip in silence.

———

They were halfway through their second beer when the sound of a boat motor ebbed into Del's consciousness. Coming to her as a distant drone, growing louder, closer, by the minute. The boat—a dinghy—made its way up the waterway toward them from the south, a spotlight on its bow lighting the way. One occupant, a man, guided the craft through the night. It passed by where they sat watching from the deck-patio, then quickly throttled back, and glided the remaining distance to the dock. The man, tall and largely built, tied the dinghy off behind a larger craft that was already docked there. And then climbed aboard the larger boat.

It was dark at the far end of the dock. Del was unable to see the man clearly. And the boat's arrival deserved no more consideration than a passing motorist or passing jogger in a park. Non-event worthy. Except that it had somehow captured Falconet's attention.

"Why so interested in the arrival, Frank?"

Falconet said nothing. But he watched as the man from the dinghy prowled about the deck of the pleasure boat for a time, then went below into the sleep cabin for a time. Soon after, he returned to the deck and took time to study the highway beyond the dock, study the neon lights at Houma Lace, as if trying to decide if he was up for a late-night lap dance or not.

Apparently deciding that he was, he stepped out onto the dock and headed toward the road and Houma Lace on foot.

"Frank?" Del said again. "What's so important about the man in the boat?"

He was still studying the vacuum left by the man's departure. "I don't know," he said, turning to face her now. "Just thinking."

"You were watching the guy like he'd just committed a felony by showing up. What is it?"

"Nothing really … I suppose … but … doesn't it strike you as odd?"

"It's a man. A boat. We're sitting next to a dock. The bayou. No. Not really."

"Well … see … the man comes up the bayou from the south, in the dinghy."

"Yeah …?"

"He ties off to the bigger boat and climbs aboard."

"So?"

"I just think that's odd is all."

Del knew Frank to have a suspicious nature. It was one of the things that made him good at his job, kept him safe on the streets where he plied his trade. She said, "I don't get it. Maybe it's his boat and he came to pick it up?"

"That's just it. If it's his boat, why wasn't he the one to dock it there? Why did he have to come pick it up?"

"I don't know, Frank. Maybe he loaned it to someone. Or maybe he rents boats and the renter abandoned it there and he had to come get it."

Falconet seemed to think about it, accept the answer for now. "Maybe," he said. "I just thought it odd is all."

"You've been working undercover too long, Frank," Del said, giving him a slight smile. "Every man on the street is up to something. Every passerby guilty of some crime. Where's your faith in humanity?"

"Like I told you, I've been shot six times on the job. Humanity has let me down. But I suppose you're right. I need to lighten up."

Falconet took up his beer and sipped it casually, his eyes back on the bayou, the peacefulness of the night. But Del could tell he hadn't completely let go of his suspicions.

She considered the possibility that he could be right. His instincts had proven themselves to be right more than once—those times back in the hills of Kentucky. She thought about it some more, but with no reasonable explanations coming to mind, she put it behind her.

Now she was back to thinking about him. Thinking about the confidence he instilled in her. Thinking about what it would be like to make love to him...

Right there, right then...on a restaurant patio...beside the bayou.

TWENTY

PAYTON HAD NEVER BEEN to Houma, never really been to Louisiana, in fact—given that he'd come to Terrebonne Key from the Gulf side, having been dropped, literally, from the sky.

All he knew of Houma—the town—was what Teddy had spoken of in one of their late night drink-and-bull sessions beneath the thatch-roofed cabana. He'd talked of a strip club, in Houma, Houma Lace, that was a kind of roadhouse affair, across the road from the dock. Dark-haired Cajun girls—*smack!* The dock he'd mentioned was next to a restaurant called The Shack.

Payton had found The Shack easily enough, by following the bayou upstream. And, he had quickly spotted the winking neon signage of Houma Lace—advertising *Girls-Nude-Girls*, across the road where Teddy said it would be.

There had been no sign of Teddy on the *Sand Castle*, Ivess's boat, or even that he might have been staying there. There was no key in the boat's ignition either. Something Payton hadn't considered in advance. Which meant—damn!—he'd have to take the dinghy back to the island. And—shit!—make up some kind of excuse why the boat was gone, try to cover until he could figure out how to get it back to the island.

Unless he found Teddy.

He was still counting on that, holding out hope that Teddy was around someplace, and all was well. What he imagined was that he would find him, probably at Houma Lace, his lap full of Houma girls, celebrating and spending their getaway money like there was no tomorrow. And Payton was fully prepared to slap his kid brother senseless—big as he was. Maybe only then give him a hug and rejoice in his being safe.

Payton crossed the road and into the parking area of Houma Lace, staying close to the lot's perimeter, close to shadow and the protection of the cars that filled the lot. The neon images were tantalizing. Inviting him to go inside, get his hands on something young and firm just this time—feel something different from Ivess's sagging flesh. Touch something soft without feeling sick to his stomach. But the risk might not be worth it, particularly at this important juncture. So close to getting off the island for good. No, there were prying eyes inside. Suspicious eyes. Best to keep his face away from public scrutiny.

Still ... he had to find out if Teddy was in there. Or, at the very least, maybe Filo, the man who had gone with Teddy to collect the ransom. Either one. Or both ...

That's what he was thinking.

Payton moved between the cars to a shadowy spot where he could watch the front entrance. His first time back in civilization for a while, it felt like eyes the of the world were on him—on the street, behind the cars.

There was no one anywhere that he could see.

Payton waited, watching the entrance for movement, wondering how the hell he was going to find Teddy without being seen.

Just then, the door to Houma Lace opened and a sleek young black woman appeared, in street clothes, carrying a bag over her shoulder. One of the dancers, off duty, headed home for the night. She was coming between the cars, headed his way.

Payton hunkered down out of sight as she made her way past to a battered little Honda Civic, two cars over. This might be it, Payton thought. The opportunity he needed.

He had a gun but didn't want to risk having to use it, draw attention. So Payton reached in his pocket for a knife he carried, slicked open the blade, and waited, as the woman fumbled in her purse for the key, came out with it, and slipped it into the lock.

Payton made his move.

He came up behind her, strong and fast, grabbing her from behind and clasping one hand across her mouth. "Scream and I'll slice you ear to ear," he said, giving her a glimpse of the knife, the blade glinting in the lights from the highway. "Understand? Nod, if you understand!"

The girl had gone rigid with fear, but now offered a nod.

"Do you know Teddy? Comes in here sometimes."

The girl nodded willingly, his hand still over her mouth.

"He inside tonight?"

The girl shook her head, no.

"What about Filo? You know him?"

Again, she nodded, trembling beneath his grip.

"Okay," Payton said, close to the girl's ear. "Here's what we're going to do. You're going to get behind the wheel, when I tell you. And I'm going to slip in behind you. You're not going to look at me, understand? I'll be right behind you, telling you what to do."

The girl nodded her consent.

Payton raised one leg and drove his heel into the sideview mirror, shattering the glass, pieces of it clattering to the pavement. The girl shrieked a muffled cry beneath his hand.

"Now, inside! No sounds! Don't look at me!" he said, easing his hand from the girl's mouth.

She dutifully complied, unlocked the door and opened it.

Payton quickly reached behind her to unlatch the rear door, and slipped in behind her as she took the driver's seat. Inside, he reached across the seat and tore the rearview mirror from its post. The knife at her throat again, he said, "Drive!"

The girl hesitantly started the engine and made a sweeping loop around the cars in the lot and out onto the highway.

Payton remained close behind her, the knife at her throat. When they were on the road and heading south, he said. "What's your name?"

"Silk," she replied.

"Silk," Payton repeated. He sat farther forward over the seat, getting a view down the girl's blouse. "I can see that." Now he asked. "You know where this Filo lives?"

"Yeah, I do," the black girl said.

"I figured you might. You do things for him?"

"I do for anybody what's got the money," Silk said. "I do for you, you won't hurt me."

"We'll talk about it," Payton said. "For now, I want you to take me to see Filo."

"You not the first one asking," she said. "Some lady came by the club asking for him earlier."

"A woman?" Payton's interest was suddenly aroused.

"Uh-huh. Pretty white girl, nice."

"You tell her where he lives?"

"Uh-uh. She asking lotsa questions. I didn't wanna say too much. Only his name."

"I'm asking lots of questions," Payton said.

"Yeah, but you got a knife. She only got a pretty face."

"You're a smart girl, you catch on fast." Payton grinned. "All right. You just keep playin' along nice and take me to him now."

They were headed south, passing occasional cars that were headed back north. Soon the rows of commercial establishments gave way to rural countryside, farmland, and sprawling wetlands. As the girl drove, Payton remained content with letting his eyes caress the flesh inside her blouse.

Soon, the Civic slowed, and Silk flipped on her blinker. "This here the place where Filo lives," Silk said.

She made the turn into a gravel drive, where a small house trailer sat amid the trees, on the bayou side of the road. There was a pickup sitting in the drive. Blue with splotches of gray primer. Payton remembered Teddy mentioning a pickup they had used to get to Arizona. If this was it, it suggested that at least one or both had returned from Arizona. *That was good.*

"Pull in behind the piece of shit," Payton said.

Silk did as she was told. She slowed the car to a stop behind the truck.

"Kill the engine," Payton said.

Silk complied.

"You're sure this is it?" Payton said, cautious.

"Where he lives," Silk said.

"All right."

They sat there in the dark for a while—Silk's eyes front and center, still fearful to make a move. Payton checked the highway behind them, surveyed their surroundings in front of them. They were right on the bayou's edge, the slow-moving water making its way toward the Gulf. The trailer itself was dark, no light escaping from within.

"We're gonna go inside," Payton said. "You're doing good. Just keep it up and do as I say."

"I will," Silk said. "I don't wanna end up on some news program."

Payton studied the situation for a moment longer, then stepped out, urging Silk out ahead of him.

He waited with her, in shadow, as a car passed by on the highway. Then moved her across the lawn and onto the tiny metal porch. The moon's reflection danced on the waters of the bayou, just twenty feet or so away. The trailer itself sat quiet.

His greatest hope—if he dared to have one—was that he would find Teddy inside, with or without Filo, shacked up, maybe after a heavy night of celebrating. Teddy, of course would have some explaining to do—"*I thought I told you to come straight back with the money!*"—and, of course, he would have some excuse or other, about how the boat had failed to start, or how he'd lost the key. *But why hadn't he called?* Payton would have to box the big dummy's ears, then give him a hug and ask, *"So, where's the money?"* But he didn't think it would go down that way. The trailer was pitch-dark inside. And, the sinking feeling that dragged at his insides was all about the woman on the phone. She had Teddy's cell phone. Why wasn't Teddy attached to it?

Or was he? He was starting to have some nagging doubts.

Payton considered knocking on the trailer door, but then tried the latch instead. The knob turned and the door eased open. Payton slipped quietly inside, guiding Silk in ahead of him.

It took a moment for his eyes to adjust to the darkness. When they did, Payton could see that the trailer was even smaller inside than it appeared from the outside. "Sit over there," he said, giving Silk a push-start toward the sofa.

He made his way stealthily through the living space—keeping one eye on the girl—all the way back, where the bedroom lay behind a curtain divider. There was no one there, nothing to see.

Payton returned to the front, where Silk was sitting with her legs crossed, arms folded. There was an open loaf of bread on the counter. He removed a slice and bit into it. Day-old, maybe, but still reasonably fresh, which further confirmed that Filo very likely had made it back from Arizona. There were dishes in the sink. A half-empty beer can on the counter—*more evidence.* And the place didn't have a completely abandoned feel to it. More like its resident had been there recently and simply stepped out for a time.

He's around someplace, Payton assured himself. *But how long before he returned?*

Payton wanted to curse his luck. Curse Teddy. Curse the forces that had brought him to this place, this *predicament*. He needed to get in and out quickly, get back to the safety of the island, and do it before Ivess discovered him gone, or sure as hell she'd make her call to the authorities, give him up to them, and then it would all be over.

He was buoyed, however, by the thought that one or both had returned from the ransom demand—no accounting for why some woman had Teddy's cell phone and how she came to know about the teen hostages. The question was becoming less and less about *What became of Teddy,* and more and more about *What became of the money?*

So, what now? Payton thought.

Payton thought of Ivess. She was an early riser, liked to see the sun come up across the statue garden. Liked to believe she was the queen of her universe—that island, that boring, mosquito-infested, fucking island. *Bitch!*

Thinking of the island caused Payton to begin imagining what he might do if Teddy couldn't be found. What if, say, Teddy had gotten picked up by authorities? What if the money was never turned over? Or, what if Teddy had gotten the money and decided to get greedy, run off with it? It was starting to be a very real concern.

A woman had answered Teddy's cell phone... *What was it Silk had said, about a woman coming into the club to ask about Filo?* Who was this woman? Could she be in Houma? Could she already be onto him?

It didn't seem possible.

One way or the other, Payton knew he needed answers, and soon, before Ivess woke up with questions of her own. And the only way to get his answers was to wait for Filo.

Okay, so wait...

Payton crossed to a recliner that faced the sofa and sank into it. He studied Silk, across from him—pretty fucking black girl—letting his eyes roam from her cleavage, across her midriff, and down the length of her slender thighs.

"You wantin' me to do something, is you?" Silk said.

Payton was already thinking, *Why not?* If he had to wait, why not take advantage of the situation?

"Why don't you get out of those jeans?" he said. "Then get over here and show me what you can do."

Silk hesitated, but only for a moment. Then she rose from the sofa and began unbuttoning her blouse.

How old is she? Payton questioned in his mind. *Twenty-one, twenty-two?* Built like a thoroughbred racehorse. It had been a long time since he'd had anything this fine, this young, this firm. And... look at that! ... packing a whole lot up top.

Ivess was suddenly back in his mind, her pruned-up expression on her face.

Screw Ivess! Payton decided. *The bitch could go to hell! Would go to hell,* if he could just get his hands on the money. Payton sat back deeper into the piling of the recliner—forgetting about Teddy, Filo, Ivess, or the money for a time—as Silk slowly pushed her jeans down her thighs.

Oh, man! Payton thought again. *A man could sure get used to this freedom thing.*

TWENTY-ONE

LISSA AWOKE FROM A strange, convoluted dream. It was just past midnight, she believed—but she had no real way of knowing. She rolled quickly out of bed and crossed to the window. Outside, the clouds that had been hanging on night after night had finally moved off. Stars filled the night skies. And a full moon had risen, laying a soft white blanket across the island.

She tried to remember the dream she'd been having but could only recapture fragments of it. Incongruous images—first of her grandfather, Edgar; then of Jacob Worley, the old-timer in the tin-type photo. Odd—they had seemed as one and the same person in the dream. *Grandfather Egan, Jacob Worley* morphed into one being. Two different people from different decades in time, bound together in dreamscape—*how was that so?*

On one hand, the dream had left her feeling guilty—guilty for forsaking her grandfather's trust, guilty for getting her friend Kendra into such difficult circumstances. On the other hand, it had left her feeling regretful—disappointed that she had not been able to fulfill her mission, her goal to at least prove the existence of the

171

Worley fortune. It seemed like such a shame, such a terrible waste. They had come all this way, had gotten so close. *It's there for the taking!* Worley had seemed to say in the dream. *Or had that been her grandfather?*

No matter, she guessed—feeling another stab of disappointment—the skies were clear, the moon was full, the door was unguarded. It was maybe time to go home.

Lissa took a last look at the night beyond the window, then crossed to the bed and began to dress. She slipped into her shorts and top, calling to Kendra in a hushed voice, her friend still sleeping, "Kendra!" She moved on to find her shoes. "Kendra!" she said, a little louder this time.

"What? What's going on?" Kendra sat up in bed.

"It's time!" Lissa said. "We're getting out of here!"

"Home?"

"What else?"

"Are you sure?" Kendra said, even as she slipped out of bed.

"The moon is out. We'll be able to see."

"What about the tigers?"

"We can't worry about them. Just hurry!"

"What about the Rougarou?"

"We can't worry about monsters either."

Lissa finished zipping and buttoning, then crossed to the nightstand to retrieve the Jacob Worley tintype. She gazed upon Worley's image for a moment in the pale light, admiring what she believed to be the genius of it. Her dream, that of her grandfather and Worley, whispered words echoing through dreamscape: *It's there for the taking!*

But we have to go! she said to herself, or perhaps to the memory of Jacob Worley.

It brought on another stab of regret.

Now she turned to the door and opened it a crack to peek out into the night.

Kendra finished dressing, slipping into her shoes and tying them. "I'm ready!" she whispered. "Tigers or no tigers, swamp monsters or no swamp monsters. I want the hell out of here."

"All right, just keep it quiet."

Lissa stepped out ahead of her friend, checking the path in both directions.

"Let's just go," Kendra said, setting off toward the path that had brought them there.

Lissa hesitated.

"What's wrong?" Kendra asked, still in a hushed tone. "Why aren't you coming?"

Lissa considered the Worley photo again, the voice in her dream. It was all too regretful. All too much of a shame. "I can't!" she said. "Not without one peek."

"Are you crazy!"

"We should look for a different way back to the kayak," she reasoned. "It's not safe going through the mangrove."

"We'll have to face the mangrove no matter what! You're making excuses. Lissa! We need to get out of here!"

Lissa knew her friend was right. But, they had come this far. How could she possibly leave without knowing? "I just want to see if it's there! It will only take a minute. I know where it's at from the printouts!"

"For the love of God! Lissa?"

"Just one look. You'll love me when I prove the treasure is there."

"I'll love it when we're off this godforsaken island!"

Lissa held her ground.

Kendra stared at her with pleading eyes. "I hate you!" she finally said.

"Come on. We'll hurry," Lissa said, already turning up the path toward the main house.

Kendra hesitated, but reluctantly followed, grumbling to herself.

They followed the path that took them up to an open area where a thatch-roofed cabana sat shrouded in moonlight. From there they could see the main house, the place where Ivess, the woman they'd heard about, lived. It was a big, stately-looking Southern-style mansion, dark and brooding in the night. They could also see a beach from there, the tide in, waves lapping at the shore, moonlight dancing on the water.

See, not so threatening, Lissa thought.

"How do you know where to look for this garden?" Kendra asked

"I've seen it from Google Earth. At least, what looks like it could be it," Lissa said. "I want to see it for myself. See the sculptures. It should be off down a path to the right of the house."

"Yeah, and what about the tigers? How do you know they don't just live in the garden at night? Maybe it's where they, like, hang out!"

"I'm sure they prefer the mangrove to hunt for food."

"Food, see! That's exactly what scares me! I bet we look a lot like food to them! Can't we just go? This is insane!"

"Just take it easy. All I want is a look at the garden, that's all. Just a quick look, and then we'll head for the kayak. Come on."

Lissa led on, past the cabana—Kendra reluctantly following— and up the path toward the house, then right at a juncture that bypassed the mansion and ran down a slight incline into a lower bottom where Lissa believed the garden to be. There she spotted a wrought-iron archway marking the entrance into the garden. The scrollwork at the top of the arch read: *WORLEY*.

"There! That's it! You see! It's really there!"

"Good! You've seen it! Now can we get to the kayak and go home?"

"Come on. I want to check it out!" Not waiting for approval, she moved off in the direction of the arch.

Kendra huffed a sigh and followed, glancing over her shoulder.

Lissa led them down through the arched opening and into the garden. It was impossibly large, she saw now. More so than it had appeared on Google Earth. The size of a football field or larger. It was rectangular in shape—just like a football field—perfectly defined by a perimeter of flowering shrubs—oleander, bougainvillea, and the like. Throughout the garden were well-tended plots of azaleas, other flowering plants and shrubs—a colorful, open area carved from the thickly tangled mangrove that snarled the rest of the island.

At intervals around the perimeter of the garden were statues—enigmatic white marble figures, staring this way and that, atop massive stone bases. *Worley's sculptures.* Exactly twelve, as Lissa now counted, same as the numbers on a clock. The play of shadow and milky moonlight seemed to give them life.

"Wow!" Lissa proclaimed. "This is it! It really does exist!"

"You gotta be kidding me!" Kendra replied, her mouth agape at the monumental statues before them. "Who are all these people?"

"They're not people. I think they're supposed to be, like, ancient Roman or Greek art or something."

Lissa moved on into the open.

Beyond the far perimeter of the garden, in a clearing at the edge of the mangrove, sat a pair of small wooden structures. Lissa believed these to be storage sheds, perhaps, for landscaping implements and equipment. Near the sheds was a pen built of strong wire mesh, a plywood top. This she considered to be a pen for the tigers when they weren't on duty or prowling the mangrove.

Lissa gave thought to the tigers now, out there roaming free. But quickly dismissed it, overwhelmed by the reality of her find ... *They were here! She and Kendra. Here in the sculpture garden that she'd long read and studied about!* She turned in place, taking in each of the marble statues in turn. "They're magnificent!" she cried. "Look at that one over there," she said to Kendra, pointing to one of the male figures. An archer with his bow drawn skyward but his eyes turned off across the garden. "And that one over there!" A water maiden, pouring from a marble vessel—her eyes looking off in yet another direction.

Lissa led them quickly to the far side of the garden, where one figure, at first glance, seemed shorter than the others. The figure, as it turned out, was of equal height but sitting lower in the ground than the others. Seated down in a hollowed depression in the earth, where the sculpture had seemingly been moved and its heavy base unearthed at sometime in the past. It was now back in place but with the ground surrounding it lower than before.

Lissa withdrew the tintype photo from her hip pocket. "See, this is the statue people believed Jacob Worley was indicating, as the place where he'd buried his fortune, by pointing to the time on his watch," she said, holding the tintype to the moonlight. "It's the statue in the two o'clock position, like the watch appears to say. It's sitting in a hole because that's where they dug." She ran her hands along the marble admiringly.

Kendra shook her head. "But they didn't find anything!"

"No," Lissa said. "See, that's what I was trying to tell you the other night. The previous people didn't take into account that the image is a negative. If you look at it that way, that would say Jacob is actually pointing to the ten o'clock position, to that statue ... right over there!"

She turned to point at the marble figure that sat opposite the sunken statue, across the wide garden, closer to the entrance.

"It's the woman pouring water from a pitcher," Kendra said. "You believe that's where the treasure is?"

"I'm sure of it!"

"I see now why they didn't want to dig up all of them," Kendra said. "The statues are huge! The bases huger! Look at them!"

Lissa considered the sculptures. It was as she'd imagined. The statues were large, and the stone bases were massive and embedded well into the earth, like the stone heads on Easter Island she'd seen photos of. It must have taken a tremendous amount of work to unearth just the one. "See," she said. "Not finding anything under the one they thought was right, they just gave up. Probably thinking that the legend of the photo was nothing more than that. A myth. A hoax. One of the articles said that most people dispelled the idea that there's actually a fortune here at all. That Worley, in reality, spent it all before he died."

"Well, there! You see! It's crazy!"

"I don't think so," Lissa said. "I believe it's still here."

Kendra seemed to consider the possibility for the first time. "Well … I guess that's all well and good … but, even if there is a treasure, how do you expect us to move the statue, move the big stone, and dig it up?"

"I don't know," Lissa said. "I guess I just wanted to see for myself. I haven't thought that far ahead yet. Let's check it out."

"Lissa, no!" Kendra said.

Lissa ignored the protest and set off across the wide garden to the ten o'clock statue of the water maiden. Kendra followed, throwing glances over her shoulder, still nervous of the dangers in the night.

"We're not going to be able to move this, Lissa!" Kendra said.

They were both at the water-maiden sculpture now, looking up at it.

"Let's see how it feels. Give me a hand."

Kendra reluctantly joined her behind the sculpture. They had to reach above shoulder height just to reach the shins of the water maiden. They braced, put their backs into it, and pushed with all their might. The statue didn't budge.

"Try again!"

More pushing, more straining, still the maiden held fast to her perch atop the massive stone base.

"This is useless!" Kendra cried.

"We need something to leverage it," Lissa said, scanning the nearby foliage for a branch, a limb, something sturdy and long, but finding nothing.

"This is crazy, Lissa! We're—" Kendra halted mid-sentence. "Oh, God!"

Somewhere off in the mangrove, one of the cats had raked off a mighty *ROWWWLLL!*

"It's okay. They're not that close," Lissa said.

"We can't do this! Please! Can't we just go back! I don't even want to find the kayak! It's too dangerous!"

"One more try." Lissa braced herself against the statue again. "Come on!"

Kendra wearily joined in.

"On three," Lissa said. "One … Two … thr …"

"Da hell!" a voice cried.

At the sound of the voice, Lissa and Kendra both jumped back a step, coming to attention.

The Cajun, Leggett, appeared at the far end of the garden, stepping out from one of the small wooden structures that Lissa now realized was not a storage shed at all, but a shack—the little man's living quarters.

"Da hell you t'ink you're doing!" Leggett scolded, then came marching their way. "My beauties, dey out there, dem!"

"We're sorry," Lissa said. "We didn't mean any harm!"

Leggett broke off a switch from the nearby oleander as if to use it on them. He whipped it against his pant leg, a show of just how serious their infraction was. "Go, youse! Both you now! Git! Back to da bungalow!" Speaking to them as if they were just two more of his cats that needed controlling. "Both you!" he commanded, whipping the switch against his pant leg again for further measure.

Lissa took a last look at the sculpture of the water maiden. Then reluctantly moved off toward the arched entrance, her head hung.

Kendra followed in her footsteps.

Somewhere off in the cypress grove one of the cats gave off another *ROWWWLL*.

Leggett urged them on, whipping his switch at the brush to keep them moving, and grumbling to himself.

Overhead the stars continued to twinkle brightly, the moon continued to glow. They had lost their one chance to get away, Lissa knew. Now, they were headed back to their bungalow prison, to whatever fate Payton might have in store for them. They might never get another moonlit night, so perfect, for crossing the island. She had committed a grievous error. Blown it for the both of them! How, Lissa thought, could her friend ever forgive her now? And, who would ever find the Worley fortune now?

TWENTY-TWO

FILO AWOKE TO FIND himself lying on the ground, looking up at the sky. He'd spent the night on the banks of the bayou, a good quarter-mile from his trailer. His fishing line was still dangling in the water, no catch on it. There was an empty bottle of Wild Turkey on the ground next to him. He had passed out sometime during the night. His tiny Coleman lantern had run out of fuel.

The presence of the woman from Arizona in Houma had rattled him, made him nervous. Best spend as little time as possible at home, he'd decided. Let her look and search, search and look. Get bored and go home. But now he was hungry, wanting only to return to his trailer and see what he could find to eat. The idea of stretching out on a real bed sounded appealing, too, even if it was for only a short time. Let the kinks settle out of his bones, the night chill work its way out of his joints.

So Filo crawled to his feet and stretched. Then gathered his fishing tackle, lantern, and pole, and headed back along the water's edge toward his little Streamline trailer.

He arrived to find a strange vehicle parked behind his pickup in the drive. But it didn't look like something an investigator would drive. It was dinted and rusting at the quarter panels. There were no signs of official-looking emblems on it—something he was sure to expect.

Then he remembered...

"Wait!" That was Silk's car, the Nigra from Houma Lace. He remembered she had driven it there on a couple of past visits, doing things for him, that she would only do for money. *So, why was she there and waiting?* Maybe behind on her rent, he figured. Wanting to see if he would like a little action, be willing to contribute to the cause. It brought a smile to Filo's face.

He hurried his step now, tossing his gear into the back of his pickup as he passed, and jauntily sprang up the steps onto the metal porch.

He'd barely stepped inside when a hand came out from behind the door and grabbed him.

Silk was there, all right—sitting half-naked on the sofa, looking up at him, her eyes wide and pleading. She wasn't there for fun, he realized.

"Who's there?" Filo cried over his shoulder, his words nearly choked off by the arm wrapped around his throat—a man's arm.

"You Filo?" the man asked.

What should he say to that? Filo wondered. But he nodded, sure that Silk would confirm it if he didn't. "Who are you?"

"I'm looking for Teddy."

Understanding struck Filo now. "You're Payton, aren't you?" he said.

"You know who I am?"

Filo nodded. "Teddy's brother."

"What else do you know?"

"Nothing," Filo said, wondering, *Why the third degree?* "Nothing at all."

"I'm looking for Teddy. He was with you, last time I talked to him. Where is he now?"

Filo understood now that Payton, locked away out there on that island, had not heard of his brother's death. He said, clearing his throat, "Yeah, well ... I'm real sorry to have to break the news to you this way, Payton, but ... Teddy's dead."

The man seemed to go rigid at his back. Then his arm tightened even tighter on Filo's throat. "Dead?"

"Yessir!"

Payton took Filo by the shoulders now and sent him sprawling onto the sofa next to Silk. The girl scooted aside, looking to put distance between them if possible.

Filo clawed his way up to a sitting position and leaned back into the sofa, trying as best he could to maintain his composure. "Yeah! The ransom exchange, Payton. It didn't go well. There was trouble. There was this storm, first, see ... then there was this woman!"

"Woman?"

"Some blonde. A looker," Filo said. "Teddy took a liking to her and ..."

Payton crossed to Filo, bent at the waist and put his face close to his, red with anger and on the verge of exploding.

"What woman?" Payton asked, insistent on answers.

Filo edged sideways in his seat. "I don't know. Some woman, showed up with the money is all. You know how Teddy is ... was ..." he said, trying to keep the whininess out of his voice. "I wanted to stay, really, I did. Wanted to make sure things went okay. But ... well ... he sent me on down the hill ahead of him. Stayed alone with the woman and the money."

The mention of money seemed to bring a new level of interest to Payton's expression. "So, you never saw the money?"

Filo was feeling exceedingly uncomfortable, the man speaking way too close. "I saw it, a bag of it ... but ... I left Teddy alone with her ... like I told you ... I don't know what came next ... I only heard about what happened on the TV news, later that night at the motel. The woman was some kind of investigator, turned out. She shot and killed Teddy. I guess the money stayed with her."

Payton's eyes drilled into him, testing him. They remained like that, hard as steel, 'til finally he said, "She killed my brother?"

Filo didn't know exactly what else to say. He'd already told Payton so.

Payton held his gaze for what seemed an eternity, then straightened, giving Filo some blessed room to breathe.

Filo took the opportunity to inch farther away along the sofa and cross his legs, in an attempt to get casual, saying, "I'm surprised to see you here, Payton. I thought you didn't ever come off the island ..."

Filo realized in that instant that he'd made a mistake talking about it, particularly in front of the stripper. Now he tried to cover, saying, "I mean, nice place and all, out there near the Gulf." *Damn!* Still saying to much. When would he learn to just keep his mouth shut?

"Well, I'm sure you can see the situation calls for exceptions," Payton said. "All this went down, and you decided to just come home, pick up your pole and go fishing, like nothing ever happened? No thought whatsoever about getting word to me. I mean, since you happen to know just where and how I live."

"I didn't know what else to do, honest! I don't own a phone. See for yourself! I thought about trying to come out to the island, inform you. But, then, I saw that woman investigator again. She's here in town, and I thought … well … better to stay lost, not lead her to where you are … see … That's what I was thinking … Thinking of you … Why I spent the night on the bayou, fishing. I was playin' it safe!"

"Whoa! Back up," Payton said, stepping closer again, the tension coming back into his muscles.

Filo wasn't sure what he'd said wrong this time, but he was sure he'd soon find out.

And he did …

Payton said, "The woman who killed Teddy is here! In Houma!"

"I couldn't believe it myself, Payton. Really! I don't have any idea how she managed to find us here. How she knew to …"

Payton turned to Silk now, asked, "The woman that came around the club asking about Filo, she a blonde, good-looking?"

Silk nodded, eyes wide. "I thought she was a dancer, you know."

Payton's hand shot out to grab Filo by the front of the shirt now, lift him partially out of his seat. "You little shit!" Payton spat, his face close again.

"Payton! Surely you're not blaming me for Teddy's death, are you? I mean … I wasn't even there at the time! I was just the transportation! A ride to and from! I wasn't even taking a cut of the ransom! Truly! I thought of it as, well, like helping out a friend, is all."

Filo had whined his words out, just the way he'd wanted not to. But what could he do? The man was inches from his face again and had the front of his shirt twisted into a knot.

Filo waited, praying.

Payton didn't respond, at first. He was back to drilling into him with his eyes and seeming to process all that he'd just learned. "Yeah, why should I blame you?" Payton finally said, letting his anger subside a bit. "You weren't even there, like you said. An innocent bystander."

Filo tried a smile.

"So, tell me, Filo ..." The hand tightened farther. "Where is this woman that you led here to me?"

"I ... I don't know. I didn't ... I saw her up the road, last evening. At the diner on up from where the strip club is. You know, Houma Lace. Please, you gotta ..."

Payton's free hand went to his pocket. The next sound Filo heard was the unmistakable sound of a knife blade, snicking into place.

Silk, on the sofa next to him, cried out and covered her mouth with her hands.

Filo only got a look at the blade for just an instant before it swept cleanly across his throat. Blood spilled down the front of his shirt, flooded into his throat.

"I ..." Filo said, but then couldn't finish.

Payton held him upright for just a moment, then shoved him back into the sofa.

Filo could hear Silk whimpering softly on the seat next to him. Could feel his strength beginning to ebb. His vision blurred—Payton's face, still glaring at him, was turning fuzzy. His strength was bleeding out through the throat wound that he tried desperately to mend with his hands. An icy finger of certainty traced down his spine. *So, this is what it's like to die,* he thought. Against his will ...

Filo felt an odd smile cross his face.

———

Payton waited until he was sure Filo was entirely gone, then turned his eyes to Silk.

"I didn't see nothing!" she said.

Payton considered what to do with her. Teddy was dead. *Dead!* And his dream of getaway money had vanished into thin air. And more immediately troubling, perhaps, was the knowledge that the woman investigator who killed Teddy and spoiled his plans was unbelievably here in Houma. Who was this woman? How long before she'd find him, and his free existence on Terrebonne Key— albeit an underprivileged existence—would be taken away?

Payton considered the woman in front of him now. She knew too much and had heard too much. All it would take would be for the female investigator to get to her again, and this Silk would lead her directly to him.

Payton hated to do it in this case; she was a saucy young thing. But there was business to be taken care of. The most important of which was finding the investigator before she found him.

Payton took Silk by the arm and drew her to her feet.

If his moment of real freedom was near an end, he was at least going to make the most of it. "Come on," he said, dragging her toward the bedroom.

"You gonna kill me?" Silk implored.

"Of course not," Payton said, already planning what to do to her.

———

Silk's Honda was sitting on empty. So, Payton collected the keys to Filo's pickup and left the trailer, closing the door behind him. It was a little after nine that morning. Teddy was dead. There was no money to be had. No near-term chance to free himself of the threats that Ivess used to hold him on Terrebonne Key. And, now, there was this new threat of the woman investigator, already in Houma. *Who was she? How had she managed to trace Teddy and Filo back to him? What did she know about the island? And, more importantly, where was she right now?*

These were the things that troubled Payton Rickey as he slid behind the wheel of Filo's pickup and started the engine.

Payton considered that, possibly, all the woman really knew of him was that he was a caller to Teddy's cell phone. She had *suggested* he was the one holding the teens, which he was. But did she really believe that, or had that just been a fishing expedition on her part, an attempt to draw him out, see how much he would admit to?

Well, he hadn't admitted to anything that he could remember. But, one thing for sure, if she'd taken Teddy down, this woman was dangerous. It also stood to reason that if she'd found her way to Houma, she was smart, too. And it would probably only be a matter of time before she would possibly find her way to Terrebonne Key. Could he take that risk?

He had two options as he saw it: return to Terrebonne Key immediately and spend the days, weeks, and months ahead—*Shit! The rest of his life!*—looking over his shoulder, or take action, go looking for this woman investigator, and get rid of her before she had the chance to discover anything more.

Payton thought of Teddy now, of the chance for freedom that had been taken from him. It was the second option that appealed most to him—find the woman. And not only find her, not only eliminate her from his life, but make her pay. *Pay dearly.*

The idea put a smile on Payton's face.

He wheeled the pickup through the yard and out onto the highway, heading back toward the boat dock. He wasn't sure how to go about finding this woman. And there was still the problem of Ivess. *Suspicious Ivess. Prying Ivess. Demanding Ivess.* It was already getting late into the morning, and once she finished her morning routine, she would start asking for him. Finding him gone, she would head for the phone to make her call to authorities. He was sure of it, *the vindictive bitch*.

But Christ! What choice did he have really?

Payton headed back north, up the highway toward Houma, sure of one thing in his mind: however he went about finding this woman, whatever he decided to do with her ... he had to do it fast.

TWENTY-THREE

THEY HAD SPENT THE night making love—Del being the aggressor this time. Wanting Falconet desperately.

From the moment they'd left the restaurant, she'd had trouble keeping her hands off him. She believed her need, in part, was fueled by the simple fact that they were back together again, the two of them. His raw masculinity was a powerful attraction at any time. But she also believed she had desperately needed release. An escape from thoughts of Louise and her granddaughter Lissa, of the other teen, Kendra; release from promises   if only momentarily.

Falconet had done his part.

Knowing her and using that knowledge, he had lifted her on wave after wave of passion ... *another ... and another ... and another ...*

Now, morning brought the world back to her doorstep. It was time to find Lissa and Kendra. Find Filbert Lohman as the next immediate step to accomplish that end.

Del was just stepping out of the shower when her cell phone rang.

It was Randall.

"What have you got?" Del answered, wrapped in a towel, her hair still damp and hanging in her face.

Falconet was just coming around, wiping sleep from his eyes, and sitting up on the edge of the bed, naked, to listen.

"And a good morning to you too," Randall said.

"Sorry, I'm just feeling anxious."

"What else is new? But I think you'll be happy to know I've got something for you, courtesy of your 'friend' at the police department. Got something to write with?"

"Hang on …"

Del found a notepad and pen on the nightstand and carried them to the desk to take a seat.

Falconet came to stand behind her, look over her shoulder.

"Okay, shoot," she said.

"Filbert Lohman, AKA Filo, lives at 8-0-0-6 Little Caillou Road."

"I'm on Little Caillou now," Del said. "That's got to be somewhere close by."

"I do my best," Randall said. "Is the Fed still with you?"

"Yeah, he's right … He's staying here in the motel," she amended.

Randall said nothing. But Del could picture him smiling to himself, knowing exactly where Frank would be. Where he was, right now, in his nakedness, his hands massaging her shoulders, as she scratched the information on the notepad.

"You watch out for yourself. And watch out for your man, while you're at it."

Her man, Del thought. *She liked the sound of it.*

Randall ended the call. Del laid her cell phone aside.

"We've got an address."

"Right?" Falconet said. "Randall's a good man."

"I've got to finish getting dressed," she said, sweeping Falconet's hands from her shoulders and heading to the bathroom to finish up.

"I'll put some clothes on and grab some coffee and a couple of danish from the breakfast bar," Falconet said. "Meet you at the car."

They found the residence of Filbert Lohman. It was a trailer on the bayou side of the road, just beyond the Houma city limits, no more than five miles from Houma Lace. Falconet had studied Del's face as she drove. She had been wildly in need of him the night before—with tears in her eyes as they coupled. Taking—*yes! yes! yes!*—but giving also. Driving him to the brink, numerous times, only to back off, spare him, for the next mad rush toward closure.

They had reached that place of glory sometime in the early morning hours.

Now, she was back to being focused, serious, her mind on the task ahead. Find Filo and pin him down. Leverage a confession from him, the location of the ransomed teens. A location that Falconet believed would also yield Payton Rickey as the *not-so-dead* fugitive.

Falconet braced, as Del slowed the Wrangler and wheeled it into the gravel drive.

There was no pickup in the driveway, as they'd both been expecting. But there was a beat-up, dark blue Toyota.

Del pulled the Wrangler in behind it and killed the engine.

"Let's just hope he's home," Del said. "I feel like the clock is ticking on Lissa and Kendra."

Falconet stepped out on his side, as Del slid out on the other. It was quiet there, away from the bustle of the commercial district. Flies buzzed. The leaves in the trees rustled gently in the summer breeze. Falconet had worn a loose-fitting white shirt this morning, tan slacks. The day was already hot and humid, the back of his shirt already damp with perspiration, sticking to him.

Del took to the porch, drawing her handgun—her Baby Eagle—from her waistband at her back. Falconet did the same, poising his service weapon alongside his leg, as Del knocked once.

No response.

Falconet stepped forward and knocked harder. "Federal investigator! Open up!" he called through the door.

Nothing.

"What do you think?" Del said.

Falconet knocked once more, ever louder this time, then tried the knob.

The doorknob turned, and Falconet nudged it open.

Del pushed in ahead of him.

On the sofa, just across from the door, lay a man. He was folded oddly backward, legs spread at an wide angle to the floor. Del could tell, without question, that it was a body, and not simply a man in the throes of a late-morning nap. She could tell, without question, it was Filo. "Goddamn it!"

"That's Filo?" Falconet asked.

"That's him! We're too fucking late!"

Falconet kept his eyes on the back hallway, but stepped to the body and checked for a pulse. "Yeah, he's dead all right . . . come on." He stepped away, moving carefully down the hallway toward the back.

There was no one in the bathroom. Falconet parted the curtain that separated the living area from the bedroom. "Shit!" he said.

Del pushed in beside him to take a look.

Sprawled across the bed naked was the beautiful black girl, Silk, who she'd talked to the night before in the club. She lay facedown, her legs spread, her eyes staring off blindly toward the wall. There was a pool of blood beneath her. Her throat had been cut.

Del lowered her gaze.

"You know this one, too?" Falconet asked.

"That's the girl from Houma Lace. The one who gave me Filo's name."

Del turned away sharply and paced back to the living area.

Falconet caught up to her, tucking his weapon away.

Del stood, shoulders slumped, her gun hanging limp in one hand. She had placed all her hopes on finding Filo, the last remaining connection to the teens. Now Filo was dead. And so was an innocent bystander.

Falconet came up behind her, put his hands on her shoulders.

"Goddamn it, Frank!" she said. "He was our last chance to find Lissa and her friend!"

"Not the last," Falconet said. "There's still whoever is holding them."

"Who! A dead man?"

He was trying to console her, she knew, but she was feeling sorry for herself, unwilling to allow herself to be consoled.

Falconet remained calm. He said, "I still believe it's Payton Rickey. I still believe he's alive and behind this entire thing."

"That does us a lot of fucking good! He's managed to stay hidden for months! We don't have months! Lissa and Kendra don't have months!"

She was crying—something she despised herself for. And she was being a bitch to Frank—something else she despised herself for. He didn't deserve it. But how could she help herself? All her hopes and prayers had been taken from her.

"We'll find Payton," Falconet said, his voice still calm. "We know he's somewhere in the area."

"You're damn right!" she said, wiping her eyes and finding a new level of resolve. "And when we do, I'm going to put a bullet in his fucking chest, just like I did his brother."

She knew she was spouting off. But Falconet had seen her this way before—that time in Nazareth Church, back there in the hills of Kentucky, two years ago, when she had learned the infuriating truth about her mother.

Frank knew how to handle her. And he knew, right now, the thing to do was to not piss her off. He said simply, "We'll find the girls."

It was just the right thing to say, the only thing that needed saying.

Del stopped her sniveling, wiped the last tears from her eyes, and put some steel in her backbone. "All right!" she said. "I got it out of my system. Let's find this bastard!"

Falconet stepped away, giving her space to deal with her emotions—on her own and in her own way.

They would get past this setback, she knew. Move on to the next step. Something new always turned up, it always did. And when it did, she'd be ready. Things had a way of working that way.

"I'll take a look around," she said. "See if I can find anything."

"I'll call local authorities," Falconet said, crossing out the door and out onto the porch—in large part, she believed, to give her time alone.

He was a good man. He was.

And she was glad he was there.

———

The Terrebonne Parish Sheriff's Department responded to the call, along with the medical examiner and her team. Del remained distant and aloof, as Falconet answered questions and posed questions of his own.

The parish sheriff himself came onto the scene—a man named Lincoln Thibodaux. Thibodaux was tall and lanky, bald on top, wearing a rumpled tan suit and tie this day. But he seemed competent to Falconet, thoughtful in his questions and responses. They were on the lawn, outside the trailer, the day hot and humid. Sweat wicked through their clothing.

"So, this could relate to those remains of the U.S. marshal we found in the swamp a few weeks back?" Thibodaux said.

"We believe so," Falconet replied. "We think it might also have to do with a pair of missing Arizona teens my partner has been hired to find." He looked around for Del to introduce her and found she was already sitting in the Wrangler, alone and still angry, but anxious to get on with the hunt. Falconet produced a photo. "Have you ever seen this man, or heard his name, Payton Rickey?"

Thibodaux looked the photo over, then shook his head. "No, can't say as I have. He someone of interest?"

"Well... again, we're not sure," Falconet said. "It's all just a lot of speculation at this point."

"All right," Thibodaux said. "My deputies have both your statements?"

"They do," Falconet confirmed.

"Then, let me know if I can help."

Thibodaux handed Falconet his card.

"Thanks, I'll stay in touch."

———

They drove back to the hotel in silence—Del doing the driving but remaining distant and quiet. She was hurting, Falconet knew, feeling down about the turn of events that had left them without a single lead to the whereabouts of Lissa Rogers and Kendra Kozak.

So, Falconet rode, staring off out the window into the distance, considering his own feelings, as he allowed her to consider hers.

They were dead in the water—the way it felt. They had combed the trailer as they'd waited for authorities to respond. But nothing they came across had offered any connection back to the missing teens. And Falconet had shown off Payton Rickey's photo, yet none of the medical examiner's people, the sheriff's deputies, nor Thibodaux himself had ever seen or heard of the man. Still, the teens were close by—*so very close by, Falconet could taste it.*

But where? An inch could feel like a mile when you had nothing to go on.

———

They arrived back at the hotel just after eleven a.m. Del wheeled the Wrangler into a parking spot close to the building. She killed the engine and sat there unmoving for a moment, her thoughts still on the teens, Falconet believed.

"We'll find Lissa," he said. "I promised before, and I promise again."

"Can you give me a minute alone?" Del said.

Falconet studied her for a moment. Then said, "Sure, I need a shower, anyway. We left in a rush this morning and I didn't get to take one. We haven't eaten anything, either."

"Go on," Del said. "I'll meet you at The Shack when you're through."

"It won't take long," he said. He leaned across the seat and gave her a peck on the cheek. It elicited a sad smile.

She would be all right, he knew—a woman who always landed on her feet, no matter how turbulent the going. Lunch, and maybe a drink, was what it would take. And talk, about what to do next.

Falconet left her there, behind the wheel of her Jeep, and made his way to the balcony and to their room.

TWENTY-FOUR

DEL REMAINED BEHIND THE wheel of her Wrangler for a time, thinking about Louise and the past, about the promise she'd made to her over her gravestone, and about her own need to find Lissa Rogers and her friend. She had placed all her hope on finding Filo. Now, having found him—having found him dead—it seemed as though all hope had run out. There were no more leads. Not even a long shot that she could see. What could possibly turn up? What stroke of luck could possibly turn things around?

She needed to think.

Del slid out from behind the wheel of the Wrangler and made her way down to the curb and across the highway to the dock. She followed the bayou upstream for several dozen yards, in the direction away from The Shack. And stood at the water's edge, looking down into the lazily meandering current. Bullfrogs croaked amid stands of cattails, seeming to question her presence there. *"Wad up? Wad up?"*

What was up was that she'd let Louise down. It didn't—couldn't—feel any other way.

She still believed, as Falconet did, that Payton Rickey was behind the ransom. But if, in fact, he was alive, he'd managed to stay under the radar and out of public view for months. What chance did she have of finding him, before he made the decision to kill Lissa and her friend and take off? There just didn't seem to be a way.

Still, Falconet had promised they would bring the girls back alive. And she trusted in him, his confidence. It just wasn't clear how that would come to pass.

Del tossed a pebble into the water and watched the ripples run away across the bayou. This was a devilish part of the world, she thought, imagining the swamps that spread off to the south, and all the secrets they surely concealed. Someone needed to pull the plug on the place and let the water run out. Maybe then they would be up to their asses in the very alligators they were looking for.

Del stuffed her hands in her pocket and slowly made her way back toward The Shack. Falconet would soon be showered and meeting her there. She could use a drink, she thought. Not a beer, this time. But a stiff one, with lots of bite to it. One to jar something loose inside. Let her grab onto the demon inside her, hang onto its tail until it reached the gates of hell.

As she reached the end of the dock, Del spotted something she hadn't seen earlier. Among the handful of other cars in the small parking area between the road and the dock was a pickup truck. It was blue—an older model, gray-primered in places. It was Filo's truck, she was sure. She had missed it, somehow, as she passed on her way to the bayou—her head not in a place to notice such things.

What the hell was it doing here?

Somewhat obvious, now, was the fact that whoever killed Filo had taken his pickup. Now the pickup was here at the dock, as though whoever took it was returning to wherever they came from...

By boat!

Del was suddenly reminded of Falconet's suspicions about the man in the dinghy the night before. The aluminum dinghy was still tied off to its bigger cousin—the pleasure boat. The pleasure boat was still moored at the dock, just yards away from where she was now standing. The *Sand Castle*, it read across its stern.

Bless his heart, Del thought. Could Falconet's incredible paranoia be the thing that would turn their pursuit around, give them another opening?

The idea seemed to fall into place logically. If the man they saw the night before was Payton Rickey, and he arrived by boat, it was possible he had been hiding out somewhere to the south, perhaps the swamps—an explanation for why no one in Houma had ever seen or heard of him. It also made sense that with Filo being the only one who could testify to his involvement, that he would need to finally come out of hiding long enough to get rid of Filo, maintain his *dead man* status.

Christ! Del thought. *Was it all that simple?*

Now, thinking of Teddy, Del remembered her encounter with him on the mountain and the keychain she'd removed from his pocket, along with his cell phone. *The* Sand Castle? *Was it possible? No way! But, then... My God!... maybe!*

Del removed the key from her pocket and considered it for a moment. It was a single key on a key ring, looking something like a car key or, say,... *a boat key.*

It was all too logical, too prophetically plain, not to be considered.

There are no coincidences, she reminded herself. *Only incidents that coincide. Shit happens for a reason!*

Del crossed to the dock, with the key in hand, to get a better look at the boat. It was a fast, sleek thing. Fiberglass hull. The helm was located behind the cabin on a short deck that extended to the stern. It had a rigid overhead shade canopy. Inboard engines. And a curved windshield, offering a line of sight across the hull. Portholes on its sides offered a view out from within. There was no one on deck, no one at the helm, and from all that she could see, no one moving about in cabin below.

So where was Payton Rickey now, she wondered?

Del threw a quick glance toward The Shack, then another back across the road to the motel. Falconet had not come out of the room yet.

Del took the key in her left hand, and reached behind her to wrap her fingers around the grip of her Baby Eagle. The familiar coolness of it offered an immediate sense of comfort. She gave it one last cautionary thought, then stepped down off the dock onto the deck of the *Sand Castle*, her weapon still secure in her waistband but at her fingertips and ready.

The cabin below was empty. And not much to speak of. There was a small galley and a small forward sleeping compartment with two adjacent bunks.

Del considered the key again. If this was the boat that Teddy originally arrived on, the key from his pocket had to be the ignition key. Del turned to the helm and sat down behind the wheel. She felt uneasy being there, as though she was attempting to steal the boat, rather than inspect it. She cast a quick look about, then attempted the key in the ignition...

The key slid easily into the lock.

She twisted...

And the key turned.

The big inboard motor sprang to life.

Holy shit!

Del quickly shut it off.

It was too much to ask for, really! But there it was! The very boat that Teddy Rickey had driven to Houma, possibly just days before he arrived in Arizona to claim a ransom.

Oh, man! Wait 'til I tell Frank about this! she thought.

Just then, a cell phone in her pocket rang, nearly startling her out of the seat. It was Teddy's phone, as if Teddy was calling from the grave to congratulate her on her ingenuity.

Del withdrew the phone and answered.

"Aren't you just one clever little bitch?" a voice on the phone said.

"Payton?"

"So you do know me," the voice said.

"Where—?"

"Don't turn around! And don't reach for the weapon you've got tucked in at your back. I've got a gun and it's pointed directly at you."

"Where are the teenagers?" Del said into the phone.

"Still on that?"

"We can make a deal," Del said, fishing for leverage.

It seemed to cause the man to hesitate. There was a moment of no response. Then Del felt the boat shift as he stepped down onto the deck.

"Don't try anything funny. Just keep the phone to your ear and the other hand where I can see it."

She felt his presence at her back now, felt the muzzle of a gun poke into her ribs.

Payton jerked her Baby Eagle from her rear waistband. Now his hand closed over the cell phone and stripped it from her hand. "Much better!" he said.

Del turned to see Payton Rickey for the first time. He was dressed in a tan safari shirt, tan shorts, and deck shoes. A ruggedly handsome man, but with cold penetrating eyes. A *killer's* eyes. He looked considerably like his brother, Teddy, only with dark hair and older by a couple of years.

"So, at last we meet," Del said.

"You made a big mistake coming here."

"What are you going to do?"

"You killed my brother. My first instinct is to put a bullet in you and drop you in the swamp. But I'm starting to like what you just said about a deal."

Del threw a hopeful glance toward the road, the hotel. Falconet was still nowhere in sight. "There's people who know you're alive. Right here in Houma. They know you killed Filo."

"Filo needed killing."

"They'll come looking for you. They'll come looking for me."

"They can look all they want," Payton said. "No one's found me yet. Now what's this about a deal?"

"You've got something I want," Del said. "I can get you something you want."

Payton considered her a moment, the gun pressed close to her midsection. "What are you offering?"

"I can't give you Teddy back. But I can arrange to get the money to you. Isn't that what you really want?"

Del watched Payton's eyes for the answer.

"You can do that?" he asked.

"I arranged it the first time. All it would take would be a phone call. You wanted fifty thousand before, I say we make it sixty this time. Something for your trouble. The girl's grandfather can afford it. I could have it wired to a bank here in minutes. I can have someone deliver it. Like ordering a pizza." Del said, ad-libbing, saying whatever came into her head, whatever she thought he wanted to hear. She cast another quick glance toward the road. Surely Frank would be coming soon.

Payton never took his eyes off her, but she could see he was considering the offer.

Just then, patrons could be heard exiting The Shack, coming out onto the dock amid loud conversation, raucous laughter.

"Get below. We'll talk more about this later," Payton said. He pushed Del off the seat and in the direction of the cabin.

Del balked.

Payton jabbed the gun painfully hard into her back and gave her another shove, sending her to the edge of the cabin portal. Another stiff shove, and she had one foot on the steps leading down.

The restaurant patrons could still be heard, coming ever closer.

Call out, Del thought. *Get their attention.*

But before she could open her mouth, Payton brought the gun down hard on the side of her head …

Negotiations ended.

TWENTY-FIVE

FALCONET CAME OUT OF the motel room, buttoning his shirt and letting the door close behind him. He had started into the shower earlier when Darius called, wanting an update. He had brought him up to speed on Filo and how he strongly believed that Payton Rickey was—yes, in fact—alive and somewhere in southern Louisiana. It had taken him fifteen minutes to get Darius off the line.

So, then he showered, hurrying through the motions, and thinking of Del. Her mood had darkened, and while he believed she needed a little time alone to sort things out, he didn't want to leave her alone too long, give her time to do something impulsive.

Now he was hustling across the landing and down the stairs to the parking lot.

Del was no longer sitting behind the wheel of her Wrangler. He quickly crossed the parking area to the road, jogged between passing cars, and hurried up the walkway to the dock. He noticed that the pleasure boat with the dinghy attached was no longer moored there.

Falconet hurried on to the restaurant and went inside.

The hostess greeted him. "Just one?" A laminated menu in her hand.

"Actually, I'm joining someone."

The hostess waited patiently as Falconet scanned the restaurant and bar area. He saw no sign of Del. "Did you see a good-looking woman with short blonde hair come in?"

The waitress puzzled on it a moment.

"She was wearing boots and jeans, about your height."

"No ... I don't think so."

Falconet turned back outside. *Where the hell was she? Had he misunderstood their plans?* He scanned the dock area and the bayou in both directions looking for her.

Falconet took out his cell phone and dialed her number. He got her voicemail. "Hey, where are you?" he said. "I thought we were meeting at The Shack? Call me." He ended the call.

He gave the area another once-over, but seeing nothing of her, returned inside. "I'll just wait at the bar," he told the hostess.

She gave him a smile and tucked the menu away.

Falconet took a seat on one of the barstools and ordered a beer.

Fifteen minutes passed ... twenty ... Falconet had sipped his way through his first beer and considered ordering another. Yet ... he couldn't imagine why Del hadn't shown up. He knew she was down, even distraught, over losing the one opportunity they had to find the teens. But he didn't think it was like her to abandon him, go off on a pout. She was more resilient than that.

Falconet ordered a second beer and sipped for another twenty minutes, becoming more anxious, more worried by the minute. Now he dialed 411 and asked for the number for Desert Sands Covert in Tucson. The operator connected him to the number and the call rang through. A pleasant receptionist answered, and he asked for Randall. When the coarse, familiar voice came on the line, he said, "Randall, this is Frank Falconet."

"What's happened to my girl?" Randall said immediately.

"No … nothing … I mean, I don't think … I was just wondering if she'd called into the office recently, if you'd talked to her?"

"Not since yesterday," Randall said. "Should I be concerned?"

"No … I don't think so … we were just supposed to meet at this restaurant here. She hasn't shown up yet."

"Well," Randall said. "She's a girl who does whatever she wants."

Falconet understood Randall's response. But, still, he didn't think Del would just stand him up. He said, "Yeah, I know she can be a handful. Just … if she calls in, have her call my cell phone. Okay? She has my number."

"And if she calls your cell phone, have her call me," Randall said. "I worry about the girl too."

"I will," Falconet said. And ended the call.

Falconet turned to face the bar, sip his beer, and wait. He supposed she would show up, sooner or later. But these situations, these *matters of the heart,* Falconet thought …

They could take the wind right out of you.

TWENTY-SIX

LEGGETT SPOTTED IVESS, THE island's matron, coming down the path from the main house toward the bungalows and thought, *"Ooo ye yi!"* She had the female cat, Gigi, with her. He'd just taken the teenage girls some food and was returning to his duties. Java was in position outside the girl's bungalow. Leggett hurried up the path to head Ivess off.

"Leggett, have you seen Payton? I've simply been looking everywhere for him," Ivess said, seeming with every intention to be on her way to investigate the bungalows for herself.

"Naw, ma'am! I been workin' all dat time!" Leggett said, placing himself in front of Ivess on the path.

"You can't tell me where Payton is? It's after noon and I haven't seen him all morning. I've asked the waitstaff, and none will confess to seeing him. He's not on the beach, not at the cabana. Come to think of it, I haven't seen his brother, Teddy, for days either. Where is my Payton? I want to know where he is this minute!"

"He all time around," Leggett said.

"Is he at the bungalow?"

Ivess attempted a step past with her tiger; Leggett crowded their way, the tiger nuzzled against him. "He naw!" Leggett said. "I just come from dere myself."

Ivess eyed him suspiciously for a long moment. "What's going on, Leggett? Why hasn't Payton come to me today?"

Leggett stalled, opting to fuss with Gigi's collar.

"Leggett? What are you not telling me?"

Leggett held out, thinking that answering to ma'am might be slightly better than answering to Payton. "He all time be 'round someplace."

Leggett couldn't bring himself to make eye contact, but he hoped to catfish she was buying it. That's when he heard the sound of a boat engine, the *Sand Castle*, returning to its moorings. He wasn't sure whether to thank God for the timing or make a run for it. It all depended on Ivess's reaction.

"Is that the boat I hear, Leggett?"

"Hmmm..." Leggett said, stalling.

"Did Payton leave this island?" The question was mostly rhetorical. She was still glaring at him, suspiciously. "There's something going on, Leggett! And I intend to get to the bottom of it! I just hope I don't find you're lying to me."

"Naw, ma'am," Leggett said.

"Well!" Ivess said, waiting for him to provide escort. "Take me to the boat grotto."

Leggett hesitated, but decided he had little choice. He expected there might be a confrontation, raised voices, if Ivess become angry with Payton. "Yaw, ma'am," he replied. He hooked a chain leash to Gigi's collar just in case, then led the two of them away.

———

Del awoke to the sound of the boat's motor roaring in her ears. Her head was pounding from the blow she'd taken. She didn't know how long she'd been out, but assumed it had been some time. She was lying in a somewhat fetal position on one of the sleep-cabin's bunks. She attempted to move and found that both her hands and her feet were bound with duct tape. Another piece was strapped across her mouth. She could see out the rear of the cabin through the small doorway that led up on deck. Payton was at the helm, one hairy leg visible to her beneath his shorts. The sun was still up—that much she could see—and there were big, puffy white clouds trailing behind them. If she craned her neck, she could see out through one of the cabin's portholes, catch glimpses of cypress trees with Spanish moss dripping from their limbs. An occasional waterfowl would take flight at the roar of the boat's big motor, and would flap off across the water. *Where was he taking her?*

Del believed she had gotten through to him, keeping his hope alive—and herself in the process—by convincing him that he could still use her to collect the ransom. Of course, even if she did, her life, and those of the teens, was no more certain. It was a ploy to buy time. Temporary at best. But she hoped, wherever it was he was taking her, it was where the teens were being held. Only then—and with a boatload of luck—might she have the chance to get them all out of there alive.

———

The island's western tip appeared across the port bow. And now the boat grotto and main house came into view. The main house was the big, old stately mansion, built by the island's previous owner—a guy named *Worley*, Payton assumed, from the iron scrollwork above the entrance to the garden. The boat grotto was wholly Ivess's doing, having it constructed to look like a natural stone outcropping, jutting out from the shoreline. The entrance resembled the mouth of a cave. In reality, it was fashioned from fiberglass and painted to give the appearance of a natural geologic formation. It was ideally situated on the leeward shore, facing back toward East Bayou and the mainland, providing shelter for the *Sand Castle* from storms that, more typically, came off the Gulf from the south and east. A beautiful piece of work, really—built and paid for by the trust that maintained Ivess's reclusive lifestyle.

Payton slowed the boat and carefully navigated it toward the entrance to the grotto. When he was in range, he cut the engines and let the boat glide on its own momentum. The dinghy followed. He worked the wheel, maneuvering the craft, deftly, so that it just made the cave entrance, bumped hard against the landing, and settled to a stop. *Perfect.* Now he jumped out to tie the boat off.

So far, so good! Payton thought, throwing a glance out through the grotto's landside doorway to the path leading up to the back of the house. *No sign of Ivess.* Now he climbed back aboard and went down into the cabin to get the woman on her feet and out of there, into hiding.

She was still lying on the bunk, conscious now, and looking up at him through ice-green eyes that were more calm than he might have expected. *This woman was something else! Smart,* he realized. He'd have to keep a close eye on her.

Payton leaned in over her, pressing his weight against her, and put his face close to hers. He peeled the tape on her mouth back partially, let her suck in a good, deep breath. "You still with me?" he said.

Del nodded.

"Good! We're going to take a little walk. To a place where you can get comfortable. I might even release your bonds. And, then, we're going to talk about you getting that money for me. The fifty... no, you're right ... sixty thousand dollars. You understand? Tell me you understand!"

"Yes," Del said.

"Good!" He stretched the tape back tight across her mouth and drew his knife from his pocket. "Now, I'm going to free your ankles, and you're going to walk with me. We'll have to cut through the mangrove, so you'll have to stay close and do what I tell you. There are things on this island you don't want to have to face alone, trust me. Are we simpatico?"

Del nodded agreement.

"All right! You play real nice!" Payton positioned the knife, ready to cut the ankle bindings, when he heard a voice that chilled his soul.

"Payyy-ton! Oh, Pay-ton, darling!"

NO, NO, NO! Payton thought. Of all times to make her presence known. *Shit! Ivess!*

"You stay right here! Don't move!" he said to Del, putting the point of the knife in her face. "Don't you make a sound!"

He got another nod from her.

"All right!" Payton rolled off top of her and went on deck.

He could see out through the doorway to the path. Ivess had not yet made it all the way down the hill, but she was coming, quicker than he would have liked. Leggett was right behind her, leading the female cat by its leash. He had to get his story straight, and quick.

Payton removed both the woman's gun and his own from is front waistband and stuffed them both in back, pulling his shirt down to conceal them. He then climbed out onto the landing and went out through the doorway just in time to head Ivess off. "Hey hey..." he called, a cheery greeting. "What are you doing down here? I could have sworn you'd be on the beach with a daiquiri by this time a' day." Payton caught up to her, catching her by the elbow to turn her back toward the house.

Ivess balked and stood her ground. "Just where have you been, Payton! I've been looking for you all morning!"

"Why ... what? ... I've been around! Been getting some things done ... fixing up ... you know!"

"I heard the boat motor!"

"Well, sure ... I was just testing it ... blowing the carbon out ... you know ... it's a nice boat. You gotta do those kinda things from time to time."

Ivess gave him a suspicious glare. "Yes, and where's that no-good brother of yours? I haven't seen him in days!"

"Teddy? ... why ... I think he's back at the cabana ... maybe ... someplace, I'm sure."

Ivess stayed with the suspicious drilling of her eyes. "There's something you're not telling me. What are you two up to?"

"Why, Ivess ... nothing ... just been a lot of things to do is all. Listen, I'm all finished up down here. Why don't you and I go back up to the house and let me fix you a drink? One of my specials." He took her elbow again and turned her back up the path.

She resisted for a second, but then allowed herself to be guided away.

Leggett—who'd been listening to the exchange and holding on to Gigi's leash with both hands—took the turn in Ivess's attitude as his dismissal from duty. He led the cat off ahead of them. All of them making their way, now, back toward the house.

Payton gave a silent sigh of relief. He'd gotten her away from the boat and from the good-looking woman he had bound below. But he wasn't out of the woods yet. *Uh-uh, not completely!* He knew he still had plenty of explaining to do, about how and what and why he had been unavailable to her for her every beck and call. The way things were shaping up, he could see his complete atonement might very well take awhile—Ivess a sponge when it came to attention, sucking it up but never giving anything in return.

And the woman down there in the boat? Well, she was just going to have to wait it out until he was finished. *All there was to it.*

"Maybe you'd like a foot rub," Payton offered, leading Ivess on.

TWENTY-SEVEN

DEL KNEW SHE COULDN'T wait for Payton to come back for her. She had to act now, while the opportunity availed. She squirmed herself around, got her feet off the edge of the bunk, and dragged herself up into a sitting position. Her hands were bound behind her back, her feet bound tightly together at the ankles. She slid off the bunk and managed to stand without toppling.

The ceiling was low. She crouched at the knees and managed to hop her way out through the galley and to the portal leading up onto the deck. She peered out.

It was into the afternoon now; she could tell by the angle of the sun. From where she stood, she could see beyond the stern and out back across the water, in the direction from which they'd come. Out there was what looked to be an endless swamp. Miles of it. Patches of land, water; more patches of land, more water. No sign of boats or people or life. She was on an island—she had heard Payton confirm at least that much.

The boat had been driven into some kind of enclosure, and she could see now that it was cavelike, a grotto of sorts, with stone walls that looked fake—formed to give the appearance of real stone. A boathouse.

Del listened outside. The voices she'd heard earlier—Payton's and that of a woman named Ivess—had drifted away. She was alone, she believed, at least for now. And she would have to make her move now if she was ever going to have one.

She turned back to the galley, wanting to find something—anything—to free herself of her bindings. On one side of the galley was a fold-up table, retracted and fastened to the wall by a latch. On the other side, a small, two-door pantry. She managed to back her way to it and use her fingers, behind her back, to pry open the door. There were canned goods, some packaged goods, and other supplies. Nothing she could see that could be used to cut her bindings. Alongside the pantry was a small refrigerator, and above it a wall-mounted cupboard. She backed her way to the refrigerator and stretched to reach the cupboard, hoping to find something sharp inside—utensils, a glass or ceramic plate she might break. Something! *Damn!* Anything! She reached, but it was too high, beyond her grasp.

Del gave up and hopped her way back to the portal.

She needed to free her hands, her feet, get the goddamn tape off her mouth so she could breath properly. She gauged the height of the first step and hopped once. Gauged again and hopped a second time, this time banging her head on the low ceiling and nearly toppling backward off the step. The bump shot a pain through her skull, reminding her that the thump Payton had given her with the barrel of his gun was not yet ready to dissipate. She managed to fight off stars and keep her balance. She measured the last step to the top more carefully, hopped, and made her way up onto the deck.

The space inside the tiny cabin had been claustrophobic. On deck, the air was fresh, a cool breeze coming off the water. She was able to stand fully erect, get the kinks out. She could hear birds. Some sounding exotic, like parrots, cockatoos, and the like. Others were more of the same haunting cries of waterfowl that she'd been hearing on the trip there. It was an odd mix, she thought—and, now she remembered Payton's warning. *"There are things on this island you don't want to have to face alone."*

What things? Del wondered.

She hopped her way across the deck scanning for something, anything, she could use to cut the tape. The key was not in the ignition—something that might have been used to saw through the tape—not to mention, serve the purpose of starting the boat and getting the hell off the island. Payton had taken it with him. Nothing else seemed to provide an obvious solution.

What? Think! Something sharp ...

That's when she noticed the landing. It ran the length of the grotto. A wooden deck, laid with planks. The planks were secured with nails. And she saw that a couple of the nails were partially backed out. Loosened, perhaps, over time, by the constant shift and sway caused by the lapping of wakes against its moorings. A couple of the nails were protruding as much as a quarter-inch or more.

Del crossed to the edge of the boat. To get on to the landing she would have to first hop up onto the side of the boat. Then she would have to hop from the boat to the landing. If at either juncture she were to lose her footing or balance, she could fall between the boat and the landing, into the water, become trapped beneath them. Not a good thing, she considered—hands and feet bound, she would likely drown. It was a very risky proposition.

Del considered the idea for a moment more but decided it was the only option she had.

She planted herself firmly on the deck, feet together, making herself aware of the wet spray that had slicked the deck's surface. She gauged the distance and made a leap of faith.

She struck the landing on the side of the boat and held on, teetering there precariously for a moment as the boat fishtailed. When she found her balance again, she considered the distance to the landing. The boat had been tied off in haste and had now drifted to the end of its rope, leaving a distance of at least two feet between her and the landing.

Del planted again, crouched, and sprang.

The boat sashayed farther backward in the water. Instead of sticking a landing, as she'd planned, she pitched forward, landing hard on one shoulder against the planking. The air punched out of her. A sharp pain shot through her side, brutalizing the ribs that were still tender from the beating she'd taken on the mountain. Del cried out—a muffled cry into the tape that still covered her mouth.

She lay there for a long minute catching her breath and urging the pain to subside. She felt grateful. Though she'd taken a fall, at the very least it was better than splashing down beneath the boat in deep water.

When she thought it was safe to move again, Del rolled herself facedown and, like an inchworm, hunched her way up into a kneeling position. Her head was still spinning, and for a moment she thought there was a chance she might yet black out and pitch backward into the water. Instead, she held on until the dizziness passed. Then she knee-walked herself to the end of the landing where the nails were protruding.

There, she sat back on her rear, her back to a protruding nail, and by Braille hooked the edges of the tape over the head of one of the nails. Bit by bit, stroke by stroke, she ripped and sawed her way through her bonds. When she felt the tape loosen, she gave a pull with all her might and the tape gave with a raw rending sound.

Thank you, God! Del offered up. Her hands were free.

Del stripped off the remaining strands of tape and used her now-free hands to peel away the tape covering her mouth. She took a deep, long breath and exhaled. So good, the cool air off the water. Next she tore loose the bindings at her ankles, and she was completely free.

She didn't hesitate. She quickly scrambled to her feet—her legs still a bit unsteady. She first checked her pockets—*empty*. Payton had taken both her cell phone and the one belonging to Teddy. He also had her gun—the Baby Eagle—and one of his own. She made her way out of the boat grotto through the doorway onto land.

The sun was low in the sky, off on the western horizon. On terra firma, now, she could see out across the open Gulf in one direction, turn and look back and peer across a wide, near-endless expanse of swamp.

Where was this? she wondered. And thought of Falconet again. *How, in God's name, would he ever possibly find her here?*

It was isolated, for sure. Off to her left was dense foliage; along the shoreline and running inward were stands of cypress, thickly tangled mangrove. She could see exotic birds in the trees, above, sitting alongside their native cousins. Up a path from the boat grotto, impossibly so, stood a stately Southern mansion. She was looking at the back of it—a door leading out from what might be the kitchen area onto a small porch. The front, she presumed, faced off across the open waters of the Gulf. There were paths leading both to the house and off to other parts of the island, telling her that there were possibly other structures, other facilities, yet to be seen.

So, now what? she considered.

Del moved quickly up the path staying close to cover, focusing on the house where she believed Payton and the unseen woman had gone. Halfway there, an alternate path led down to a high wrought-iron arch. It gave entrance into what appeared to be a well-maintained garden, surrounded by marble statues. Beyond the garden, in a clearing amid the tangled mangrove, sat a pair of aging structures. One, a shanty of some sort, possibly sleeping quarters for a gardener. The second she believed to be a tool shed—a place to store the implements used to maintain the grounds.

Del moved on toward the back of the house. There she put her back to the wall and listened. It was mostly quiet inside, but for the sounds of kitchen noises coming from behind the screen door—house staff, possibly, going about their afternoon chores.

Staying low, she slid stealthily along the wall to the corner of the house and peered out into the yard. From there Del could see past the front corner of the house, and out, down a path that led to a small sand beach, where a pair of beach chairs and umbrellas were arranged facing the open waters of the Gulf—a startling view. A stand of palm trees—possibly imported—gave the impression that one might be vacationing on some island paradise. Not a bad layout, she thought, once you got past the swamp.

But Del was anything but vacationing.

Another path led away from the side of the house, back down through the trees. Far down from where she stood, she could see what might be a cabana of some type. It had a thatch roof; party lights were strung about. Beyond that, more trees, possibly more amenities to the island she hadn't discovered yet. Thus far, she hadn't seen anything that might suggest where the teens were being held.

It was a nice enough setup, Del thought. She could imagine Payton Rickey hiding out here. Private. Self-contained. And possibly with an island mistress to provide for him, help secure his anonymity. That was why none of the locals back in Houma had ever seen him. And, perhaps, the ransom of the teens was his way of preparing his next move—wishing, maybe, to escape his exile, no matter how much self-imposed.

It was all just speculation, of course. And none of it really mattered anymore. She was here. And she believed Lissa and Kendra to be here too, someplace. The only questions left were *where* and *how* to get them off the island.

Del heard a door bang open, around at the front of the house, and a man's voice talking in oddly conjoined words and sentences. The man's dialect was Cajun, she believed. He came into view at the far corner of the house—a little man in tan work pants and shirt, carrying a tray of food.

Food for the hostages? Del considered.

Even more interesting—and totally unbelievable—was that he was leading a beautiful but fierce-looking white tiger. The tiger milled and circled at the end of its leash, but overall kept pace. The Cajun continued talking to it as he went, speaking to it as if it were a child. Referring to the beast as "Gigi," and saying things like, "Da's my beauty! Come on! We gaw find your brother!"

Its brother? Del thought. *Another tiger on the island?*

Was this what Payton had warned about? "*Things on this island you'd rather not face alone?*" What kind of fairytale land had Lissa and her friend stumbled into? What other surprises were awaiting?

Del drew back into the shadows, as the Cajun made his way around the side of the house and down the path toward the cabana.

It was the first real encouraging news Del had received in some time. Lissa Rogers and Kendra Kozak were seemingly still alive and being held here. Possibly hidden away in some guest house or outbuilding, or some other building somewhere, where the Cajun and his cat were headed.

Del took a glance back at the kitchen door, checked the path ahead, then followed, keeping a safe distance, sticking to the security of the surrounding foliage.

The Cajun continued on down the path.

Del drew to a stop at the cabana, taking cover behind a corner of the rectangular bar.

The Cajun continued on, eventually arriving at a pair of bungalows—Del could see now—set apart from each other, within another small clearing, amid the trees. At the front of one of the bungalows, near the door, Del saw what she now knew to be the brother of the first tiger. This one was even bigger and more magnificent than the first. And easily twice as fierce-looking. It lay at the end of a long chain. *A sentry*, Del realized. *This is where the girls are being held*. One big, bad guard dog to watch the door.

The Cajun clipped the female's leash to that of the chain that secured the male. Then he proceeded with the food tray to the entrance. He knocked once before entering and disappeared inside, leaving the cats outside to stand guard.

Damn! Del thought. How was she supposed to get past that?

The good news was she now believed she knew where Lissa and her friend were being held. And that they appeared to be alive and well and being cared for. The bad news was they were all still stuck here on the island, with vicious tigers and a violent fugitive. Either of which would not hesitate to take their lives if given the chance. Del had to get them out of there and quick, she knew. The only question was *how*?

The sun was dropping low on the horizon, and dark clouds were forming off to the south, forewarning of possible rain sometime into the evening hours. And before long, Payton Rickey would return to the boathouse to discover her gone. Then all hell would break loose again ... time was running out.

Del continued to watch the bungalow from the cover of the cabana. Only a few minutes passed, then the Cajun was back out of the bungalow, his hands free this time. She watched as he unhooked the leashes of both cats, got a firm grip on the male's chain, and started back up the path, her way.

Oh, shit! Del thought.

Her first instinct was to find a place to hide. But if the tigers caught her scent on the wind in passing, they would likely react, give up her hiding place. *Then what?*

She had to move fast, keep distance between herself and the trio. Without hesitating, Del bolted from her cover behind the bar and raced back up the path toward the main house.

From the kitchen door at the rear, one of the house staff had come out onto the porch, shaking out a throw rug; several more rugs were piled at her feet, her work only just begun.

Del wasn't sure who she could trust. The island mistress she'd heard earlier didn't sound as if she had knowledge of the captive teens, but what would be her reaction if she found out? What would be Payton's reaction if she did? He was violent, reactive as nitroglycerin. She couldn't risk being seen.

The Cajun was still coming with the tigers. Del had to think fast. With her way back along the path blocked, the Cajun and the tigers closing in from the opposite direction, Del had no choice. She thrashed off the path and into the brush, moving fast. Limbs grazed her face; broad leaves slaked at her thighs. She could only hope the tigers did not detect her, or that the sounds of her beating a fast path through the trees didn't alert the Cajun or others.

The foliage gave way somewhat quickly, and Del found herself in the garden she had seen earlier. She had entered it from the side, between a pair of marble statues. There were eleven more, Del counted, spaced some twenty yards apart, around the perimeter.

From there she could see back past the arched entrance to the back of the house. The maid was still on the rear porch. And she couldn't return to the boat grotto—soon Payton would free himself from the island mistress and come looking for her on the boat. She couldn't allow him to find her there.

And now she spotted the Cajun and the cats coming off the path near the back of the house and making the turn toward the garden. They were still coming her way. Del turned quickly off along the perimeter, passing statue after statue until she reached the far end of the garden. Some thirty more yards ahead was the clearing where the shanty and tool shed sat. She could also now see a large pen with a plywood roof covering, a place to keep the tigers when they weren't at the ends of their leashes. Beyond lay densely thicketed mangrove. Hard going, impossible to penetrate with any kind of stealth.

Del threw a glance back to see the Cajun and the cats still coming. They were on the path leading down beneath the arch. There was only one thing left to do, and do it fast. Del burst across the clearing and to the tool shed, hoping to hell she wouldn't find it locked.

It wasn't, thank God!

There she slipped inside, feeling relief that she was out of sight for now and that she apparently hadn't been spotted.

Inside she waited, catching her breath until she heard the Cajun approaching, the man still talking baby talk to his kittens. A small knothole in one of the planks offered a view outside. Del peeked through as the Cajun led the cats to their pen and corralled them inside. He then closed the pen and crossed to the shanty.

Thank God the tigers are out of the equation for now, she thought. But what about the man?

Del watched, praying for him to go inside his quarters and close the door. Only then could she perhaps slip out and make her way back to the bungalows.

Instead, the man sat down on a small bench outside the shack, leaned back against the planking, and withdrew a harmonica from his shirt pocket.

"My beauties like to hear a little music?" he asked, as if expecting them to answer. Then, placing his mouth to the harp, he began to play.

The sounds were sad and mournful.

Just great! Del thought. *Mood music!*

She watched the man, and listened, for a moment longer, then stepped away to study her surroundings for the first time. It was, as she had surmised, a tool shed for gardening equipment. There was a good-sized riding mower, various trimming and edging tools, other handyman tools hanging from posts and nails. A dirt floor.

Outside, the Cajun continued his mournful refrain.

There was nothing she could do, she knew, but get comfortable and wait. She found a place on the dirt floor, alongside the mower, and leaned back against the wall.

"I've found them, Louise," she said inside her head. "But I'm stuck here for a while."

The thing about the devil, Del, is the devil knows how to wait. You just have to be as good at it as he is.

As outside the harmonica moaned, Del thought about Lissa and Kendra in the bungalow, having a dinner she wished she could share. And she thought about Frank, back in Houma, going crazy with concern and worry by now. Would he come looking for her —

her knight in shining armor? Would there be any clues at all he could follow? Del didn't believe so. After just reuniting with Frank again, and starting to believe in the idea of partnership, she was all alone in this thing anyway.

TWENTY-EIGHT

FALCONET WAS WAY PAST worry. He was convinced now that something bad had happened to Del. They'd become separated after only a short time together. The night before and the nights before that had been great—loving and tender—both of them excited about being reunited. She wouldn't just take off, leave him hanging. *So, what had happened? Where could she be?*

It was close to dinner time, and he needed to think. Falconet crossed the road to The Shack again and ordered a drink—this time a shot of hard liquor to clear his head. Filbert Lohman had been murdered. Someone had gotten to him. There was only one reason, he believed, for someone to do so. And that was to shut him up. Filo had been on the mountain the day Del had shot and killed Teddy Rickey. It stood to reason that whoever was holding the teenagers captive would want to keep that knowledge secret. And Falconet now believed he knew exactly who that was for sure. *Alive and well.* Payton Rickey.

Falconet downed his drink and ordered another.

No one in Houma had seemingly ever seen Payton. So, where was he hiding? There were endless miles of swamp to the south. That was a possibility. But how did you begin to look for a man in the countless miles of wetland?

A thought suddenly popped into Falconet's head, a tucked-away suspicion that now suddenly inserted itself into his consciousness. The dinghy, which caught his attention the night before ... the man who had arrived to tie off to the pleasure boat, then leave on foot ... both the boat and the dinghy were now gone. What if ... Falconet began to speculate ... What if, the man he'd seen the night before had actually been Payton himself? One could reason that Teddy Rickey had initially come by boat to Houma, met Filo, and continued on to Arizona to eventually get himself killed. In order to eliminate Filo and retrieve the boat, Payton Rickey would then have been forced to some other means of transportation—such as the dinghy. And, now, let's say, what if Del had somehow stumbled onto the same conclusion this morning, come to the dock, and wound up a victim of Payton? If so, where would he take her? What would he do with her? Falconet didn't want to consider the possibilities. But he knew he had to find Del, and fast. It was time to get off his ass and act.

Without waiting for the bartender to serve his second shot, Falconet threw some cash on the bar and headed out. Over his shoulder, he heard the bartender calling to him, "Hey! Don't you want your drink?"

He didn't. And didn't bother to respond. He pushed out the entrance onto the dock and walked down to where the boat had last been moored. He scanned the bayou in both directions but considered strongly the direction from which the dinghy had arrived. *South.*

From what he'd learned from maps, the Little Caillou Bayou flowed that direction, eventually emptying into East Bayou. There he remembered the water spreading out in all directions, into a spider web of twisting, turning ways. All of which ultimately found their way into the Gulf of Mexico. So—*Christ!*—where did he begin?

It was possible he was jumping to conclusions. Looking for ghosts under the bed. But, then, as Falconet turned from dock to leave, he spotted a blue and gray-primered pickup among the cars in the parking area. He crossed quickly to it. The doors were unlocked, no key in the ignition. Falconet rummaged inside. There was not much to be found. But the registration above the visor confirmed that it was owned by none other than . . .

Filbert Lohman.

He turned his eyes back to the dock. There was no speculation left. This was Filo's truck, and Payton Rickey had used it to get back to the boat after killing him. The boat he now believed Del had been swept away on.

Damn it!

Falconet tossed the registration certificate onto the seat and headed back across the road to the motel parking lot. He knew Del to keep a spare key somewhere on the vehicle. He searched the wheel wells and—*Eureka!*—came out with a small magnetic tin containing the spare. He slid behind the wheel, cranked the engine, and set out down Little Caillou Road heading south. He didn't have a boat but knew the road ran parallel to the water. Worse case, he would take it to its end and find out where it went; best case, he would spot some sign of the *Sand Castle* somewhere farther down the bayou.

He drove for more than forty minutes, seeing nothing of the boat, but seeing fewer and fewer commercial establishments, more sprawling grazing plains and wetland.

There was a long stretch of road where there wasn't much of anything but the occasional house trailer, water-logged trees, and swamp grass. The road continued on—the Little Caillou Bayou continuously just outside his window.

Eventually, he came to the town of Cocodrie, and the road came to an abrupt end at a large marina. Boats of all types sat lined, shoulder to shoulder, in slips along a wooden boardwalk. There was a boat ramp, for launching small craft. There was a wide parking area, loosely populated with vehicles. Commercial businesses sat clustered about the marina—a bait shop; several craft and souvenir shops; and a restaurant, Le Bord de l'Eau Café, sitting right at the water's edge. Beyond the marina, the Little Caillou Bayou spread out quickly in all directions, forming the vast swampland of East Bayou. Falconet pulled Del's Wrangler off into the parking area and stepped out.

For a time, he stood looking out at the vast wetlands. It was a foreign landscape—at least to a man from the city. It was vast and isolated. A cypress swamp, full of secrets. He thought of Del and tried to imagine her out there somewhere. Then thought of her again and tried *not* to imagine.

Payton had possibly taken her with him, to the place where he had remained in hiding. The two teenage girls were possibly out there too. Where was *there*?

Falconet left the Wrangler and walked over to the marina. He strolled the boardwalk, checking out the boats moored at water's edge. There were all types, from fishing boats to pleasure boats to impressive yachts. None of them was the *Sand Castle*.

He considered the open waters of the bayou again, a dull and achy longing in his heart, then crossed over the boardwalk to Le Bord de l'Eau Café.

Inside—looking perhaps a bit like a lost puppy—he considered the patrons. They were mostly locals, he believed: fishermen, yachtsmen. A waitress came in a kitschy little sailor's uniform. "Can I help you?"

Falconet realized he didn't know what to say. Where did he begin? "Where does the water go once you leave the marina?" he asked.

The waitress looked at him like she didn't understand the question. "You sure I can't get you a table or something?"

"No…" Falconet said. "Sorry, not now."

Falconet turned and left the restaurant.

He'd come to realize just what a fishing expedition he was on. The swamp was vast, the pathways of navigation endless. He also had very little to go on, but some pieced-together hunch, any assumptive point of which, being wrong, could take the logic in a completely different direction. He was *pissing up a rope,* the way he saw it now.

Falconet stood at the entrance for a time, trying to reason his way through to *What to do next?* Coming up with nothing, he left and followed the walk back to the parking area and to the Wrangler.

He had just reached for the door handle when he noticed a vehicle sitting all by itself down at the far end of the lot near the boat launch. It was a late-model Land Rover. From that distance, it gave off the impression of having been sitting there for quite a while, abandoned maybe. Falconet left the Wrangler and crossed the parking area to get a better look.

On closer inspection, it was obvious the Land Rover had not been driven in some time. It was covered in caked dust. There were leaves collected in the roof rack, lodged beneath the wiper blades.

The entire body was peppered with bird droppings. The right front tire was low on air. And, the license plate was from Arizona.

Right? Falconet said beneath his breath.

The doors were locked. He cupped his face to the driver side window and peered inside. There was a graduation tassel hanging from the rearview mirror, various hair clips and combs lying in the tray in the center console. There were music CDs sticking out of the pockets in the door panels. The steering wheel had a pink, fuzzy steering cover.

Falconet gave a conspiratorial look around. Then, seeing no one, used his elbow, in a sharp punch, to bust in the driver's side window. He reached through and unlocked the door and let himself inside.

From the driver's seat, he inspected above both visors and found nothing. He considered the personal effects in the tray. Then leaned across and popped the glove compartment to rummage through a collection of tissue packets and lipstick cartridges to find the vehicle registration. The vehicle was registered to Lissa Rogers of Tucson, Arizona.

Bada bing! Falconet thought. He had hit the jackpot.

It stood to reason that the girls had driven to road's end, then had likely taken a small craft into East Bayou. What was further obvious was that the girls had not returned.

What demise had befallen them? Had they motored or paddled off into the swamp, become hijacked by another boat? Or had they gone off to some specific destination, only to stumble onto Payton Rickey's hiding place.

The latter seemed more likely.

Falconet slumped back in the seat to think. Where exactly had they gone?

The possibilities were endless.

He rubbed his temples, trying to ease the throbbing that had come into them. When he dropped his hands, he noticed something he hadn't seen before. A manila folder, stuffed down between the seats. He drew it out and perused its contents.

Inside the folder were various printouts from the Internet—Google searches and the like. Some were street maps of Houma, the surrounding countryside. Others were Google Earth aerial views of East Bayou and its spider-veined waterways, stretching out to form the swamp.

Other printouts were that of various Internet articles. Some told of the history of the area, of life along the bayou. One article in particular, however, caught Falconet's eye. It was an article titled "Jacob Worley's Treasure."

Falconet took time to read the article.

It told the legend of a man named Jacob Worley, a recluse living on the island of Terrebonne Key, located far out in East Bayou. It was told that Worley had died after a long bout with dementia, leaving behind a treasure trove of gold and silver somewhere on the island, with no instructions to its whereabouts other than a curiously posed tintype photo, which was also presumed lost to history, and references to a sculpture garden where the alleged treasure was believed to be hidden.

Right? Falconet thought. He didn't see a tintype among the mix of papers. But had the teens gone off on some foolish Nancy Drew treasure hunt? Had they gone looking for legendary gold and by chance stumbled onto the hideout of Payton Rickey?

No! Falconet first thought. But, then, thought … *Well, maybe.* It was all very plausible.

Falconet thumbed the printouts again, coming back to the aerial map of Terrebonne Key. He spread it out on the steering column in front of him. Terrebonne was a fairly sizable patch of land compared to the thousands of spotty mangrove islands that populated the swamp. It sat at the far reaches of Bayou East where the swamp gave onto the Gulf of Mexico.

Falconet let his eyes move from the map, out across the very real waters of East Bayou to the horizon shrouded in late-afternoon marine layer, cloud cover now beginning to form. His mind made the leap to Payton Rickey again. The plane carrying him had gone down somewhere in the Gulf, somewhere out there, possibly not altogether far from Terrebonne Key. *There are no coincidences,* he remembered Del saying. *Only incidents that coincide!*

So they do, Falconet thought to himself.

Now he thought of Del again. Could she be out there with the teens, held captive on Terrebonne Key?

Falconet couldn't be absolutely sure. But he believed he needed to find out.

TWENTY-NINE

It was dusk by the time Payton shook free of Ivess. He hustled back to the boat grotto to check on his charge, only to find the tatters of her tape bindings scattered across the landing. *No, no, no!* Payton lamented.

He climbed quickly aboard the *Sand Castle* and checked the cabin.

Goddamn it! She was gone.

Payton silently cursed Ivess—the woman had a knack for screwing up his plans. *Well, all right,* he thought, he'd just have to find this female investigator again. It shouldn't be hard, as long as she didn't somehow get off the island.

He considered that very real possibility and spotted the dinghy still tied off at the stern of the *Sand Castle*. At least she had chosen not to make a break for it, but had foolishly opted for carrying on her search for the teens. So, let her find them. *So what?* Sooner or later he would catch up to her and she'd have to bargain for each of their lives, maybe worth more in the end.

235

Payton went to the stern and gathered the line by which the dinghy was tethered. He undid it and dragged the dinghy close, then maneuvered it around to get the bow pointed off toward the swamp. He gave it a shove, hard, and watched it go. It glided smoothly for a ways, then the wind from the southeast caught its tail and the boat slowly drifted off toward the swamp. *That settles that,* Payton thought, a smile crossing his face. *Now we go and find the woman.*

Payton went back outside and scanned the foliage for signs of her. He ran his eyes back toward the house and to the path leading down to the garden. She was out there somewhere, night closing in, possibly rain on the way. *Could she get off the island before nightfall?* He didn't think so. He had scuttled the dinghy and still had the keys to the *Sand Castle* in his pocket. So, okay, it was a matter of going to the bungalows first, checking on the teens, making sure they were still secure. Then start his search, track her down, but not let her get away.

Payton started back up the path, aiming to do just as he'd planned. But then he spotted Leggett, down beyond the garden, outside his quarters, as he sometimes sat before dark, playing his music. His time, Payton figured, before he let the cats off their leash to make their nightly hunt. He couldn't let that happen tonight. If he was to find the woman and keep her alive long enough to secure the ransom, then he didn't need Gigi, or in particular, Java, the mean-ass male, out there in the bush with her.

Payton diverted from his plan to go down through the garden, to where Leggett sat with his harmonica to his mouth. The Cajun stopped playing at his approach.

"What bring you this way?" Leggett said.

"Just checking. The girls still in the bungalow?"

"Took dem some dinner," Leggett said.

"But you brought the male back with you?"

"Pischouettes? They not goin' anywhere, dem."

"Yeah, well…" He was thinking of the woman, the door unguarded from the outside now. Payton gazed over at the tigers—the female lying down, the male prowling the pen. "It's looking like it's going to rain. You gonna keep the cats in their pen tonight?"

"My beauties don't care 'bout wet," Leggett said. "Java, he like the rain."

"Well, do me a favor. Keep them both locked up tonight, okay? Feed them if you have to."

"What 'bout dem girls?" Leggett asked. "You gonna keep your own eye on them."

Hmmmm? Payton thought about it now. Maybe that wasn't such a bad idea after all. Instead of traipsing around in the rain looking for the woman. Sit back and wait for her to come looking for the teens. He said, "I'll see to the teens. You just make sure you keep the cats in their cage."

Leggett gave him a suspicious look, but he didn't question further. He put the harmonica to his mouth and began to play again, telling Payton he was no opposition to whatever plans he might have.

Good! Payton thought.

He left the Cajun with his cats and his music, and headed off toward the bungalows.

———

Del had heard Payton's voice and returned to the knothole to see him come out from the garden to confront Leggett. She was able to hear the conversation and learned that Payton was instructing the Cajun—whom she now knew as *Leggett*—to keep the cats contained for the night. He had discovered her missing, she knew, and was planning his search to find her. There was both good news and bad news in that. The good news was that she wouldn't have to contend with two prowling tigers in her quest to get to the teens. The bad news was that Payton wouldn't leave them unguarded, and he was just about as dangerous as the beasts. Maybe more so. And it also sounded like rain was headed this way.

Leggett went back to playing again.

Confound it! she complained to herself. She really needed to get out of this shed.

Del settled back on the floor, once again, and listened as Leggett continued to play.

She would have to wait it out. Wait … and hope the little man didn't decide to sit there all night.

———

Payton made his way back to the bungalows, stopping by the cabana long enough to grab a bottle of Old Granddad and take it with him. He'd been thinking about the woman, and was starting to like the idea of sitting back and waiting for her more and more. The clouds were rolling in heavy now—a rain, maybe a good one, on its way. It would be insane to be out there looking for her. Besides, she had nowhere to go. No one knew to look for her there.

Time was completely on his side.

Payton went by the bungalow and checked first on the teens, peeking in through the window to see them both sitting on the bed, thumbing through magazines Leggett had supplied them. Okay, so everything was secure.

He crossed now to the edge of the clearing and scanned the mangrove for signs of the woman. Nothing yet. But she was out there somewhere—that much was for sure.

He turned back to his own bungalow and went inside. His doorway faced the other bungalow at a slight angle. He could leave the door open and lie in bed, suck on Old Granddad—if you dared think about it that way—and keep an eye on the teens. Nothing to do but wait.

Payton left the door ajar and made his way to the bed with his bottle and lay back. He was still hurting about Teddy, and angered by his death. The arrogance of this woman. *Christ!* He wanted nothing more than to put a bullet in her brain, almost regretting not having done so at the dock. But, then ... well ... there was still the money to consider. Still Ivess. And, still, this—fucking!—island. With or without Teddy, if he could get his hands on the ransom money, he could flee this place, live out his life in some exotic paradise a free man. That's what he needed to do, he reminded himself. That's why he had to be patient and wait.

Payton uncapped the bottle and took a big swig. The taste of it was good, the feel of it a rush, burning its way down. The breeze through the door brought more good feelings, confident feelings, the heat of the day dissipating, temperature dropping, as the clouds accumulated.

Let the woman hang out in the rain, he thought ... *there was no big rush.*

THIRTY

"Payton is back," Kendra said, this time her turn at the window, looking out into the growing gloom. "The door to his bungalow is open. He has the light on. I can see him lying back on his bed."

The last of the day's sun had disappeared beyond the main house. Dark rainclouds had rolled in, darkness had settled. She'd been thinking about home, such as it was, wanting more than anything to get out of there, off the island, and out of this depressing part of the world.

Lissa rolled off the bed to join her at the window and look out into the night. "Is he alone?"

"I think so. He left his door open, I'm sure, so he can keep an eye on us."

Lissa turned her gaze to a starless sky. "It's gonna rain. Maybe Leggett won't be letting the tigers out tonight, maybe that's why."

"Please, tell me you're not planning another midnight trip to the garden!"

"No," Lissa said, a resigned tone in her voice. She crossed back to the bed and sat down, lowering her gaze. "I can see it was a mistake coming here. We can't get to any treasure without help. I know that now. I should have just taken the tintype to someone who could help."

"Maybe we still can," Kendra said, feeling a pang of regret for her friend. "Maybe someone that's … like … I don't know … important or something. Get them to come back with us."

"You're not mad at me?" Lissa asked.

Kendra thought about it. She'd never really been able to stay mad at Lissa for long, even with the crazy situations she got them into. *Well*, this being a pretty bad one. But still. She crossed to the bed and gave her friend a hug. "I'm not mad. But I do want to go home."

"We can't leave until Payton leaves or falls asleep. It's also going to be pitch-black out with the clouds and all. We'd never be able to find our way back to the kayak in the dark."

Kendra seemed to consider it. "Maybe we could just go to him. Ask him to let us go?"

"Don't even think about it! If he was going to release us, he'd have already done so."

"What do you think he'll do to us, then?"

"I don't know," Lissa said. "But I think you're right. We need to try to make a break for it. Grandpa has got to be worried sick."

"Maybe he's sent someone to look for us."

"Maybe."

"You think we can leave tonight?"

"I don't know. Maybe, if Payton falls asleep. Maybe if it doesn't rain and the skies clear. A lot of maybes. And we still don't know if the cats are out or not."

Kendra turned her gaze back out the window, to Payton's open doorway—the man in there, the light still on. "*I just want to go home,*" she said quietly to herself …

"*I just want to go home.*"

241

Lissa studied her friend. She could almost hear the wheels of desperation turning in her. She could see the effects the stress of their incarceration was having, dragging Kendra's spirit down, weighing on her.

Lissa lay back on the bed, turning her gaze to the ceiling and beyond. The intrigue of finding the Jacob Worley fortune was still with her. It played powerfully on her mind. But she knew now that there was no way the two of them could acquire it. Not alone. It would take someone with the ability and resources to move the statues and exhume the heavy stone bases they sat on. It would take workmen, shovels and implements, maybe heavy equipment, to peel back the earth. Whatever made her think they could do it alone? It was crazy, she realized.

She considered the idea that Kendra had brought up, that perhaps her grandfather, being concerned, would send someone to look for them. He loved her, she knew. Would do anything he had to, to get her back. But could they count on anyone actually finding them? Could they try to wait it out and see what happened?

More importantly, she thought, could Kendra hold out ...

And not do anything stupid.

THIRTY-ONE

LEGGETT PLAYED HIS HARMONICA, mournfully, well past the setting of the sun and into nightfall. But now it was time to feed Java and Gigi. He could see them pacing anxiously back and forth. So, he finished up a refrain, then rose—tucking his harmonica into his shirt pocket—and stretched to get the kinks out. Clouds had socked in heavy, and the first few drops of rain could be felt, patting intermittently off his face and hands.

In the pen, Gigi—more gentle and tame—settled quietly, aware that Leggett was now ready to attend to them. While Java, always nervous, always anxious, continued to prowl the cage, pacing first one way, then the other.

Leggett retrieved their leashes from a hook at the corner of the pen. "I gonna come," he said.

Java raked off a harsh *ROWLLLL!* As if to say, *Be quick about it.*

"We gonna take a little walk to the house, so you just hold onto dem horses." He undid the cage latch, and stepped inside with the cats.

Gigi came to her feet, while Java continued to pace. He hooked the leash to her collar, then crossed to Java, first working him toward a corner of the cage, clapping his hands once, calling "Java!" to initiate control.

The cat seemed to obey, slowing his pace. But, then, as Leggett attempted to latch the chain leash to its collar, the big cat rose up on its back feet and balked. Leggett grabbed for him, getting one hand on his collar, but, then, lost his footing in the loose-sand bedding inside the cage.

Java made an impressive leap over top Leggett, and shot out through the open gate into the night. "Java!" Leggett called after him.

It was too late.

The cat raced for the mangrove, into the bush, and was gone from sight.

"Ooo ye yi!" Leggett lamented. He remembered Payton's instructions, not to let the cats out this night. But what could he do? There was nothing. Not now. Not until daybreak and after the rains cleared. Whatever reasons the man might have had for wanting the cats inside meant little now. He would round Java up come morning, lying idle and content over some late-night kill. And he would return him to duty outside the girls' bungalow. All would be fine…

At least he hoped so.

"Mais…" Leggett said, collecting Gigi by the leash, resigned. "You my good *pischouette*. Let's get you some' to eat."

––––––

Del had watched the entire episode take place through the knothole from inside the shack. She wasn't crazy about the big male tiger being loose in the brush, but at least the Cajun had finally left his position outside the door and she was free to gain her freedom again.

She had lost well over an hour, trapped inside, listening to Leggett blow his sad refrains, wondering if he was ever going to give it up, go inside, leave, fall asleep—hell die, for Godsake!

Finally!

Del stepped out into darkness, feeling the first few drops of rain on her face. *Great!* Just what she needed, she thought—one more thing to complicate her mission.

It was hard to see, but Del knew the way out into the garden. She crossed along the back sides of the marble statues and found the spot where she had earlier entered the garden from out of the brush. Here a small amount of light filtered down from the porch light at the back of the house. She could see Leggett up there behind the house, feeding the female cat. She would have to avoid the path that circled around behind the house, and shortcut her way back to the cabana.

Del set off into the brush, picking her way one step at a time.

The light drops of rain continued to fall. Soon, she could tell, however … she would be dealing with a downpour.

THIRTY-TWO

By THE TIME KENDRA came to terms with what she was about to
do, the rain was clattering off the roof of the bungalow and rushing in torrents off the eaves. Lissa was sleeping soundly next to her.
She had thought about it long and hard, somewhat sickened by
the idea. But, it was the only way, she believed, to get off the island,
out of this terrible situation.

Their one attempt to leave hadn't been an attempt at all. It had
turned out to be simply Lissa's chance to see what she came to see.
Leggett had found them and brought them back. But who were they
kidding anyway? There was no way they would make it through the
mangrove with tigers roaming loose. It would be suicide. Ridiculous! More crazy than going to look for the treasure itself.

No.

There was only one way to get out of this, she believed. Go to
Payton and convince him to let them go. No matter what it took.

Kendra slipped quietly from the bed and crossed the room to
the window. It was hard to see through the downpour, but the

door to Payton's bungalow was still open, and he was still in there lying back on the bed, the light on.

She stood for a time, still hesitant, working up her nerve to go through with it. She was already feeling naked—dressed in nothing but her panties and the knit top she'd come to the island in. The thought of what she was about to do was humiliating. But humiliating, tinged with a certain naughty excitement. The timing was right—the door was unguarded, Lissa was asleep, and Payton was all alone. It was now or never. And *never* was starting to feel like not an option.

Kendra took a deep breath to buck up her courage, let it out slowly. Then crossed to the door and slipped out into the rain, closing the door softly behind her. She padded, quickly, barefoot, across the path between the bungalows.

In the short distance to his door, she was already soaked to the bone—her hair drenched, her flimsy clothing sopping wet. She blinked back the water that ran into her eyes.

Payton was lying propped against the headboard, dressed in only his boxer shorts. His hard, angular face was shadowy, unshaven. He had a bottle tucked under his arm. A darkly masculine pose, almost sexy, she thought—if only he were closer to her age.

She couldn't tell if he had seen her there, or if he was even awake or sleeping. His eyes appeared to be closed. She was just one step from the doorway, front-lit by the light spilling out from inside. He hadn't reacted to her being there.

Kendra threw a quick glance back toward the bungalow where Lissa slept, second thoughts urging her to *Go back! Don't do this!*

All remained quiet.

For a moment—only a moment—she considered listening to her inner voice, turning around, and going back to the bungalow before it was too late. But *it was now or never,* she told herself again. Putting on a stiff upper lip, she braced her shoulders and rapped softly on the door jamb.

Payton still didn't respond.

She rapped again, louder this time.

Payton's eyes snapped open. "Yeah … what … who …?" His voice was raspy with sleep. He cleared it now, seeing her there.

Kendra stepped inside.

"What the fu … What are you doing out of your bungalow?"

Kendra stepped farther into the room, closing the door behind her. He seemed more suspicious, initially, than turned on—a reaction she hadn't anticipated. "I couldn't sleep," she said. "I saw your light on and thought you might want some company."

His eyes moved up and down the length of her—panties and top soaking wet and clinging, hair dripping. "You need to go back," he said.

His words were saying one thing, Kendra realized, but his eyes were saying something else. "Can't we just … talk?" she said with a girlish little shrug of her shoulders.

His eyes found the place between her thighs, a dark triangle, barely concealed beneath the wet, sheer fabric.

Kendra let him look for a moment, then she reached for the light switch and flipped it off. Now, she crossed in darkness, wet feet padding, to the bed where Payton lay.

He allowed it.

A light from behind the nearby bathroom door, cast just enough glow for her to see him, for him to see her. She sat down on the edge of the bed next to him and waited.

"Well …" he said, his voice catching in his throat.

Kendra moved one hand to rest it gently upon his shoulder.

Sex was not something new to her. She'd been with any number of boys from school—on the back seats of cars, mostly, in back bedrooms at parties, some. But Payton was not a boy. He was a grown man, someone taboo. The reaction in his eyes, seeing her nearly naked at the door, had sent little waves of excitement through her loins, overriding her reservations, betraying her inner feelings. *She could go through with this*, she now thought. *She could do what she had to do.*

Kendra let her fingers trail through the hair on his chest.

He was strong, powerfully built, his chest covered with a thick, dark mat. There was something so wrong, so incredibly illicit, about the things she was doing, the things she was feeling. Being here in the dark with him, alone, was such a dark and dirty secret. She felt a shudder of welcome excitement ripple through her.

Payton reached for her without saying a word and pulled her down on top of him.

"So, you're feeling just a little frisky, are you? Away from the boys too long." He pressed the whiskey bottle into her hand. "Maybe you'd like a drink?"

Kendra accepted the bottle and took a sip. The liquor burned its way down her throat, causing her to choke. She felt tears well up in her eyes.

"Go on. Take a real hit," he urged. "This one will go down much easier, I promise."

She took another sip, and he was right. This time the alcohol burned less, slid down her throat in smooth relief, and left her feeling tingly, wired for whatever was to come.

Kendra handed the bottle back to him.

He took a slug for himself, capped it, and laid it aside.

His expression became serious now, darker. He let his eyes run along the length of her, across the curve of her hip, and down her thighs.

"I've been drunk before," Kendra said, not sure why she felt the need to tell him.

Payton studied her in the dim light a moment longer, then reached out and cupped one of her breasts, squeezed a little.

She felt another ripple of pleasure course through her. "I want to go home," she said. "If I'm real nice, will you let us go home?"

"So, that's what this is about?"

"I'll do whatever you want!" she said. "I'll let you do whatever you want."

"Whatever I want?" Payton said, an amused smile crossing his face.

Kendra didn't need to say more. She could already feel his body responding. She sat up to straddle his thighs, and peeled her wet top off over her head. She tossed it to the floor; it landed with a soppy *phlatt*. She could see his rugged face in the shadowy glow of light from the bathroom door. "Please? You'll let us go?" she asked, cooing the words and leaning in to plant a first wet kiss on Payton's cheek. "No one ever has to know."

Without waiting for an answer, Kendra began a trail of wet kisses down the side of his neck and onto his chest. "I promise," she said, softly. And continued her journey down, never taking her eyes off his.

Payton leaned his head back and closed his eyes in anticipation. He said, "I guess we'll have to think on it."

THIRTY-THREE

Del reached the cabana, coming out of the brush wet and shivering. The night air had turned cool. And—having missed breakfast and lunch and now dinner—her stomach was growling, she was hungry. There were more important things to consider. She knew where the girls were being held. If she could get to them, she could at least send them off toward land, and out of harm's way. As for herself, sooner or later, she would have to face off against Payton Rickey, make him pay for all the crimes he'd committed.

She made her way from the cabana, on toward the bungalows. Thankfully she had not encountered the male tiger. And there was no one else in sight. The main house was dark, but for the kitchen porch light where Leggett was occupied with his cat. Payton was the wild card. She had no idea where he might be.

Both of the bungalows were dark when she reached them.

Del studied them for a moment, feeling uneasy about the unguarded nature of either. The teens likely knew of the cats being on the prowl at night, and were likely afraid to venture an escape. But where was Payton? Why hadn't he shown his face again?

Del studied the bungalows a minute longer, thinking of Falconet now, thinking just how much she really needed him. How much she depended on him for strength. How much she loved him. She remembered the challenges they'd faced, the last time they were together—there in the hills of Kentucky, in Nazareth Church: the cold, reproachful clannishness of the people; the treachery of the community's religious leader. Falconet had been there to watch her back, pick her up when she fell, offer love. She wished he were here now. Wished he could put his arms around her and make the feelings of loneliness and fear go away. Be there, to balance the scales.

Ah, but those were wishes for another day. Tonight she would have to act alone.

The rain was coming down hard. Del wiped it from her eyes, knowing she could wait no longer. It was time to act. Get Lissa and Kendra out of there while the moment was right.

Staying low, Del moved quickly up the path to the bungalow where she knew the teens to be. She took a peek through the window, but could see little through the darkness within. She moved to the door. It was unlocked. She quietly eased it open.

A lone female figure was asleep on the bed, breath coming in soft rises and falls. Del crossed to peer close into the face. The room was dark, but she could tell by the fine features that this was indeed Lissa Rogers, no doubt.

"*Lissa!*" Del called in a hushed tone, simultaneously clamping a hand over the girl's mouth, to prevent her from crying out in surprise.

Lissa awoke with a start, eyes wide. She tried to scream, but Del kept her hand clamped tightly across her mouth. "Shhh, shhh, shhh," she said, not trusting to release her hand just yet. "Lissa, I'm Del Shannon. Your grandfather sent me."

The sound of *grandfather* seemed to strike a chord. It took a second, but Del could see understanding register in Lissa's eyes. She held on until Lissa gave her a nod. Only then did he remove her hand.

"Don't make a sound, okay?"

Lissa nodded again.

"Listen to me carefully. Are you okay to walk?"

"Yeah. I'm fine," Lissa whispered, going along. "Gramps sent you? How'd you find us?"

"It's a long story. He's worried about you. Come on! Get dressed! I'm going to get you out of here!"

Lissa obeyed, rolling out of bed to find her clothes and begin dressing. "Where are we going?"

"I'm not sure, just yet. Off this island, if possible." Del moved to the window to check the night outside. The opposite bungalow was still dark.

"Wait!" Lissa suddenly said, aware, only then, of her friend's absence. "Where's Kendra?"

"I found you here alone," Del said.

"Oh, crap!" Lissa said, rushing to the window to peer out. "She's in the other bungalow with Payton. I know it."

"What? Why?" Del wasn't completely comprehending.

"She's been acting funny for a couple of days now. I knew she was up to something. I think she thinks if she's nice to Payton, he'll let us go."

"He won't!" Del said. "Trust me!"

"I know, I tried to warn her."

"We've got to move fast. Finish dressing."

"But what about Kendra? She's with him!"

"We can't worry about that now. I'll get you out of here and I'll come back for her, I promise. You have to trust me."

Del moved to the door and cracked it open to peer out.

"The cats might be out there," Lissa said.

"One of them is," Del said. "The male."

"He's the mean one."

"Actually, I didn't like the look of either of them. Now hurry."

Lissa finished dressing.

Del checked her quickly for fitness—shorts and top, running shoes. She was dressed and ready to go. "All right," she said. "Stay close, we're going to be moving fast."

Del slipped out into the rain again, leading Lissa by the hand. The opposite bungalow lay quiet. The two of them headed off up the path, toward the cabana, darkness surrounding them. When they reached the cabana, Del brought them to a stop.

The light was still on at the back of the house, but the Cajun and the female cat were no longer there. Del waited, studying the situation, rain streaming into her eyes, draining off both of them. "Leggett must have gone back to his quarters," she said. "That's a good thing."

"Where are we going? How are we going to get out of here?"

"There's a boathouse down the hill from the house. We don't have the key to the big boat, but there's a dinghy. I'm going to put you in it and send you back toward the mainland. You think you can find your way?"

"I guess," Lissa said. "What about you?"

"I don't know. I'll have to try to find a way to free Kendra, then … well, we'll just have to see what happens. But, you get to Houma, find help. Send them this way. Police, sheriff. Anyone who will listen. Can you do that?"

"I'll try," Lissa said.

"Good girl! Your grandm—" Del quickly amended her thought, scolding herself for her near slip of the tongue. "Your grand*father* will be very proud."

It was okay for her to be working on Louise's behalf, Del thought. But Edgar Egan was the only grandparent Lissa had ever known. She didn't want to spoil the love Lissa had for him.

Lissa gave Del a troubled smile.

Del gave her a reassuring smile back.

The girl was worried but ready to get off the island, Del believed. She gathered Lissa by the hand again and led on, the light from the back of the house making it easier to see.

They skirted behind the main house. Del considered for one moment making contact with the woman who lived there, appealing to her for help. But she couldn't afford the possibility that the woman was part of the ransom scheme. Or, at least, opposed to any of them being on the island. One scream—one word—from her, and the house staff, the Cajun, and probably Payton himself would be on them in a heartbeat. Better play the odds, she concluded. Stay on the move and out of sight.

At the juncture to the path leading down to the sculpture garden, Lissa hesitated.

"What?" Del inquired.

"Nothing," Lissa said. "Just thinking."

Rain continued pouring.

"Well, come on," Del said, with a tug. "You'll have plenty of time to think in the boat on your way back to Houma."

Lissa followed. But Del noted her reluctance. Something about the sculpture garden intrigued the girl.

They reached the boat grotto as the wind picked up and the rain began coming in sideways. Del led them inside through the side opening and across the landing to the boat. She was glad to be out of the drenching downpour, but there was still no time to spare. She climbed aboard the *Sand Castle*, leading Lissa on board with her.

It was dark inside the grotto. "There might be some towels in the cabin," Del said. "Why don't you go below and check, turn a light on while you're down there, so we can see."

Del watched as Lissa fumbled her way below in the dark. A second later a light came on below, casting its glow onto the deck— just enough of it, emitting from the cabin, to allow her to move about the deck, but not so much that it would penetrate beyond the walls of the grotto. *Good!*

Del moved to the stern and searched the shadows for the dinghy. She couldn't see it out there. She searched a hand along the side, feeling for the tether line that secured it. It was nowhere to be found. "Damn it!" Del cursed aloud.

Lissa appeared back on deck, drying her hair with a towel. "What's wrong?" she asked.

"The dinghy's gone! Payton must have scuttled it, or cut it loose. We're stuck!"

Lissa handed a second towel to Del. "What do we do now?"

Del considered for a moment, hanging onto the towel but doing nothing about the water that dripped from her hair. "How did you and Kendra get here?" she asked.

"By kayak. But that was way at the other end of the island. We'll sure never get there in the dark. It's a mile of thick mangrove. And you said Java is out there."

Del had to think about it, weigh the benefits against the risk. Payton was tied up with Kendra for now. And he probably wouldn't come looking for her at the boathouse, since he knew she'd already fled that location. So...

"I suppose we'll have to stay here until first light," Del said. "There are a couple of bunks down below. Maybe we can find some food in the pantry."

"What about Payton?"

"Well, this might not be our best choice. But, with a little luck, Payton won't come looking again until morning."

"And Kendra?" Lissa asked.

Del thought of the second teen, thus far almost a footnote in her mind to her concerns for Lissa, Louise's granddaughter. But now she felt a rightful pang of regret for her, too. The girl was foolishly giving herself away to a man who would use her, then think nothing of killing her and discarding her body like so much trash—the way he'd left Silk, back at Filo's trailer.

"I'll do my best to get to her, honey," Del said. "I promise."

She had made a lot of promises of late. Promises that she had yet to fully keep. She had found Lissa, that much she could avow. But what now? How could she possibly follow through and get her and Kendra back safely.

Del gave Lissa's head a stroke. The girl looked pitiful with her damp hair hanging in limp strands. Del imagined herself to look the same way.

Lissa gave her what passed for a smile. She seemed resigned to following Del's lead. That was at least one good thing.

"Come on," Del said, urging Lissa ahead of her. "Let's get below. We need to get out of these wet clothes and get some rest. We'll want to be up with the dawn tomorrow. Everything will work out fine, you'll see."

Her words of comfort were meant to provide Lissa reassurance. *But what about her? Could she count on Falconet to bring reassurance to her?*

Del wasn't sure ... and the night was still full of dangers.

THIRTY-FOUR

THE NIGHT PROGRESSED WITH the rain continuing steadily, clattering against the top of the grotto. Below, in the small cabin, Del and Lissa slipped out of their wet clothing and hung the pieces in various places in the galley to let them dry. They found a box of breakfast bars in the pantry, sharing a pair and saving the rest for morning. It all wasn't so bad—the air warm enough this summer night, the snack bars tasty, and the bunks reasonably comfortable.

Wrapped in towels, the two of them sat cross-legged facing each other across the bunks, talking about all that had transpired and how Lissa and Kendra had been seized the moment they first set foot on the island. What Del had yet to learn was just why they had come to Terrebonne Key in the first place.

"Tell me something. Back there at the entrance to the garden," Del said. "You seemed to hesitate. What was that all about?"

Lissa lowered her eyes. "I don't know, just something about the place."

"Lissa, listen…" Del said, giving a second for the girl to look up at her. "This is a very serious situation we're in. I really need you to understand that."

"I know."

"What brought you here? I mean, this is not your typical summer outing, showing up on a private island occupied by a dangerous fugitive. There was something you came looking for. What is it?"

Lissa was still having trouble holding her gaze. But then she relented. "I'll show you." she said, and clambered off the bunk to cross to her shorts, hanging from a knob on the cabinet door. She fished in the back pocket, a look of stark surprise coming onto her face. "Oh, no!"

"What?" Del asked, stepping off the bunk to join her.

"The tintype… the Jacob Worley photo… I left it at the bungalow!"

"Jacob Worley?" Del remembered seeing the name enshrined in the iron scrollwork over the entrance to the garden.

Lissa tossed her shorts to the floor and crossed back to the bunk to frump down on it.

Del rejoined her. "What's this about a photo?"

Lissa held onto her pout a moment longer, then relented with a sigh. "It's why we came… why I came, anyway. It's all about the Jacob Worley photo and the fortune he left behind."

"Fortune?" Del said, still trying to come to terms with this teen who ventured so blindly. It made her wonder if Louise would have been adventurous as a teen. She believed she might have been.

"All right," Lissa said. "Here it is…"

Del sat listening as Lissa laid out the story for her. How she had come to learn of the legend of Jacob Worley's riches. How she'd discovered that the very tintype photo that many had long believed to contain the secret to the trove was right there in her grandfather's collection. How she'd researched and studied every story and article she could find on the subject. How the photo was linked to the sculpture garden they'd passed earlier that night. And how she had come to believe that she alone had rightly figured out about the photo what others had wrongly assumed. "So, that's why I came here," she said finally. "To see if I could find it. Or, at least see for myself that the story was true."

"Wow!" Del said. "That's some tale. And, so, Kendra didn't really know anything about why you were coming here?"

"No, not really. Not until after we got here. I feel bad about getting her into all this."

"And the photo is still back at the bungalow?"

Lissa nodded. "I guess I've decided, even if I'm right about the treasure, I can't get to it. It would be too difficult. But I would still need the photo to try to explain it to someone else."

"Well, maybe we'll be able to come back for it some other day, once this is over. But, for now, we need to get ourselves and Kendra off the island. Understand?"

"Yes."

They both grew quiet then. "We need to get some rest," Del finally said.

Lissa nodded and returned to her bunk.

Her head had hardly hit the pillow when it sprang back up. "Did you hear that!"

Del had heard it—the low sustained growl of a jungle cat.

Lissa came to her knees and put her face to the porthole and peered out. "It's Java!" she cried. He's coming! Oh, God!"

Del felt the boat rock as the weight of the beast landed on the side of the boat. Then rock back as the cat KALUMPED! down heavily onto the deck.

Lissa let out a scream.

Del sprang for the door to the cabin that was hanging open. For a brief instant, she and Java locked eyes, as the big cat slinked into a low stance, let off a sustained growl, and stalked her way. Del slammed the door shut, just as the cat lunged.

Her back braced against the door, Del felt the weight of the tiger smash against the other side. She held tight, her legs locked at the knees and straining. The tiger scratched and pawed, its claws, like nails on blackboard, giving off spine-grating sounds.

Lissa's cries had turned to whimpering. She had backed against the farthest corner of the berth, tears streaming down her face.

Del held on.

The onslaught continued for several long seconds; then the cat ceased its barrage on the cabin door. Del, once again, felt the boat shift, as it paced back and forth, side to side. Then, in the same way it had arrived, the cat leaped back out onto the landing and slipped away quickly through the archway and into the night.

"He's gone!" Lissa cried, her face to the porthole again, her words coming out in sobs of relief. "He went back out! He's leaving!"

Del let her breath out in a long rush and slumped to the floor, still keeping her back to the door. Her legs were shaking, along with her hands. Her arms had gone limp. There were tears of fear and joy, mingled together in her eyes. It felt as if every ounce of her blood had drained to her feet.

She had faced men with knives, men with guns, men with grips powerful enough to snap her spine. But never before had she faced such a wild and magnificent beast as the one who'd come to call this night. "*Whew!*" she said, letting it out.

Lissa still had her face glued to the porthole.

"It's over. You can relax now," Del said, though she was far from convinced herself.

Lissa seemed to melt back onto the bunk. She lay there quivering.

"I'm sure glad we decided to stay on the boat tonight," Del said. "I don't want to think what might have happened if we'd have run into him in the dark. But, first thing, come daylight, we're heading down to where you left the kayak and we're getting you out of here, pronto."

Lissa didn't put up an argument. She rolled face down on the bunk, and closed her eyes.

Del could see she was crying.

Del remained sitting, back against the cabin door, for some time. Had the tiger really retreated, she wondered? Or was it playing some kind of cat-and-mouse game with them, waiting for them to drop their guard? She wasn't taking any chances.

She thought of Falconet again, now, and wondered what his response had been to finding her gone. Had he written her off as having dumped him again? Or was he searching for her this very moment, scrambling to come to her rescue? She prayed that he hadn't found the island this night in the dark. As relieved as she would be to know he'd come, she didn't want him stumbling around out there in the dark with Java on the prowl. He was a tough guy, but not that tough. She prayed only that he had figured things out and was making plans to come find her by early light.

And, she decided the very next time she saw him that she wasn't going to let him out of her sight so easily.

She missed him badly, just now ... she wanted to be with him.

THIRTY-FIVE

THREE IN THE MORNING, Kendra slipped out of Payton's bed and searched for her panties, bunched somewhere on the floor. She pulled them on and found her top somewhere nearby. "You'll let us go now?" she asked, untangling the top.

Payton was watching her; she could see the smug smile he was giving her in the dim glow of light coming from behind the bathroom door. "Go? We're just now getting to know each other." He reached for the bottle and took a hit off it.

"But, you said, if—"

"No, *you* said!" Payton corrected sharply.

Kendra was feeling sick. She'd given herself over to him for hours on end. Giving what she could bring herself to give, taking all that he had to dish out. And it had been a lot.

Sex with him had not been pleasurable, as she had first conceived it might be. It had been rough and demeaning. At times humiliating. And she felt ashamed, now, for those first warm, tingly feelings she'd allowed. The man was incredibly strong and had the stamina of a bull. He'd done things to her—forced her to do things to him—that she had neither planned nor imagined. Some of it painful and humiliating, all of it sick and disgusting. But she'd endured, telling herself that it had to be done. That, given all that she'd allowed, he would surely, now, let them go, give them passage back to Cocodrie and the mainland.

Now he seemed to be reneging, going back on the deal she thought they'd made. "You have to let us go now!" she said. "You have to!"

"I don't have to do anything," Payton said, taking another hit on the bottle.

Kendra slipped her top on over her head—the material damp and cold. She searched her mind for some comeback, something to tip the scale of the argument back her direction. She said, "I'll … I'll go to that woman … Ivers … Ivess … or something. I've heard you and Leggett talk about her. She owns this island. And you're afraid of her, I can tell!"

Payton flashed a steely look at her from behind the upturned bottle. "What did you say?"

Kendra pulled her shoulders back and stood her ground, confident in her position now. "I'll tell," she said simply.

Payton sprang from the bed with such surprising speed that Kendra had no time to react. She let out a timid little shriek, as he grabbed her wrist and wrenched her close.

"You think you're in control here! Want to tattle on me like some little schoolgirl? Stupid little bitch! I still haven't yet decided whether not to kill you right this minute. Dump your chunky-ass body in the swamp. Or maybe just feed you to the fucking tigers. I believe they'd like that!"

"You're hurting me!" Kendra whined.

Payton tightened his grip and put his face close to hers. Kendra could smell the liquor on his breath once more. She let out a whimper.

"Jesus Christ!" Payton said, almost to himself, in disbelief. "You don't know the half of it. Are you too stupid to realize that you're only *alive* because I thought you had some value! But with the woman here, I don't need you anymore! You or your skinny little friend!"

Kendra wasn't sure what he meant by a woman being there. She only knew that the look in his eyes had grown hard as stone.

"*Please...*" Kendra whimpered.

Payton grabbed the neckline of her top and yanked hard, rending the fabric all the way down, parting the front, exposing her breasts to him once more. A blush of red still lingered on one of them, from where he'd squeezed and twisted hard enough, earlier, to bring tears to her eyes.

Kendra cried out in humiliation this time. She tried vainly to cover herself.

"Get the fuck back over there, stupid little twit!"

Payton flung her by the arm, back across the room. She hit the bed wildly, arms and legs sprawling. She bounced once, banging her head against the far wall, and landed face down. She tried to roll to face her attacker, but, once again, he was too quick for her. He was on her again, between her legs from behind, shoving her face into the mattress with one hand, wedging his other hand between her thighs.

It had been brutal before; it would be violent now, Kendra knew. "*Don't! Please!*" she whimpered.

There was no deterring him with words, no resisting him by force.

Payton drew his fist back and punched her hard in the back of the head.

Kendra saw stars, her head spinning toward unconsciousness. Go ahead, black out, she told herself, leave this ugly place for a time. But she didn't. Couldn't. Her mind swirled, her senses all too aware of the pain—pain she felt now, pain she imagined to come.

She could feel him positioning himself at her back. She wanted to cry out again, but, then, her mind locked on something...

"I CAN TELL YOU SOMETHING!" she cried out, not quite knowing how or why the idea had come to her.

Her words had no immediate affect—the man was too enraged, to consider reason, too mindlessly set on brutalizing her.

"GOLD!" she cried. "I KNOW WHERE THERE'S GOLD!"

With this, Payton eased off. "The fuck you talking about?"

Kendra wanted to cry. She wasn't sure she could find gold, or if there was any in fact to be found. But it had stopped Payton's assault for now.

"I know where there's a treasure," she said, more calmly now.

"What are you trying to pull?" There was suspicion in his voice. He sat back.

"It's why we came here," she said, feeling a stab of guilt, at betraying Lissa's confidence. "Lissa! My friend. She knew where a treasure is buried, in the sculpture garden. Gold and silver! Lots of it! Millions perhaps!"

Payton withdrew. He rolled her over beneath him, pinning her wrists behind her head. "Talk to me."

"She found it. There's this legend, about ... I don't know ... some old guy. Who buried his treasure in the garden. Lissa figured out exactly where. We were down there the other night! She showed me, exactly where! I can take you to it!"

"Who else knows?" Payton asked, seeming interested, but not entirely buying into it as yet.

"Nobody! I promise! She didn't even tell me. Not until we got here."

He was still looking at her with guarded suspicion. "This for real? Not some stupid kids' game?"

"It's real! It's been this secret for a long time, years and years. But that's what that old photo was about. The one you saw the day you caught us on the island. It's the secret to where the fortune is buried!"

Payton searched her eyes. Appearing at least somewhat satisfied, he rolled off of her and dragged her up into a sitting position against the wall. "All right!" he said. "If what you say is true, I guess I can cut you a little slack. Maybe find you a way to get home. But, come daylight, first thing, you'd better produce some hard evidence, or that'll be your last chance, sister."

"You'll let us go then?"

"Of course! Why wouldn't I? I mean, a sweet girl like you," Payton said.

Kendra wasn't sure if she should believe him, but it had gotten him to ease up on her for now. For that she was grateful. "What are you going to do now?" she asked. "Can I go back to the bungalow?"

"Oh, no," Payton said. "You and I have some making up to do."

Payton placed a hand at the back of her neck and drew her to him. He kissed her long and hard, tasting her deeply.

"See there. I can be nice," he said. Now he pushed her down onto the mattress again and crawled on top of her.

Kendra wasn't sure exactly what he had in mind. But she prayed that it didn't involve more punching and slapping. As long as he was tender about it, she could close her eyes and pretend—endure whatever was to come. Then, morning would roll around, and she could lead him to the sculpture garden, tell him what he wanted to know, and she and Lissa could get back in their kayak and row away, putting all of this mess behind them. He would let them…

Wouldn't he?

THIRTY-SIX

THE REMAINDER OF THE night passed in relative calm. Java had not returned. And Payton Rickey had not come looking for them. The sun had just breached the eastern horizon, and it was time to go. Del was already dressed, having slept fitfully on the floor beside the cabin door.

Lissa was still sleeping.

"Lissa!" Del said, shaking her awake. "It's time to go!"

Lissa came around slowly, blinking her eyes to get the sleep out. "It's morning already?"

"It is. And we need to get moving. Eat these," she said, handing Lissa the last two remaining snack bars from the box. "I've already had mine. They're the last two."

"Is Java still gone?"

"I hope so," Del said. "Either way we can't stay here."

Lissa sat up and began unwrapping her meager rations to take a bite. Del leaned across to the porthole and checked outside.

When Lissa had finished eating, Del said, "Get dressed. The clothes are still a little damp, but they'll have to do. What does the Cajun usually do with the cats come morning?"

"He usually takes the female, Gigi, to stay with Ivess during the day ... That's the woman who owns the island ... Java, he usually brings to the bungalow and ties him up outside so we won't go anywhere. After seeing Java last night, I guess you can understand why we stayed put."

"Yeah, I can appreciate that, for sure," Del said, remembering the sheer terror she'd experienced the night before, the big cat clawing at the cabin door. She'd rather face off with Payton any day.

Del went on deck and stood staring out at the bayou beyond the stern of the boat, giving Lissa a chance to dress. She wanted to imagine that if she concentrated hard enough on where she was, she could somehow conjure up psychic vibrations, send them out across the water, and then Falconet, thinking hard on her at that very moment too, would somehow receive her distress call and know just where to find her. He had once said to her, that time back in the hills: *I could find you in space.* She hoped that it was true.

Dressed, Lissa came on deck to join her. "I'm ready. What about Kendra?"

"I'm afraid she'll have to wait it out, sweetie! But as soon as we get you into the kayak and on your way across the water, I'll come back for her. The best thing we can do for her right now is to get word to the outside world. Can you take me to where you stashed the kayak?"

"It's that way, all the way at the other end of the island," she said, pointing east, toward the sunrise.

"I think it's best we stick to the shoreline. It will be harder going, I suspect, but I don't think we can risk going back along the path."

Lissa became pensive now. "You sure we can't go back for the Jacob Worley photo?"

"I'm sorry, we just can't risk it," Del said.

The comment drew a pouty look.

"Come on. You ready?"

Lissa hung onto her pout but nodded her head.

"Good," Del said. "Let's go!"

And, so, together they climbed from the boat and set out along the shoreline, east.

The going was rough—even more so than Del had imagined. They zigzagged around brackish marshy areas, pushed through nearly impenetrable thickets of mangrove, detoured around downed trees, sometimes waded ankle deep in water. At one point, they even had to cut a wide berth around an alligator who had come onto the shoreline to sun itself. There were other things to avoid, too—slithery things that disappeared beneath the waters, only to surface in some other secretive nook.

Del kept them moving, thinking of Falconet as she did. Where was he? Was he coming? How long would it take him to get there?

The sun rose hot; the morning wore on.

———

Falconet had spent his night in restless worry over Del.

At the marina, the evening before, he had looked into renting a boat. He was told bluntly that they wouldn't rent the boats out after four p.m. And that only a damned fool would go swashbuckling off into the swamp at night. The good ol' bayou boys behind the rental counter there were two of them—had poked fun at the whole ludicrous idea. And at his Jersey accent, wanting to know where exactly he was from. *"Let me tell you, boy. Bayou East is not the Hudson River!"* One of them had chided, nudging his partner to bring him into the discourse.

Falconet had taken their good-natured ribbing. And their advice—knowing that if he lost his way in the swamp, he would be of no use to Del or the teens.

Then, rain had come.

Right around dusk, the dark clouds over the bayou had broken loose. Visibility was cut to nothing. And—the good ol' boys possibly right—Falconet pictured himself boat wrecked on some patch of swamp grass in the glade, fending off alligators, had he failed to heed their advice.

He had also placed a call to the Terrebonne Parish Sheriff's office and left word for Sheriff Thibodaux—the man he had met at the Filo crime scene. "Have him call me," he had told the answering party. "It's important."

He knew he would not get enough support from deputies to act on what was still only a hunch on his part—asking them to risk the weather and the swamp at night on a notion that hostages were being held on Terrebonne Key, a privately owned island. But he had felt if he talked to Thibodaux, personally—one lawman to another—he might be able to win him over, get his help.

He didn't hear back from him.

And so Falconet had spent a tortured night back at the hotel in Houma, waiting for morning to arrive and the rain to end.

Now at first light, Falconet was just leaving the hotel with the intention of heading back to Cocodrie to rent the boat he could not get the night before, when his cell phone rang.

"This is Sheriff Thibodaux," the voice on the other end of the line said. "You called?"

Falconet reminded the sheriff of the conversation they'd had at the trailer the day before. "You remember the woman that was with me, the investigator from Arizona?"

"The good-looking one?"

"There was only one," Falconet said, mildly annoyed. "But yeah ... I've got reason to believe she's been kidnapped and taken out to Terrebonne Key."

"That old place?"

"If you say so," Falconet said.

"You say this relates to that case you were working on? The fugitive, the missing teens?

"It's all part and parcel," Falconet said, not wanting to have to explain all the ways the dots connected.

There was a moment of silence on the line, where Falconet believed Thibodaux was preparing a response to reject his plea.

"Where are you?" he said finally.

"At the motel next to Houma Lace," Falconet said.

"I'll meet you at the dock across the road," Thibodaux said "Twenty minutes."

Falconet hung up feeling grateful. He hadn't been thrilled by the prospect of heading out into East Bayou alone. He needed some good-ol'-boy expertise just now, someone with boating experience and an intimate knowledge of the swamp. He was, after all, a Jersey boy ... *the hell* did he know about anything?

Falconet's thoughts turned back to Del. Were his hunches correct? Or was he just wasting his own time and that of the parish sheriff's department?

Falconet wasn't sure. But he had nothing better than a hunch to go on. He had relied on his gut before, and it had always served him well. They would find Del and the teens on Terrebonne Key. The only question was ... would they find them before it was too late?

THIRTY-SEVEN

Ivess DeMarco came out of the house early morning and headed straight down the path toward the cabana. She was still in her bathrobe, a pair of house slippers of her feet, and her hair was in seismic disarray. The rain had stopped; the sun was out; and the day was promising to be a cheery one. But Ivess wasn't feeling cheery. She was in a terrible, angry mood, and she wanted someone to know it. That someone being Payton.

She had awakened to a fuzzy recollection about the evening before. Vague snippets of their last conversation. *What had happened?* She remembered querying Payton about being at the boat grotto, the boat motor running. He had claimed he was working on the boat, *blowing it out* or something? She didn't believe it. In all the time he'd been on the island, seven months now, he'd never worked at anything she hadn't had to nag him about. And she sure as heck hadn't been nagging him about "blowing out the motor." She also remembered the evasive way he'd answered her when she'd asked about Teddy. Where had the brother been keeping himself? Just what was he up to? Why hadn't she seen him these past few days? These things she deserved to know.

Payton had lied to her then, too, she believed, telling her that "Teddy was around and busy, he'd been working on cleaning up the garden, hauling some brush down to the pit to burn." *Psssh!* The worthless brother did even less than Payton! Nothing at all really! And why hadn't she seen him? But Payton had plied her with brandy—being suspiciously jovial. He'd rubbed her feet, paid her compliments—something he never did. *"What have you done with your hair? It looks nice today. You using something new on your skin?"* What kind of tripe was that?

She had fallen asleep in the parlor chair, as she vaguely recalled. Awakened in her bed this morning. She didn't remember dozing off. Couldn't remember anything, really, past late evening yesterday. *What had he given her? And why? What was he hiding? What was he covering up?*

Well! She was going to get to the bottom of it this morning! That's all there was to it! She was going down to that bungalow and find out once and for all!

Then we'll see!

———

Payton woke suddenly with the awareness of morning sunlight streaming into his bungalow. *Fuck! What time is it!*—his first cohesive thought.

The naked teen was still next to him. He'd taken her at his pleasure until early light. Then, with the weighty delirium of alcohol working on him, he had tucked her under his arm for safekeeping and they both had fallen fast asleep.

Payton rubbed his eyes and opened them for the first time.

That's when he saw her standing in the open doorway.

"Ivess—?" he started to say, his head suddenly feeling like it might explode.

"*How could you!*" she shrieked, her voice clawing into his brain like that of a burrowing badger.

The cat, Gigi, was not yet with her—he could be grateful for that. "Now, hang on! It's not what you're thinking!" he heard himself saying, though he supposed it was exactly what she was thinking.

"I trusted you! I took you in! I mended your wounds! I cared for you! I brought you to my bed! And this is how you repay me! You make me sick!" Ivess turned on her heels and headed back out the door.

"Now wait!" Payton rolled the girl aside and sprang out of bed, grabbing his pants in the process, hopping on one foot to get first one leg in to them, then the other. "Ivess! Come on now!" he called.

"I'll have you back in jail before you can get your goddamn pants on!" he heard her say, already some twenty yards up the path toward the cabana.

"Fuck!"

Payton stumbled toward the door and, then, in an afterthought, came back for his gun and the woman's gun, both lying on the nightstand next to the bed, saying to the girl, "You stay right the fuck where you're at. You so much as move while I'm gone, I'll come back and put a bullet in you."

Eyes wide, Kendra gave him a nod.

Payton stuffed both weapons into his waistband and headed out the door, giving chase, barefoot and shirtless, up the path.

Ivess was already to the cabana and making the turn onto the path that led to the house. "Stop! Goddamn it! I can explain!"

Resolute, Ivess quickened her pace.

"Stop, goddamn it!"

Payton stubbed his toe as he made the turn. "Mother fu …!" he cried out, cursing a root that had grown into the pathway. "Shit!" He hopped on one foot, assuaging the pain briefly with his free hand.

Ivess continued striding. She was nearly to the house now, where she would slam and lock the door, then find her cell phone and make her call. There was no talking her out of it, Payton realized. "Stop!" he called one last time. Then drew his gun from his waistband, aimed, and fired one shot.

The report echoed across the island. The slug struck Ivess between the shoulder blades and knocked her forward to the ground.

Payton hurried to catch up to her now, ignoring the pain in his toe.

Ivess was on her hands and knees, still crawling toward the house—the fucking determined bitch!—still insistent on making him pay.

"I told you to fucking stop!" Payton said. He pointed the gun at her again, and this time shot her once in the back of the head.

Ivess dropped in her tracks without so much as a grunt.

"Bitch!" he said again.

The killing of Ivess, while spontaneous, wasn't altogether unpremeditated. He had been thinking about getting rid of her for months now. Waiting for the right time—a time when he didn't need her as his lifeline on Terrebonne Key. But what would he need her for now, if he had the treasure? She would just be an impediment to his freedom.

It had occurred to him, also, that with the money and no Ivess, he maybe wouldn't need to leave the island at all. Sure, use the fortune to build his own private sanctuary, his way. Turn Purgatory

Key into Paradise Key. Bring over some girls from Houma Lace, move them into the bungalows and make them a permanent part of life on the island. Hell, start his own harem. Why not? Maybe hire a full-time bartender for the cabana, keep him busy mixing drinks for him and the girls. Use the boat for fishing excursions, get some real use out of the damn thing. Turn it into a party boat, hell... a party island. Everybody stays, everybody plays. *Hell, yes!*

Now, the time had come. Of course, Ivess—as with all things— had intervened a bit too soon, before he'd really had time to think it all out. But... all right then... there it was! *Show time!* Time to put the fantasy into action.

Payton took a quick look around. The loud gun pops, he knew, would bring Leggett running with his tigers. They were likely down near the pens for their early morning remedial training. For sure, Leggett had heard. And surely he would come.

Despite the lingering pain in his toe, Payton turned back down the path at a dead run.

At the bungalow, Kendra had heard the shots, too. She was at the window, nose pressed against the pane, looking out, her eyes wide with fear. Payton burst through the door.

He quickly found his shoes and slipped them on. Found a shirt and slipped it on over his head. Now he fished under the bed and came out with an automatic rifle—the AR-15 Teddy had managed to pick up for just such occasions. He checked the magazine, then slung in over his shoulder by its strap. "Let's go!" he said, grabbing the girl by her wrist and dragging to the door—ignoring her whiny protests.

Outside, he dragged her to the opposite bungalow. There he kicked through the door and pushed inside.

"Sonofabitch!" he cried, finding the bungalow empty.

"Where's Lissa?" Kendra cried.

"Smartass bitch! She's gone, can't you see that! Come with me!" Payton grabbed Kendra by the hair this time and slung her out the door.

"Owww! Where're you taking me?"

"You're going to show me where that treasure is hidden!"

"Now?"

"Yes! Right now!" Payton gave her another shove to get her going.

Payton hurried the girl up the path. He was thinking about the woman, the investigator who had killed his brother and poked her nose into his business—another smartass bitch! It seemed obvious that she had come during the night while he was occupied, grabbed the other teen, and whisked her away. Or had the girl seized the opportunity to escape on her own? Didn't matter, he guessed. They were both out there somewhere, no real way to get off the island. What mattered was that they stayed out of his way long enough for him to find that treasure and hit the road for Brazil ... Paraguay ... Uruguay! ... Someplace! ... Anyplace!

His plan—conjured overnight, but forced into action only minutes ago—was to make the girl show him the location of the treasure. Then lay waste to everyone on the island. Anyone who might serve witness to him being alive—the teens, the woman investigator, Leggett, even Ivess's house staff. Anyone who offered even the most remote possibility of informing on him. From there it was just a matter of jumping in the boat—the *Sand Castle*—and cruising off into the sunset. *To where?* The hell did it matter? As long as he had the treasure.

"Keep moving," Payton said to the girl, prodding her toward the sculpture garden.

They got as far as the cabana before Leggett appeared, coming hurriedly down the path toward them. He had both the cats with him. The smell of Ivess's blood was on the wind—both the cats agitated, excited. They snarled and pulled at their chains, as Leggett led. Leggett was forced to hang onto them mightily, hustle along, just to keep from being dragged. "Java! Gigi!" he shouted at them, repeatedly jerking at their chains to try to slow their pace. Now he managed them to a stop on the path. The cats, still nervous, milled anxiously, entangling their chains, refusing to settle. "Java! Gigi!" The cats settled only a bit, still highly agitated, ready to react at the slightest provocation.

Leggett spotted the gun in Payton's hand now, the second gun in his waistband, the automatic rifle slung over his shoulder. He turned his eyes to the girl—the teen, nearly naked in just her panties and torn top.

"You keep them cats away from me!" Payton said.

"Dey frightened by the shots, dem. See! I might naw be able to hold 'em. I saw ma'am Ivess. You do this?" Leggett glared at him, wanting answers.

"Yeah, I killed the old whore. So what?" Payton said. "And if you don't keep those cats settled, I'll put a bullet in both of them too."

"Don't hurt my beauties! What for you want?"

Payton had yet to consider this. What did he want from the little Cajun? He would prefer Leggett take the cats back and lock them in their pen for now. Eventually, perhaps, they could be of some use in finding the woman and the other girl. He might also need the man—for now—to help with the digging. No telling what he might run into, what kind of effort it might take to uncover the treasure. So, he said to Leggett, "Grab a couple of shovels from the tool shed and any other digging implements you can find. Then meet me back in the sculpture garden. Just keep those beasts of yours under control. Do as I say, and you can have the whole fucking island to yourself! Just you and your tigers! … Oh, and take her with you," he said, shoving the girl off in the Cajun's direction. "She can help carry some things. I've got another quick job to do."

Leggett hesitated, studying first Payton, then the girl. But he nodded and turned off to do his bidding, the girl following behind. "Things now going to be the same," Leggett said over his shoulder. "Why you have to come here?"

Payton watched the Cajun go, ignoring his comments and realizing just how much the man loved his life here on Terrebonne Key. How much he loved his cats. And he realized that his own earlier fantasy of turning the island into his personal playground was just that—a fantasy. The place was way too close to the mainland for comfort. Getting out held far more promise. And Brazil was still at the top of his list. So, maybe spare Leggett. Bequeath the island to the him in exchange for his promise of silence. Let him stay behind to dispose of the bodies. Dispose of the evidence. What did he care, really? He would soon have all the money and freedom he needed.

Payton watched until the man and the girl were well on their way to the tool shed; then, hoisting the AR-15 higher on his shoulder, he crossed to the kitchen door and went inside.

———

It took only two more shots from the handgun to lay waste to the house staff. One to take down the matronly cook, hiding inside the pantry—having heard the earlier shots. And a second, to take down Alonda—the fat-bitch housekeeper he'd been fucking—as she fled through the parlor toward the front entrance. *Pop!* and *Pop!* All there was to it. Now on to digging for gold.

Payton met up with Leggett and the girl out in the open center of the garden. The girl was carrying two shovels. Leggett was carrying a posthole digger, a pick, and—looky there!—three sticks of dynamite. The little man knew what he was doing, Payton thought.

"All right," Payton said to the girl, relieving her of the shovels and taking her by the arm again. "It's time for you to earn your keep. Where's this treasure you were telling me about?"

Leggett gave him a quick look, suddenly interested in their mission.

"That's right, I said treasure! But, don't worry your head about it! I'll see you get a share." Now he turned back to the girl. "And, you! You just better pray your little friend is right about the treasure. I would hate to actually say what would happen if this is all just one big tease." Payton waited. "So! Where is it?"

"Well . . ."

"Don't fuck with me!"

"It's supposedly under the water-maiden sculpture," Kendra said, pointing to the statue in the ten o'clock position in the garden.

Payton looked to the maiden sculpture. "You're sure?"

"It's what Lissa believes. We sneaked down here one night to look at it."

"Dat dey did," Leggett said. "Caught 'em down here myself, dem."

"Why didn't you tell me?"

"Just some foolishness," Leggett said. "I run 'em both back to the bungalow."

"He did," Kendra said. "Lissa had the photo with her that night. It's how we came to know which statue the fortune is under."

Payton remembered the tintype—having seen it the morning the girls showed up on the island—the yellowing image of an old man, taken in what could very well have been this very garden a hundred years ago. He crossed to the water-maiden sculpture and ran his hand along the smooth marble, over the little lady's thighs. "What your friend believes but doesn't know," he said, sizing up the maiden and the massive base on which she knelt.

"Take a whole lotta work to move this," Leggett said

"That's why she better be fucking right," Payton said.

Payton rubbed his chin as he considered the stone sculpture. *All right,* he thought. He supposed he could imagine it. Take your gold and silver and bury it under the bitch, her heavy stone base, let all these other figures stand watch for you. But it was going the take some work, as the Cajun pointed out, getting to it. "Put the cats in their pen for now," Payton said. "Then hurry back and let's get started."

Leggett unburdened himself of the implements and the sticks of dynamite, fishing a Bic lighter from his pocket and placing it next to them on the ground. Then he led the tigers off through the garden toward the pen.

Payton watched him go, seeing that the cats had calmed down some. Still, they circled in place a couple of times when Leggett got them inside, before settling down on their haunches.

Now, the little Cajun was heading back to the garden.

"I just hope, for your sake, you're right about this treasure," Payton said to the girl, who had remained off to the side, sad and small, looking like some half-naked orphan waiting in a soup line for something to eat.

Payton moved behind the maiden statue, testing its stability. It was a heavy bitch, he realized. When Leggett returned, he said, "Give me a hand."

Leggett joined him, and together they braced their hands against the statue and began to push.

The stone sculpture by itself was monstrously heavy. They managed to rock it once … twice … then, on the count of three … they doubled their efforts. The sculpture teetered off its equilibrium and toppled, hitting the rain-softened ground with a *thuck* sound. Despite the soft ground, the statue broke into three sections.

Payton examined the pieces. "It's solid, nothing inside." Now he turned back to the base. "That means it's probably under this mother, like the girl figured. We're going to have to blow this sonofabitch out of the ground. You got the dynamite?"

"Blow dat rock, then what?" Leggett asked.

"Then we dig," Payton said. "'Less you've got a better suggestion."

Leggett crossed to where the sticks of dynamite were lying in the grass. He selected two of the tree sticks and the Bic lighter and returned with them, handing them over to Payton. "Two shaw be enough," Leggett said.

"Yeah, we don't want to pull a Butch Cassidy now, do we?" Payton said, remembering a scene from the movie *Butch Cassidy and the Sundance Kid*, where they used too much dynamite to blow the safe in the train car—Butch and Sundance, money raining down from the sky all around them.

Leggett said nothing, apparently knowing shit about movies.

Payton took up a shovel and dug out some of the grass and soil from beneath the edge of the massive stone. Then he stuffed the two sticks of dynamite under it. He warned the girl and Leggett back, then lit the fuse. And they all made a run for the trees, the girl squealing all the way.

The blast shattered the base, sending rock debris raining down on the garden. Off in the pen, the cats came to their feet and let out a roar.

When the smoke cleared, all three of them tentatively made their way back to the sculpture. A massive crater had been opened in the earth. The stone base itself was demolished, reduced to chunks and particles of dust covering an area of some thirty feet surrounding the pit. Payton, the girl, and Leggett gaped at the hole, wide-eyed, for a time. There was no immediate sign of treasure—greenbacks, gold, or silver.

"You think it's dere?" Leggett said, seemingly somewhat disappointed.

"There's only one way to find out, Tiger Man."

Payton retrieved the pair of shovels. He handed one to Leggett and stepped down into the crater.

"Let's get started," he said.

Leggett joined him.

And together they began to dig for gold.

THIRTY-EIGHT

THE MORNING SUN HAD risen well into the sky. Del continued along the shoreline toward the eastern end of the island. Lissa followed, hanging back, seeming tired. The going was tough, more so than Del had imagined. At times they were forced to hack their way through the dense mangrove, slog through water and mud. She had wished they could have taken a path along higher ground, follow one of the trails. But the shoreline with its dense foliage offered better cover—the trails themselves being risky.

It had taken them nearly two hours to cover what Del estimated should have taken no more than forty minutes. And, still, they had some distance to go—according to Lissa—zigging and zagging around cypress stumps, impenetrable masses of foliage, and climbing over downed trees—toward the inlet where the kayak was stowed.

She had heard shots earlier, coming from back across the island. First one. Then, seconds later, another. It was very disconcerting. It unnerved her and troubled her thoughts, knowing that she was faced with going back for Kendra Kozak. Del kept them moving.

Sometime later, there had come an even more disruptive report—a sound of a huge blast echoing from the west, the same general area as the shots.

Lissa had let out a shriek. "What was that?" she'd cried.

Del—not knowing—had consoled her and urged her on.

From the shoreline of Terrebonne Key, Del could see across the expansive bayou. She could imagine how difficult it might be to navigate the swamp if you weren't long familiar with it or didn't know precisely where you were going. She thought of Falconet again and wondered just how on earth he would ever find them. No, there would likely be no Falconet-led cavalry, metaphorical or otherwise, riding in over the hill. She was on her own, and against some pretty stiff odds.

"How much farther?" Del asked, still in the lead.

Lissa had fallen farther behind.

"Not far," Lissa called ahead. "Just up around that next bend, I believe. Keep going. This is starting to look familiar."

Del trudged on.

She continued to talk, thinking it the best way to keep Lissa moving, keep her distracted from the difficulties of managing their way through the mangrove. But then...

It suddenly felt to Del as though she was talking to herself—minutes had passed since Lissa had last responded. She turned to see Lissa nowhere behind.

"Lissa! ... *Lissa!*" Del called.

Where was she? Why wasn't she there?

Del now remembered the photo, the Jacob Worley tintype, which Lissa was so anxious to recover. *Was she willing to risk all to get it back?*

Damn it!

Del scanned back through the mangrove to the trail they'd just blazed. But it was all too painfully obvious. For whatever foolish reason, Lissa had given her the slip.

The gods—or someone—must be punishing her, Del thought. Maybe it was some kind of karmic retribution for sending Andray Moton face-first to the concrete. She didn't know. But she knew one thing, her job here had just gotten one hell of a lot tougher. And the prospect of acquiring help had just evaporated on the cool Gulf breeze.

Suck it up! she told herself.

She had yet to reach the kayak, but that would have to wait. With the shots, the explosion—something bad was going down on Terrebonne Key…

And she couldn't leave Lissa or Kendra alone to face it.

————

Lissa had never completely forgotten about the Worley tintype. She had continued to think about it from the time she started dressing that morning, to their trek along the shoreline. She was thinking about it now.

She had heard the gunshots and the blast, and for one brief moment had considered the reasonable response of not going back for it. But, as she thought about it—about how long she'd planned, how far they'd come—to let the photo slip back into history, or worse yet, perhaps, fall into someone else's hands seemed unthinkable. How could she possibly leave without it? She knew going back for it was a risky thing to do.

Lissa followed the trail that she and Kendra had taken their very first day on the island, hurrying, making the best time she could possibly make. She knew exactly where the Worley tintype photo was—provided no one had taken it. It was still back at the bungalow, inside the nightstand, next to the bed, where she had tucked it for safekeeping.

She felt bad about skipping out on Del—Ms. Shannon—the woman who had been hired by her grandfather. She was someone who had risked her own life to find her. That made her actions all the more unconscionable. She'd also come to simply like the woman, feeling something of a bond with her—both having survived the Java incident together. Del was dedicated—you could tell that about her. Her mind always seemed to be working, thinking, plotting, Smart. She would by now have discovered her gone and would be coming after her again. Lissa felt guilty about putting her through all this.

But...

She had to have that Worley photo. *Had to!* How else would she ever be able to convince anyone of her theory, get their help in proving the fortune?

She was being selfish, she knew.

She thought of Kendra. One consolation might be that Kendra had returned to their room. Maybe the tiger wasn't in position yet, and Payton had gone off someplace. All these ifs... And maybe she could grab Kendra and the photo and head back together. Run into Ms. Shannon on the trail and all three of them get off the island together. She wasn't sure how that would work, exactly, how all three would fit in the kayak. But the idea of it made her feel a little better about betraying her rescuer.

Lissa put it all out of her mind for the time. Right now, her only hope was that Payton would not be there waiting.

Her only prayer was... that he had not already found the Worley photo.

———

They dug for what must have been forty minutes—the girl sitting bored on the ground nearby, her back against a section of toppled statue. The crater had grown significantly deeper, but still there was no sign of buried treasure. Payton paused for a breather. "You damn sure this is the right spot?" he asked Kendra.

"It's the one, what she said! I'm sure!"

There seemed to be a new and surprising level of defiance in the girl's tone, Payton noted. He wanted to stride across to where she was sitting and kick the shit out of her, just because. Instead, he wiped his brow and went back to digging, chunking his spade down into the earth and leveraging up another shovelful. He spaded up another ... and another ...

Still nothing.

"Goddamn it!" Payton cried. He threw his shovel aside in frustration and climbed back out of the hole. Leggett continued to dig.

Payton crossed to the girl.

She flinched when she saw him coming, drawing her knees up in defense.

Payton grabbed her by the wrist and dragged her to her feet. "There's not a goddamn thing down there! What kind of fucking game are you playing?"

Leggett quit shoveling, stopping to see what might happen next.

"It's all I know!" Kendra cried. "It's where the photo said it would be!"

"Where's the damn photo now! Show me!"

"She kept it in the nightstand at the bungalow! I guess it's there!"

Leggett came out of the hole with his shovel now to lean against it and hear things out.

Payton studied the empty hole, studied the garden itself, and studied the remaining marble sculptures. They couldn't dig all of them up, and there wasn't enough dynamite in all of Terrebonne

Parish to blast them. And, at any rate, it would take days, weeks—hell, months! Time Payton didn't feel he had now. Ivess was dead, the staff was dead. That fucking woman and the girl were out there working against him, trying their best to get off the island. How much longer before they found a way?

Payton now considered the very real possibility that there was no treasure here at all. What if it was all some big fairytale, some worthless fable passed down from generation to generation, the tale growing bigger and bigger over time? What if the teens had just been suckered into some wise-ass tale? There was no way to know, unless he had the tintype photo and could see for himself.

"Goddamn it!" he cursed.

"Dere's treasure, naw?" Leggett asked.

"*I don't know!*" Payton snapped. He was frustrated and showing it. "I guess there's only one way to find out. We gotta find the other girl and find that photo. Gather the cats and follow me; we may need them. We're going back to the bungalow."

"What about the pischouette?"

"Her?"

Payton considered putting a bullet in the girl's head, leaving her for dead. "Screw it! Leave her!" he said. He didn't want to drag her all over the island, and he might still need her if he didn't find the other girl. He said to the teen, "Don't think about going anyplace! Understand?"

She nodded.

"Get the cats," he said to Leggett again.

Leggett hurried off toward the pen.

Payton collected both handguns and stuffed them into his waistband, slung the AR-15 over his shoulder, then retrieved the remaining stick of dynamite and stuffed it into his back pocket, along with the Bic lighter—not knowing what he might need it for but liking the idea of having it with him. Payton headed off out of the garden, through the arched entrance. He was anxious, not wanting to wait for anything. Having to gimp along on only one good leg, Leggett would catch up to him, he knew.

Payton took the path that led up the incline toward the house. It was starting to feel to him as though things were coming to a hard end. Teddy was dead. Ivess and her house staff were dead. There was no staying on Terrebonne Key now. And he sure as hell didn't want to go on the run without the treasure. Life was hard out there with no money in your pocket and no one to watch your back. His chances of evading the law would be slim to none if penniless. No, his only last hope was that the photo would tell him something.

It just damn well better be there!

THIRTY-NINE

THERE WAS NO SIGN of the tigers when Lissa got to the bungalow, no sign of Payton or Leggett or the island's mistress. That was all looking pretty good. She could only hope that Kendra was back inside the room. All she wanted was the photo; then she and Kendra could leave together, get back into the kayak and paddle away. Same way they got here.

Lissa studied the bungalow for one last moment, then raced from the security of the foliage to the door of the bungalow and slipped inside. *No, no, no* ... Kendra was not there. *"Kendra, where are you?"* Lissa said beneath her breath.

She took another look out the window to the other bungalow. The door was closed, no way of knowing if Kendra was still in there with Payton. Or if Payton himself was there, with or without Kendra. She couldn't risk knocking. All she could do was grab the photo and go.

Lissa set aside thoughts of her friend for the moment and crossed to the nightstand. To her relief the tintype was still right there where she had left it—the sad, sick old man, looking back, his index finger forever pointing to his watch. She grabbed it up and took another second to consider him. "I want to say you caused a lot of trouble, Jacob Worley," Lissa murmured. "But this was all my fault, not yours."

It had all been intended as just some summer adventure. But now … it wasn't like that. Her heart ached. *Where was Kendra? What had Payton done to her?*

She knew now she could not leave without her. Wherever she was. Whether with Payton or not. Whatever the outcome. She had to do something to try to get her back.

Lissa cradled the Jacob Worley photo to her chest and crossed back to the doorway. She stole a glance outside. There was no sign of the woman, Del, coming up the path to find her, no sign of Payton, or Kendra. The island had become deathly quiet. *Too quiet,* she realized.

The dreaded calm before the storm.

———

Payton gimped his way along the path at the back of the house, moving as fast as he could on his bum leg. Leggett had caught up to him with the cats. They were trailing several paces behind him now.

"Java! Gigi!" Leggett was calling to them, dragging at their leashes to hold them back. They were anxious, excited again.

Ivess's body was still lying there in the sun, collecting flies. Payton gave her only a courtesy glance and continued on. Leggett had to drag at the cats to keep them from pawing at the corpse. He and the cats continued to follow.

Payton's leg was feeling particularly unstable, he noticed. All that heavy digging—it had taken its toll. But there was no time to rest. Things were coming to a head, and he had to remain focused on the job.

He believed now that the woman investigator would never give in to pressures for another ransom demand. She had offered that only as a diversion, a means of staying alive until she could find her window of opportunity. *Well, she had found it, hadn't she?* Ivess provided that window when she came to the boat giotto unannounced. He could rule out any chance of money coming from that direction. Which meant that the old man's fortune was his last slim ray of hope. And it would seem that the key to that fortune resided somehow in the tintype photo.

He had just reached the path leading down toward the cabana, when—*look at that!*—the Rogers girl was coming up the path toward him. She was no more than thirty yards away. She hadn't noticed him yet—she had the tintype clutched in both her hands, considering it as she walked.

"HEY!" Payton called, reacting in surprise without thinking.

The girl looked up. Spotting him, she froze mid-stride, a deer-in-the-headlights look on her face. Then, comprehending, she turned quickly to run. She had only taken three or four steps, when she tripped—ironically over the same protruding root that Payton had stubbed his foot on earlier—and went sprawling face first into the shrubbery at the side of the path. She struggled to regain her feet, but all efforts to untangle herself only seemed to snare her more completely.

It's my lucky day! Payton thought. And started gimping forward as fast as he could.

But, now, the woman investigator—*Goddamn it!*

She appeared, coming fast up the path behind the girl, rushing to grab the girl and drag her free.

Payton felt his leg suddenly give, and he went down in his own sprawling heap. "Fuck!" he cried out.

Now, the woman had the girl on her feet and was prodding her to run. They bolted off together, down the path in the direction of the bungalows.

Payton dragged himself to his feet, cursing as he did.

The woman and girl had already made the turn near the cabana and were racing off toward the bungalows and the trail leading toward the eastern end of the island. *Fleet-footed, both of them.*

Payton decided, then and there, he wasn't going to play the chase game. Not if he could help it. He pulled the woman's nine-millimeter handgun from his waistband, leveled it and pulled off one shot … two …

The shorts went wide, one zinging off through the underbrush, the other catching the corner of the cabana, splintering off shards of its wooden framework.

The woman and girl ducked out of sight down the trail and were gone.

"Damn it!" Payton cursed again.

Behind him the cats had become unsettled again by the loud pops of the gun. Leggett struggled against their leashes.

Payton crossed around, giving the cats a wide berth, to stand behind Leggett, placing the Cajun between him and the anxious beasts. "Let 'em loose!" he said.

"But … what 'bout the woman? The pischouette?" Leggett objected.

"I don't give a damn about the woman or the girl! As long as those cats don't eat the damn photo. Now send them out there! Let 'em run the two of them to the sea if they have to! Just bring them down."

The cats were already dragging mightily at their chains, anxious to be free.

Leggett hesitated a moment longer, giving Payton a plaintive look.

"Do it, goddamn it!" Payton lifted the gun and pointed it at the big male tiger. "Or I'll drop him right where he stands!"

Leggett hesitated only a moment more, then reached down and unleashed the cats, one after the other. They tore loose instantly and bolted off into the brush.

"All right then!" Payton said with a grin. "Time to go collect the leftovers!"

Payton pushed past Leggett and headed off, gimping along as fast as he could manage, the devilish grin still pulling at the corners of his mouth. He'd never actually seen what the tigers could do to human flesh. But what the hell . . .

He was interested in finding out.

———

Del ran, urging Lissa ahead of her. The girl was fit and she could fly—something Del was grateful for just now. They raced down the path, brushing through overgrowth that sometimes crowded the way. She had caught a glimpse of the cats as she snatched Lissa from the brush. And she'd heard Payton give the dreaded order, *Let 'em go!*

My God! Del thought.

They had gotten a head start, but how could they possibly stay ahead of these predators?

"Don't slow down! " she continued to urge. "Keep running!"

She needn't have wasted her breath. Lissa was racing well ahead of her on tan, young legs, a trained swimmer with plenty of endurance, crying as she ran.

Frank! Frank! Frank! Del thought to herself, mentally calling to him across space and time. *If you ever plan to be here, now would be a good time!* "Get to the kayak!" she called to Lissa. "It's our only chance!"

They reached the eastern end of the island, ahead of Payton and the tigers, racing into the clearing at the edge of the shoreline, where Lissa had led them. Lissa drew to a stop, seemingly confused now.

"Where is it?" Del cried.

"I don't know! I thought it was . . . THERE!" she said now, getting her bearings. "The inlet!"

They raced together to the narrow inlet of water, Lissa rushing down into the ankle-deep stream without hesitation. Del splashed in right behind her.

"It's gone," Lissa cried. "We left it right here, on the bank of this inlet!"

"Are you sure!"

"I'm positive!"

"Damn!" Del said. "The rain, last night, must have flooded the inlet, washed it out to sea."

"What do we do? They're coming!" Lissa was whimpering now, ready to unravel.

Del tried to think. There was no shelter, no cover left. They were trapped with their backs to the sea; tigers and a maniac with guns ahead. "We're stuck," she said. "We're out of options."

Payton appeared far back along the trail they'd just arrived on. He had the automatic rifle slung across his shoulder, one of two handguns in his hand. He didn't bother with small talk. He lifted the handgun, Del's own nine-millimeter, she saw, and fired off a shot. The bullet zinged past her and tore through the trees clipping off leaves and tiny limbs in its path.

"You're done!" Payton called. He gimped forward, closing in as fast as he could manage.

300

Del edged farther back down the inlet, spreading her arms protectively, keeping Lissa at her back. "You won't get away with it," Del said. "There are people who know I'm here!"

"Nice try!" Payton said. "Once I have the photo and the old man's fortune, I'll be out of here! And with the cats on the prowl, there won't be much of either of you left to find."

Del continued edging Lissa backward toward the water. Payton continued closing the distance between them.

When he was within thirty yards, he stopped and lifted Del's handgun again.

There was no place left to go, nothing to stop him from putting an end to them here.

"Say your last goodbyes," he said.

Lissa shrieked, burying her face in the small of Del's back. Del drew a deep, quick breath, preparing herself for what she'd always believed her life would one day come down to. And ...

The harsh, hard blast of a boat's air horn suddenly disrupted the island's calm. It stopped Payton in his tracks, stunned, his finger frozen on the trigger.

Del's heart lurched.

The sound of a boat's motor could now be heard, closing fast.

"PUT THE GUN DOWN AND RAISE YOUR HANDS!" a voice said, coming to them through a bullhorn.

Del didn't have to guess who was behind the warning. It was her knight in armor, Falconet. She turned to see him standing tall on the bow of the boat, the bullhorn in one hand, hanging on to the boat's windshield with the other, his hair whipping in the wind. The boat was that of the Terrebonne Parish Sheriff's Water Patrol.

Falconet issued another warning. "DROP THE WEAPON!"

The pilot of the speedboat kept the boat bearing down on the island, cutting the engines only when they were within ramming distance from the shore. The boat made landfall, sliding onto the banks of Terrebonne Key; Falconet timed his heroic leap to coincide, the momentum of the boat catapulting him off onto land within a few feet of where Del and Lissa were still standing in ankle-deep water. He managed a few churning steps, then drove into them with a body tackle that took them both off their feet and to the safety of nearby brush.

Sheriff Thibodaux, who'd come along for the ride, raised his service revolver and fired off a couple of rounds in Payton's direction, offering cover.

Payton had remained frozen, too surprised and stunned to move. But now the direct assault brought him back to reality. He tossed Del's nine-millimeter to the ground and swung the automatic rifle into position. He let loose a volley that sprayed the brush over Del and Falconet's heads, and sent Thibodaux and his deputies scrambling for cover inside the boat.

"I thought I'd never see you again," Falconet said into Del's ear, his body still pinning her and Lissa to the ground.

Another round of automatic weapon fire tore at the brush around them.

"Let's get this sonofabitch, Frank!" Del said.

"You got it!" Falconet said, rolling aside to free her and Lissa.

By the time they'd reached a crouched position, Payton was lighting what appeared to be a stick of dynamite. He allowed the fuse to catch, then hurled it in their direction.

"Duck!" Falconet said. And they all dove for cover once more.

The dynamite erupted in a monumental explosion, sending earth, water, and shredded tree limbs raining down around them and the sheriff's deputies on the boat.

When the smoke cleared, Thibodaux came piling off the boat onto land, gun at the ready.

Payton had fled.

Falconet came to his feet; Del rose, bringing Lissa with her.

"You all right?" Falconet asked.

"I think so," Del said, checking Lissa for injuries.

"You remember Sheriff Thibodaux?" Falconet said.

"This one of the teens you were talking about?" Thibodaux asked, looking Lissa over.

"This is Lissa Rogers," Del said. "She and her friend have been held captive here."

"What about the gunslinger? That the fugitive you were looking for?"

"That's him," Falconet said.

"There's still the other teen on the island," Del said. "Payton will head for the boat grotto at the west end of the island. Frank and I will try to catch up to him, but it's best you take the boat and try to head him off at the water."

"If we can get the boat off the sand," Thibodaux said. "We landed pretty hard."

"Frank and I will have to move fast. I'm leaving Lissa with you. Take care of her."

"Will you find Kendra?" Lissa said, more of a plea than a question.

"Don't worry, sweetie. I made a promise to you, and I plan to keep it." Del turned Lissa over to Thibodaux, then crossed to collect her weapon from the ground, check the magazine. There were still rounds remaining. "Ready?" she asked Falconet.

Falconet joined her. "Just like old times, isn't it?"

"Yes, Frank," Del said. "But we didn't have tigers in Kentucky."

"Tigers?" Falconet inquired.

FORTY

"*I could find you in space,*" Falconet had said to her. But she could hardly believe he'd practically done so. Not only had he found her way out here, on this secluded island at the edge of nowhere, but he had arrived just in the nick of time to save her. Now they were together again. A team. And they were going after Payton Rickey together.

They crossed the island back toward the boathouse where they knew Payton would be headed, coming out of the trees at the far end of the garden where Leggett's little shack and the storage unit sat. There had been no sign of the tigers. No sign of Leggett.

They spotted Payton ahead of them, out in the open middle of the garden some seventy-five yards ahead of them. "He's headed for the boat all right," Del said.

"Payton!" Del called.

Payton turned the assault rifle on them and fired off a burst of bullets.

Del and Falconet dodged for cover behind the first of the marble statues.

Falconet got off an ineffective round. They were still too far away, out of range for their handguns.

Payton released another quick burst of fire. Bullets zipped by and pinged off the marble.

"We've got to get in closer," Falconet said.

"Let's do it!" Del said.

They broke from cover, dodging along the line of statues at the perimeter, using the marble figures for cover.

Ahead, Payton gimped along, seeming to have more and more trouble with his leg. He was all but hobbling now.

"Give it up, Payton! Sheriff's deputies are on their way!"

Payton fired off two more rounds across his shoulder and kept moving.

Falconet returned a round for good measure. They had closed the distance, but were still just shy of effective handgun range. Payton had reached the far end of the garden, where one of the statues lay toppled next to an open hole in the ground. He was gimping steadily toward the arched entrance and the path leading down to the boathouse.

Del dodged quickly to the next statue, Falconet fell in behind.

They were closing in, and Del knew Payton could feel it. He attempted to quicken his pace but struggled weakly with his leg.

They had come into range, Del readying herself to take Payton down if need be.

But now appearing, within feet of Payton, was the other teen, Kendra. She had been lying in a fetal position alongside the downed marble sections of statue where Payton had left her, nearly naked and in shock or just too traumatized to move.

She was coming to her feet, crying out to them, "Help me!"

Payton saw his opportunity and grabbed the girl, dragging her around in front of him as a human shield. "Back off!" he said. He tossed the automatic rifle and drew his handgun from his waistband and put it to her temple.

Del could see now the savagery Payton had inflicted on the girl. Her hair was in disarray. Her top was torn down the middle, leaving her breasts exposed. She wore only panties below the waist. Her legs and arms and face were streaked with dirt. She looked to be at her emotional end, just one quick snap from slipping over the edge and into some catatonic state.

"Give it up Payton!" Falconet called from behind the marble statue. "Sheriff's deputies are on their way. You've got nowhere to go."

"Back off or I put a bullet in the little whore's brain," Payton called back.

Del studied the situation. There was still no sign of the Sheriff's deputies. Payton was still some thirty yards way—competition distance for all the prize money.

"I can't make this shot," Falconet said. "I'm just not that good."

"But I am!" Del said.

She had made this shot many times at the range. Without further thought, she stepped from behind the statue, brought her nine-millimeter up in one clean motion, and squeezed off one sure round.

The Baby Eagle boomed; the girl cried out.

The shot struck Payton in the right shoulder, only inches above and to the left of Kendra's head. It snapped him back a step, and Kendra broke free, fleeing in Del's direction, shrieking at the top of her lungs. Del tried to position for the final shot, but Kendra was in the direct line of fire now, running, arms flailing, preventing either Del or Falconet from getting off another shot.

Payton fired off an ineffective round as he turned and fled from the garden and into the brush beyond the garden perimeter—taking the shortest path between his pursuers and the boathouse.

Kendra fell into Del's arms and clung there for support, body shaking, sobbing out her deep, relentless anguish.

Falconet rushed into the open, hoping for another shot. But Payton had managed to slip from sight into the dense foliage at the edge of the garden. "We have to stop him," he said. "The Water Patrol is apparently having trouble getting the boat dislodged from the sand."

"Come on," Del said, pulling Kendra with her. "I'm not letting you out of my sight."

They took the path of least resistance—all three of them—racing through the arched entrance and along the path that led to the boathouse. Payton had already cleared free of the brush and was now making his way toward the entrance to the grotto.

"We can't let him get to the boat," Del said, dragging the lolling girl behind her, trying to urge her faster.

Just then, in their path appeared the female tiger, Gigi. The gunfire had her nervous and agitated. Her eyes were narrowed to a steely glint. Her shoulders were lowered. She stalked closer, emitting a deep but very audible sustained growl.

"Tigers," Falconet said simply, his understanding complete now.

All three took a reflexive step backward.

The cat had seemingly zeroed in on Del as the alpha female in the pack. It stalked nearer, never taking its eyes off her.

Del backed another step.

Slowly, step by slow liquid step, it drew closer.

It was close enough, now, that Del could see that its eyes were a beautiful icy shade of blue. It didn't detract from the menace in them, however. For the second time in less than half and hour, Del braced for the inevitability of death.

Falconet slowly but deliberately raised his gun. Then...

"*Gigi!*" a voice called, accompanied by a sharp clap of the hands.

Leggett appeared on the path behind them, coming quickly to their defense.

He called again, "*Gigi!*"

The cat refused to back down. It stopped stalking, but never took its eyes off Del.

"*Gigi!*" Leggett called again, with another loud clap, a greater sense of authority.

The cat, realizing its master's voice, finally broke focus. The sinews in its muscles relaxed, and its gaze turned off indifferently, as if to say, *Okay, but it's still my decision.*

Del let her breath out in one long, slow release.

Leggett came forward to intercept the cat, grab it by its collar and jerk. "*Gigi!*" he scolded. "We naw eat the pretty lady!" He jerked hard on the leash again. Now, he knelt and hugged his arm around the cat's thick neck and began to whisper in its ear, stroke and coax the beast into settling. Slowly the cat calmed and became, for all appearances to Del, a big, lovable kitty.

Del turned her attention back to Payton now. He had reached the entrance to the grotto and had slipped inside.

"Is it okay to go?" Del asked. She wanted to thank the Cajun for saving them, but there wasn't time, and she wasn't sure she had the voice for it.

"My pischouette is okay," Leggett said. "I still naw see Java. He is one to watch."

The three of them moved off, still giving the tiger lots of room, and rushed down the slope to the boathouse.

———

The boat's motors could be heard starting, and a belch of start-up exhaust rolled from the rear entrance of the grotto. Payton was on the move.

Falconet let Del take the lead. It was still her show now, and he didn't want to steal even one tiny bit of her thunder from her. Truth was, he trusted her to finish the job. Tough, resilient. Smart and courageous. And—damn!—she was sexy. Fast and trim. In boots and jeans, gun in hand. Dragging the girl—her charge—along with her, as she closed in. She wasn't about to let Payton Rickey get away.

They made their way to the grotto doorway and stole a look inside.

Payton fired off a shot from behind the helm of the *Sand Castle* to stay them, as he backed the boat toward the exit.

Del drew Kendra to a safe spot beside the doorway, coaxed her to the ground, warning her not to move.

The girl wasn't going anywhere, Falconet realized. She allowed herself to be managed, like a rag doll, to whatever fate Del was preparing for her.

They took up positions on either side of the entrance, as the boat backed from the landing. They were looking for one opportunity, just one.

But Payton was gunning the powerful engines, and the sleek boat was responding, accelerating backward free of its moorings. He fired off another round in their direction, as he expertly wheeled the boat around and jammed the gearshift into drive. He was some twenty feet beyond the faux-rock outcropping.

"You want this one," Del said, sighting down the barrel of her Baby Eagle.

"You're doing just fine," Falconet said.

Payton gunned the engines and the big boat hunkered down in the water for one brief instant before launching forward.

Del took a breath and held it, her finger tightening on the trigger.

But before she could get a shot off...

A white-and-black, striped blur flashed before her. It was Java—leaping from the top of the rocky grotto, sailing through midair, sun glinting off its magnificent striped coat. It cleanly cleared the distance to the boat—its superbly engineered body reaching, claws and jaws opened wide.

Payton had only one brief instant, to see and understand. His mouth opened wide, in a would-be scream, as the cat landed on him, knocking him off his seat and to the deck. The scream did come, an agonized shriek, as the cat's sharp claws dug in. The scream was then cut silent as Java's wide jaws clamped tight around Payton's throat in a classic feline kill.

The boat sped forward on its own now, out of control, no one at the helm. It careened off the back end of the grotto, made a twirling, uncontrolled 360 turn, and sped directly for the shoreline. It rammed onto land hard, the engines choking, then dying.

The island fell quiet.

Off in the near distance, the Sheriff's Water Patrol could be seen and heard making its way rapidly along the north shoreline toward them. The *Sand Castle* sat still, half-in, half-out of water. Java remained over the body, glaring.

"Whew!"

Del and Falconet had watched the entire event go down, as if from some out-of-body state. Now, they turned to look at each other, mouths still agape.

"I didn't see that coming, did you?" Falconet said.

"No ..." Del said, having to force the words out. "But in some ways it was so much more satisfying then just shooting the man, don't you think?"

"Yeah ..." Falconet said. "Satisfying."

They were both still in shock.

FORTY-ONE

THE CRIME SCENE ON Terrebonne Key took two days to process. The bodies of Ivess DeMarco, the two house staff, and Payton Rickey—confirmed dead for real this time—were turned over to the Terrebonne Parish medical examiner. Statements from the survivors were taken and police reports were generated. Leggett De-Noux was exonerated from any charges in the matter, on a word from Del that he had been instrumental in saving their lives. Falconet corroborated her claim.

A document uncovered in a desk drawer at the mansion turned out to be Ivess's will. It bequeathed the island and all properties to Leggett, with the provision that he remain on the island and continue to care for Java and Gigi—Ivess's beloved white tigers—and create a conservancy for the other wildlife, both exotic and indigenous. The trust fund that had sustained Ivess's lifestyle now passed to Leggett.

As for the others:

Kendra Kozak was treated at a local hospital, and it was determined that her physical wounds were not life-threatening, but that she should seek counseling for those wounds that were not so visible.

Both girls were admonished for their foolishness—though everyone privately acknowledged that Lissa had been the one primarily responsible for their foolish adventure.

The days remained sunny, the air warm.

No treasure had been found.

Falconet placed a call to Darius Lemon at FBI regional headquarters in Cincinnati, putting Del on the line to say hello and add her commentary. He told Darius that his assignment was over; the case of Payton Rickey could now be closed. And to tell him that he wouldn't be seeing him for a time, that he could reach him in the near future in Tucson, where the air was a hell of a lot dryer and folks didn't all smell like fish.

Del had also called Randall to ease his mind. And, lastly, placed a call to the gentlemanly old Western writer Edgar Egan. Egan—as was his way—was overly expressive of his joy at the news his granddaughter and her friend were safe and sound. He lavished Del with praise and assured her that her company would be well and promptly compensated for its time and trouble—*her* time, *her* trouble. He would see them in a couple of days.

There was still Louise to inform.

The fourteen-hundred-mile trip back to Arizona took a full two-and-half days. Del did most of the driving, with Falconet in the passenger seat. The two girls followed in the Land Rover. It had been cleaned up and the window replaced, all tires properly inflated. They arrived back in Tucson, going first to Egan's hacienda to deliver the teens—alive and safe, as Del had promised.

Now, they were all gathered in the comfortable living area—Del, Falconet, the two teens, and Egan himself—Gerda staying busy shuffling back and forth to the kitchen, supplying hot appetizers and refilling wine and soda glasses.

The tintype photo of Jacob Worley sat ceremoniously on the coffee table in front of them, along with the stack of Google printouts that Falconet had salvaged from the Land Rover.

Egan couldn't stop expressing his gratitude, nor stop lavishing Del with praise- –referring to her as "one tough cowgirl, worthy of being a character in any of his books."

The night was filled with sociable cheer, relief for the blessed outcome of the girls' ordeal, and discussions about the reality of the Jacob Worley legend.

"It was a foolish thing you did," Egan said, scolding both his granddaughter and her friend. "But I suppose I can see the appeal, to such adventurous young minds."

"Not my mind," Kendra corrected. "This was all Lissa's brainstorm." She was smiling as she said it and gave her friend a playful nudge.

"I still don't understand," Lissa said. "I could have sworn the treasure would have been under the water-maiden sculpture. I don't know how I could have been so wrong. I was positive."

"What made you so sure of your conclusions?" Falconet asked. "I mean, just asking. Haven't many others tried to figure it out?"

"Yeah, sure. But, I figured I'd seen something none of the others had." Lissa was sitting on the floor alongside the coffee table next to the photo and printouts. She took up the tintype photo in its etched silver frame and presented it to the gathering. "See, everyone believed that the photo was Worley's message to the world ... maybe to himself, as he was going senile ... he was pointing to his watch to say the treasure is in the two o'clock position."

"Sounds simple enough," Falconet said.

"Yeah, that's what folks thought. But, see, what old Jacob either didn't consider, or as part of his secretive puzzle, was that tintypes are negative images. They are the reverse image of what is actually there. Jacob was going nuts. I figured it's possible he got it wrong himself and no one else considered the possibility."

"Except you," Del said.

"Yeah, that's what I thought, at least!"

"But it wasn't there?" Egan questioned.

"No," Lissa said, flushing a bit with embarrassment.

Del had heard the explanation before, but now had the chance to study the tintype up close for the first time. There was something they all were overlooking, perhaps, even Lissa. "Maybe he's not pointing to something in the photo," Del said.

It got everyone's attention.

"What are you suggesting, my dear?" Egan asked.

"Well … what if Worley is not pointing to his watch at all, but off-photo to a spot on the frame?"

"Right?" Falconet said. "What's that supposed to mean?"

Del reached for the tintype and Lissa handed it to her. Everyone seated leaned closer. Even Gerda—interested now—paused in the doorway to listen.

"Look at the silver frame holding the tintype, the scrollwork around its border," she said, tracing the edges of the frame with one finger. "The scrollwork is a series of Indian arrowheads, pointing this way and that, around the entire border of the frame. What if they're not decorative, but actually pointers? Worley was a silversmith, right? He etched the frame himself, I think you told me."

"Yeah …?" Lissa said, hesitantly affirming, but not yet sure where Del was headed.

"They don't point to anything," Falconet said. "They all point in different directions."

"That's just my point." Del said. "When I was in the garden I noticed that all the statues seemed to be looking in different directions, but more precisely, one to the other."

"So?" Kendra said. "What's that do?"

"Do you have a marker, Gerda?" Del asked of the matron.

Gerda retrieved a black marker from a nearby desk drawer and handed it to Del.

"See…" Del said, drawing attention to the aerial photo. "Ignore the pocket watch and look to the arrowhead where Jacob is pointing… the one on the right side of the frame. Now follow the line of the arrowhead to the next arrowhead it points to. And the line of that arrowhead to the next, and so on. Then look at the statues in the aerial photo. Start with the statue in that same location and follow its line of sight to the next statue… then the line of sight of that statue to the next. It matches the arrowheads etched in the frame."

"Hmmm…" Egan said, trying to follow the logic.

"I'm just saying," Del said, "what if he's not pointing to the location of the treasure, but rather to the 'starting point' of the puzzle that eventually leads you to the statue where the fortune is buried?"

"That's fascinating, my dear," Egan said.

"Del's right!" Lissa said, suddenly seeing the connection for herself. She took the tintype from Del and began following the arrowheads, with her finger, one to the other, until she had touched all twelve, arriving on the very last one. "Here," she said.

"That's not the water maiden at all!" Kendra said.

And it wasn't. Her finger had come to rest on the arrowhead that was in the five o'clock position on the frame, far removed from previous speculations. Now she looked at the aerial photo to the corresponding sculpture. "This sculpture is the only one that doesn't face any of the other statues," she said, wonderment in her voice.

317

"Its head is lowered, facing down, as if pointing with its eyes to the treasure."

"Unbelievable!" Egan exclaimed.

"Right?" Falconet added.

They all remained in wide-eyed wonderment.

Del rose and slid back into her chair, collecting her wine glass, a somewhat wry smile on her face. "Just saying…" she said, taking a sip of wine.

"My God!" Egan said. "That's got to be it! You're not only a tough cookie, but smart! Very smart!"

"Lissa did all the groundwork," Del said, modestly deferring to the teenager, who was still looking at the aerial image with amazement.

"It's so simple!" Lissa said. She then popped to her feet. "Well! We just have to get back to Terrebonne Key! We have to!"

Kendra groaned.

Egan shook his head despairingly.

"Well, this is all very fascinating, but I think our work here is done," Falconet said, lifting himself out of his chair, a bit tipsy from the drink. "It's time for us to go."

He offered a hand to Del.

She rose and said her goodbyes all around, getting a hug from both Lissa and Kendra.

Egan escorted the two of them to the front entrance, wheeling along ahead of them. "Have your boss, Randall, send me an invoice for your time and trouble," he said.

"I'm sure he will," Del said.

"And thanks again! Really! I can't tell you how grateful I am to have my granddaughter back safe and sound. Kendra too. I just hope she's not serious about returning to Terrebonne. But… if she gets it in her head to do so … well…"

"Like someone else I know," Falconet said.

"It was my pleasure," Del said. She considered a handshake, but then on impulse bent and kissed Egan on the forehead, thinking not so much of him but of Louise and what Louise would do if she were here, being grateful that the old man had ultimately provided for her granddaughter's safe return.

It drew a big smile from the old Western writer. "Take care of yourself, my dear," he said. "And, you too, young man."

Falconet gave a wave over his shoulder as he headed off into the afternoon sunlight.

Del took a moment to consider Falconet and all that they'd been through together—this time and the time two years ago. She knew he'd be waiting to talk to her, find the right time, and get back to the unanswered questions soon to be at hand again.

Would she have an answer for him this time?

———

They arrived at the offices of Desert Sands Covert—coming off the elevator and through the glass double doors just before the close of business, a Monday, now. Patti, the receptionist, was at her station behind the reception desk.

"Patti, this is Frank Falconet, working with the FBI," Del said.

Falconet reached a hand to her and gave her a smile.

Patti visibly swooned. She seemed to have trouble releasing the hand she held in both of hers.

Falconet seemed to be taken with her.

"Come on, Frank. Before you get yourself in trouble," Del said, dragging Falconet away.

Randall was just coming out of his office when they stepped into the bullpen area.

"Randall, this is Frank Falconet, ATF. Frank, this is my boss Randall."

"Yeah, we spoke on the phone, good to finally meet you in person," Randall said, being uncharacteristically nice in front of her male partner. "I see you brought our girl back safe and sound."

"Maybe it's the other way around," Falconet said. "Nice to meet you, too."

Randall was pumping Falconet's hand, maybe a little too exuberantly. And Del could see that there was true respect and admiration on Randall's face. It was maybe the first male friend, out of all the male friends Del had ever introduced Randall to, that he actually seemed to approve of. Will miracles never cease?

"I understand you were with Navy Intelligence at one time," Falconet said, making small talk, giving Randall a chance to crow. "Must have been pretty challenging."

"Ah! That was a long time ago," Randall said, waving it off. "I let the youngsters like Del have all the fun these days. I just move papers around my desk and try to keep track of where she's at, at any given time. That's challenging enough."

"Right?" Falconet said.

That was about all they could think of to say to each other, but it was a start. Del said, "Well, we just wanted to say hi."

Randall asked, "Have you stopped by to see Louise?"

They had.

They had stopped at the cemetery before returning to the office, giving Del the chance to inform Louise. *"Lissa's back safe,"* she had said to the grave. *"I'll keep an eye on her from here on out."*

"She'd be proud of you," Falconet had told Del, coming to stand close behind, offer comfort, reassurance, a hand on each of her shoulders.

"I think she'd approve of you too, Frank," Del said, knowing as soon as she said it, that it was an opening for the discussion to come.

Falconet didn't take the lead, not just then anyway--maybe being respectful of the moment. Instead, he gathered her hand in his and together they walked off, out of the cemetery together.

That had been earlier.

Now, Randall was saying, "Oh, by the way. Your man Andray Moton missed his court appearance, skipped out on his bail again. Just thought you would want to know."

"Thanks, Randall," Del said.

"Sure. Now, don't bother coming into the office tomorrow. You two kids deserve some time together. Go! Go have some fun!"

Del said, "We'll be sure to do that. But I think first there's a little something that needs taken care of."

Falconet said, "Something? What something?"

Randall gave her a knowing smile. "You have a nice day," he said.

In the elevator, Falconet asked, "So, you didn't answer my question? What's this little something?"

Del was holding Falconet's hand as the elevator descended. She gave his hand a squeeze now. "You remember bringing up the question of us being together? Maybe working together, somehow?"

"I've been dreaming about it for two years," Falconet said.

"Well…" she said, as the elevator reached the bottom and the doors dinged open. "Now's your chance to get your answer."

"What's that supposed to mean?"

———

Del considered the little, faded white house that sat back from the street. Pieces of siding were missing from front of the house; the paint was scaling. The rain gutter that ran the length of the front porch was sagging. A hull of a rusted-out clothes dryer sat on the front lawn. There were rusted car parts and other refuse scattered about. It was just after dusk, the neighborhood quiet. A fearful edge to the silence. No light showing from behind the blinds, no sounds of life from within.

This time Del allowed her weapon to remain holstered in her waistband at the small of her back. She crossed through the gate and onto the porch, not bothering to muffle her footsteps. She considered the darkened window, then wrapped twice on the door and waited.

The door opened a crack.

"Where's Andray, Roselle?"

"He ain't here!" Roselle said, her standard response.

Del let her eyes move pass Roselle to the darkened space beyond. "I'm coming in, Andray!" Del called inside. She waited, hearing frantic movement from within, muttered cursing. Then a door banging open and shut at the back of the house.

A second later there was even louder cursing and a not-so-muffled *Ka-thump!*

Del gave Roselle a smile, then casually pushed her way inside, gun still holstered in her waistband.

She crossed through the living room at a leisurely pace and made her way down the hallway to the kitchen door and onto the rear porch.

There, Falconet had Andray face down, his hands cuffed behind his back. Andray calling him the kinds of names he'd once called her. *"Bitch!"*

"How you doing, Andray?" Del said.

Falconet dragged Andray to his feet, the man still cursing and complaining.

"Always on me, bitch!" he spat at her.

"Well, don't say I didn't warn you."

"Let's go, tough guy," Falconet said, turning Andray toward the steps leading down.

"Bitch! I'm gonna get you! Next time! I'll be waitin'! You believe it, girl! I'll make your skinny ass—!"

Andray didn't get the chance to finish his last epithet. As they reached the top step, Falconet stuck his foot out and caught Andray mid-stride. Andray tripped, pitched forward, headfirst, off the porch, hands still cuffed behind his back. He smacked face down, hard, on the concrete sidewalk.

"You need to watch that first step," Falconet said. "It's a doozy."

They collected Andray together and led him through the yard to the Wrangler, where they folded him into the space behind the seats and drove the three miles to the Southside Tucson Police precinct and turned him in.

In the parking lot, sliding back inside the Wrangler, Del said, "Well, you did good back there, Frank."

Falconet asked, "So, is that my answer?"

Del cranked the engine. "You're such a guy! Come on, Frank. Let's get a drink and talk about it."

She wheeled the Wrangler out, into traffic, thinking of Randall, the respect he'd shown Falconet earlier. She had to admit, it was kind of nice having Randall's approval. Nice having someone to back her up. Maybe she'd tell him… "*Sure … why not.*"

THE END

ACKNOWLEDGMENTS

Thanks to Bobby Heege for his expert help with the Cajun dialect and for just being a great pal.

ABOUT THE AUTHOR

Darrell James lives in Arizona. His stories have appeared in numerous mystery magazines and book anthologies and have garnered a
number of awards; his latest story appears in the MWA Lee Child
anthology *Vengeance*. His debut novel, *Nazareth Child*, the first
in the Del Shannon series, was the winner of the 2012 Left Coast
Crime Eureka Award for best first novel and nominated for both
the Anthony and Macavity Awards. The second novel in the Del
Shannon series is *Sonora Crossing*.

Please visit him online at www.darrelljames.com.